Spear of Victory

United in Magic

The Four Keys

Book Four

J.C. Lucas

Copywrite

IF YOU'D LIKE TO BE one of the first to know about new releases or sales, click below to sign up for J.C.'s newsletter. Just click the link below, subscribe and you'll get all the news! As a bonus for signing up, you'll also get a free download of the prequel, The Four Keys!

https://landing.mailerlite.com/webforms/landing/h1f5i7[1]

---

1. https://landing.mailerlite.com/webforms/landing/h1f5i7?fbclid=IwAR1rntmBvudk-JTJH7zQQ7fN1zZrEZfZU__LspFhZ8ihLtg-1e4SviFJ9bo

Dedication

THIS BOOK IS DEDICATED to all of my readers, friends and family who have had faith in me and my dreams. Without your support, cheering me on and the excitement you've shown me, I don't think I would have had the strength to make it happen. A special shout out to my ARC team. You are simply the best! And Makarena, thank you for contributing your wonderful ideas to make this final journey for Andie perfect! Lots of love to you!

Here's to having faith and following your dreams!

May you touch fireflies and stars, dance with fairies, and talk to the man in the moon.

-Unknown

Prologue

Darkness filled me up, no matter how much I tried to push it down.
Fear that it would consume me was my new normal.
I tried to pretend that all was right with the world, that I could do
and be all the things that everyone wanted of me... but the oily
blackness that slithered inside of me had other plans.

Chapter One

I WASN'T CUT OUT FOR this.

The meetings, the looks that the witches and warlocks gave me. The disdain barely hidden from their faces as I bumbled through making decisions that I honestly felt I shouldn't be making. Why had the Fates deemed me worthy?

A long sigh sounded near my ear as Eira arranged my hair into a loose updo, with curly wisps hanging down in haphazard fashion. I didn't see why my appearance was such a big deal. We had much bigger issues at hand now, and the least of my worries was how stylish my hair was, or how perfect my makeup was applied.

What I wanted and the figure that Celeste and Aine said I needed to portray, were on vastly different sides of the spectrum.

I was front and center, being watched by the entire magical world. I had a feeling that some of them were waiting for me to fail.

I understood it, I really did. I was also waiting to fail. Not that I wanted to. *God*, I didn't want to. But seriously? I'm a seventeen-year-old girl. Yes, I've garnered some serious magical powers, but I didn't even know how strong they really were, or what I could do with them. Every day was a learning curve for me.

I tried to stay positive. I mean, I have so much more now than when I was thrown into this fairytale world. My dad, Celeste and Hunter had all come back to me after I thought I'd never have them in my life again. That alone was enough to celebrate and feed my happiness. A life that now seemed endless and full of possibilities.

That is, if we could rid it of Helios and his minions, the Fomori.

The creak of the door roused me from my thoughts, and Eira twirled in the air to look behind us.

"Don't mind me," a smooth voice sounded, and I smiled. Turning slowly my eyes met Hunters. The lift in the corner of his mouth, and the quirk of his eyebrow sent tingles over my arms and down my legs.

His gaze fell from my head to my feet, and then back up and his steely eyes twinkled as he gazed into mine.

"You look beautiful, but then again, you're gorgeous in your leggings and hoodie too."

I bit my lip to stop the full-blown grin that threatened to surface. Schooling my face with a slight scowl that I was sure he could see right through, I stared at the red heels Celeste insisted I wear. They were ridiculously high, and I just knew I'd make a fool of myself in front of everyone.

Eira spun through the air toward Hunter. Her new dress made of pink rose petals swirled around her tiny legs. She landed on his shoulder and plopped down, her legs dangling over the front of him.

"She's hated every minute of this," she whispered to him, knowing full well I could hear her. "But me? I've enjoyed having someone to dress up again. It's been ages. She's going to be the belle of the ball, and if you don't watch it, she may just steal someone else's heart."

She winked at him, and his eyebrows furrowed, a frown twisting his lips before he turned that look on me, and a soft growl rumbled low in his chest.

I rolled my eyes.

"Eira, stop that. No one cares what I look like. All they want is for me to tell them what to do and lead them. Well, the ones who believe I can, anyway," I huffed, turning around to look out the window at the rain. It poured from the sky as if to wash away all the evil that surrounded us. "And besides, there's only one person my heart belongs to. No one else can hold a candle to him."

His hand slipped around my waist, pulling me back against his hard chest, and I leaned into him as his breath tickled my ear.

"It will always be me and you, Andie," he whispered, and I shivered as he kissed my neck. The current that ran between us when we touched shot electricity back and forth through our veins. I didn't have to look to know his were lit with gold fire, and his eyes swirled with molten lava.

Too soon he released me and backed up as I turned. Eira hovered near the door, and I knew she'd been eavesdropping by the way her hands clasped to her heart, and a goofy look covered her face.

Again, I rolled my eyes and brushed past Hunter.

"Let's get this show on the road."

Star skittered up my body to wind herself around my shoulders as I walked down the hall in Aine's castle, Hunter behind me, always, while Eira flew beside me. Annoyed sighs came from her as she adjusted her wings to my slow pace. I ignored them, though as my mind drifted.

The past month I had spent more time than I ever imagined I would be learning proper etiquette. Celeste and Aine felt I needed to know it all in order to get the Fae world to take me seriously. They thought it would be something worthwhile to know so I could lead the rest of the Fae. And to say that they had their hands full with me would be an understatement. I tried, I did, *so hard*. But it was a daily struggle to not get frustrated with them.

I thought to myself many times, still do, that if the Fates had deemed me worthy, why change me? I'd even voiced that to them, and they had patiently explained that the covens and packs wouldn't care what the Fates deemed unless I met their standards. I had to earn their trust if I hadn't already. Then, and only then, would they follow. And I desperately needed them. The *world* needed them.

A conversation that I had with a particular foreign Warlock came to mind. He hadn't minced words, effectively telling me that there was no way that I could lead the Fae. That I was immature and incompetent. That had been my first meeting so far, *and* my last. It hadn't turned out well.

The blackness that had settled in my stomach rose up after his brash words, burning and squirming its way into my brain, just as it did now when I descended the stairs. I don't know what I said to him at the time. I'd barely been able to turn away before he saw the blackness slide over the white of my eyes.

I only remembered the pain as I'd fought with all I had to push it back down. And it had gone away, but not before he gasped behind me and his body fell to the floor, footsteps rushing to him.

I still hadn't been able to look back. Not until an hour later, after Celeste pleaded for me to let her help. By that time, I'd gathered my wits and felt more myself again, albeit quite exhausted and worn out.

She'd looked at me strangely as she wrapped her arm around my shoulder and guided me to my room.

The next day was when the training began.

Chapter Two

MUSIC FILTERED THROUGH my thoughts, and I looked around for Neo. He had greeted me with excitement the first day I arrived back in Fairy, all too proud that he would be the DJ at the ball being thrown in my honor before my first Faction meeting. All of the clans and covens from around the world had one of their leaders here to discuss how we would rid the world of Helios and the Fomori.

Neo waved from the music booth, his smile wide and stretching from ear to ear. I felt the darkness fade away as his exuberance hit me across the room. Smiling back, I gave him a slight nod, and Star purred next to my ear.

Per my training, I was *not* to be overly excited. I was to be demure but stern. Strong but thoughtful. And definitely never rash in my decision making.

So not fun.

When we reached the bottom of the stairs, the Titans who were waiting for us surrounded me, their tall bodies obscuring my vision. All I could see were broad backs outfitted in designer suits.

My bodyguards were assigned by none other than my favorite one who stood so close beside me now that his arm pressed into mine.

With a quick glance up, my eyes met his.

He knew about the encounter with the Warlock, yet he'd never asked me about it. I had a feeling he felt the darkness that resided in me, but he wasn't yet willing to speak of it. The fact that I could barely get him to leave my side told me he worried more than he let on.

He gave me a small smile before his eyes hardened and he looked around the room slowly. Our group stood still until he gave the go ahead, and then I was shuffled between them across the wide expanse.

It was ridiculous. *Seriously*. How did anyone live like this? I didn't want to fear anything, least of all my own people.

And I didn't. Everyone was just being overly cautious and paranoid.

It was then that my stupid heel caught on the gauzy hem of my dress and I pitched forward, my fear of embarrassing myself rising up full throttle.

A firm hand caught me before I had a chance to fall into the big back of the guard in front of me. Steadying me, Hunter reached down to unhook the material.

My hand rested on his shoulder as he did, and his eyes met mine. "I'll always be here to catch you if you fall." That boyish grin that was few and far between sparkled up at me. It was a little corny, but oh so sweet.

Maybe being moved around inside of this group, obscured from observers, and rescued by a cute guy wasn't *so* bad.

I smiled coyly back at him. "And I you."

We began our shuffle once again until our group came to a stop on the other side of the ballroom. The bodies in front of me parted, awarding me a view of a large table where none other than Teagan's parents, Hunter's dad, Celeste, and various other dignitaries were seated. They all stood then, watching to see what I would do. Celeste's calm smile eased the tension that rose in my shoulders.

I remembered her instructions, and slightly tilted my head. They all reciprocated, but with a slight bow of their bodies. I moved forward and the chair in front of me was pulled out immediately. Hunter took my right hand as I slid into it, and then seated himself beside me. The Titans moved to stand off to the side, but not too far. Their eyes continuously scanned the room.

My left hand was gently taken into a warm one, and I had no idea how I'd missed the fact that my dad sat there so quietly. His eyes sparkled as he leaned in and kissed my cheek.

Etiquette be damned when it came to him and a few select others. I'd soak up all the love I could while I had it.

"You look stunning," he said as he pushed a stray piece of hair behind my ear. "Just take a deep breath, and handle this just like you do with everything else. Strength."

He'd said the last out of hearing of the others who still watched us. I patted his hand and leaned back, clearing my throat.

"Thank you for joining us tonight."

I grabbed ahold of the crystal glass in front of me, filled with dark liquid, and held it up. The rest at the table followed suit, and once I took a sip of mine, they did as well.

Then dinner was served, and thankfully it saved me from further conversation as everyone turned to their food, chatting with their companions. I took that time to observe.

Celeste looked regal and beautiful as always. Dad seemed more relaxed than he had been in a while, and Hunter was tense and on alert. Always looking for threats.

A few others I hadn't had the pleasure of meeting yet enjoyed their drinks way too much, and their voices grew louder as dinner dragged on.

Teagan's parents remained quiet throughout the meal. Toni barely picked at her food, while Logan hovered over her, urging her on. I could see the weariness that lined their faces, and I knew that there wasn't one minute they didn't stop agonizing over Teagan.

It had been a monumental task to try and drown out my thoughts about him too. I couldn't imagine what they were going through.

There was still no word on where he'd disappeared to. No one knew if he was alive or dead. The wolves had put a bounty on his head after the murderous actions he'd taken against one of their clans, killing each and every one of them with the evil hellfire.

I still held out hope that we could get him back and release him from the hold that had taken him over. My Teagan would have never in a million years killed innocent people like that.

"It's time," a voice beside my ear squeaked, and I glanced at Eira as she hovered next to me as the churning in my stomach began.

I'd never been good at speaking in front of large crowds, but my new position required it.

Hunter pulled out my chair and I gathered my dress as I stood up. Star wanted no part of the spotlight and chose to hop onto my abandoned chair where she sat like a prissy little girl.

The hundreds of people spread out at various tables before me was overwhelming. I'd been spared earlier, tucked in the protective Titan bubble, but now I could see them all, and my anxiety ratcheted up.

Hunter took my arm as the Titans flanked us, and I squared my shoulders. Taking a deep breath, I lifted my chin as he walked with me to the platform that had been constructed at the front of the room.

Aine stood in front of a podium made of crystal. Flowers in fall colors were arranged all around it. I listened to her speak as we waited off to the side and took in the room that I hadn't paid any attention to before.

She had outdone herself again. It was November, and the entire room was decked out in crisp autumn colors. Oranges and reds. Browns and blacks. In the air, high above us, pumpkins bounced and mums of every color twirled. I wondered what it looked like at Halloween.

She finished her speech, telling all of the attendees thank you for coming, and then she introduced me.

There was no clapping as I made my way to her and everyone stood waiting silently. Hunter's warm arm slipped from where it rested around me, and I instantly missed his warmth.

Aine leaned forward and kissed both of my cheeks before giving me the stage.

Everyone took their seats again and stared up at me expectantly. I'd rehearsed what I was going to say a million times, but it still didn't seem good enough.

I cleared my throat and began, hoping they had some grace to give me a pass if I screwed this up.

"Hi everyone." I gave a half wave at the audience in front of me and immediately felt stupid for doing so. I quickly lowered my hand, but not before Coeus give a little smirk to Hunter, who just shook his head and smiled at me.

Clearing my throat and straightening my shoulders, I stared over the crowd and at the wall behind the crowd.

"I want to thank you for coming today. It's important that we use the time while you're here to get to know one another and devise a plan to stop the evil that is infiltrating our world."

There was some murmuring coming from where the clan from England sat, but I ignored them and soldiered on.

"I know that many of you have doubts about my leadership. To be honest with you, I've had them too. But I pledge to you that I will do everything within my power to lead in the way that you expect. To prove to you that the Fates bestowed this honor on me for a reason."

My voice grew stronger with each word, and I glanced at Celeste, who proudly looked on. Relief filled me as I realized that she was happy so far with my performance.

I glanced around the silent room, and everyone seemed to sit up a little taller, their eyes all staring back at mine. Only a few still looked skeptical.

"I wish to speak with each and every one of you. I want to know your worries, your fears, what you think is a good course forward, and all of your suggestions. No matter how small or trivial you think they may be, I want to know them. Working together is the only way that we can defeat the madness that is set out to destroy us. Together we are stronger. We can't defeat evil with uncertainty and fear. We must come together, put any differences aside and work as one."

Before I could go on, I heard soft clapping begin from the corner where Neo hovered. And like the ripple of a wave, the clapping began to catch on, swirling through the room until it became a roar.

One by one, the dignitaries stood, and I stared at them in wonder.

Aine had given me a speech to go over, but while I'd been up there, it had felt so clinical and detached, that I decided to throw caution to the wind and just go with what was in my heart.

I hadn't expected this reaction.

I was further floored as I watched the same table of witches and warlocks from Europe move forward in a line to stand before me. One by one, they kneeled or curtsied. They placed their hand over their heart before standing back up and moving away, only to be replaced with another group that did the same.

I felt Aine's presence behind me, but I didn't turn. I calmly stood there, and as each group pledged their fealty to me, I put my hand to my heart just as they did. I hoped they understood that I was pledging myself to them as well.

When the last group stood before me, my group, my family, each of them beamed up at me. Their light and love lit me from the inside, and I watched as they kneeled together, their eyes never leaving mine as their fists thumped their chests, and their hands shot out in synchrony. Magic shot from their fingertips to swirl across the distance to where I stood.

Sparkles twirled and danced, surrounding me as I stood still, wondering what exactly they were doing. Gentle heat emanated from my scalp as I felt something settle itself on my head.

I wanted to reach up and touch it, but I refrained. I knew what it was. I had adamantly disagreed with Celeste about needing a crown. But now she and the others had found a way where I couldn't refuse it.

Her turquoise eyes glittered up at me as Coeus reached for her hand to help her stand. *Well played Celeste, well played.*

I inclined my head to her as she and the others turned away to join the rest of the room in the evening's festivities.

"She got you good, didn't she?" Aine murmured as I turned around, joy lighting her face as she stared at the top of my head.

"And she outdid herself too." She wrapped her arm around my waist as we walked off the platform and toward the Titans that waited. "Moonbeams are a special gift that the Moon Goddess has never bestowed on anyone before. You are extremely lucky."

I glanced at her as she moved away, Hunter taking her place. I wanted to ask exactly why moonbeams were a good thing, and I itched to find a mirror to see what the crown looked like.

I could feel the hum of energy that radiated from it, and that same sense of peace that Celeste had given to me when I had first arrived at her home a year ago.

Hunter's warm hand pressed against my back as he steered me through the crowd gave me that same feeling as well, and I relaxed into it.

I acknowledged everyone who we passed, but he didn't allow me a moment to stop and chat. Instead, he moved me to a table laden with drinks. Wine, water, tea, and coffee lined the beautifully decorated display, hints of marigolds peeking out between the crystal goblets and ceramic mugs.

He reached forward, his hand never leaving me and plucked up one of the glasses that was filled to the brim with a light pink wine.

My eyebrows rose as he handed it to me, and his lips curved as he laughed a little.

"You do realize that I'm not old enough to be drinking this, right?" I stared at the sparkling liquid before turning my gaze to him as he picked another one for himself.

"I really don't think that matters anymore," he chuckled, "You're now the leader of our world, and you've earned it. We're celebrating tonight."

His dark eyes twinkled as he clinked his glass to mine and took a sip. I did the same, pulling my gaze from his before I got lost in it.

I looked around us and realized that the dancing had begun. Soft music drifted on the air, and the bright lights had been turned down. Fairies danced above us, their little lights moving in a graceful pattern.

It was beautiful, and I felt lightness in my heart that was rare these days.

The wine was light and fruity, and it immediately warmed me up. I laughed as I watched Eira grab Neo's hand and pull him into the air to dance with the others, much to his dismay.

"This is nice," I whispered, but Hunter still heard me.

I wouldn't have had to even say a word and he would have heard me. I felt his agreement as he leaned closer while we observed the happiness that surrounded us.

If only it would last.

Chapter Three

We slipped outside onto a balcony. I knew the other Titans were near, but thankfully they stayed out of sight to give us at least the feeling of privacy. And really, what was privacy anymore? My new role seemed to afford me none of it.

I was just thankful to have a moment alone with my shifter. *My Titan god.* I giggled as he looked down at me, his brows raised.

"Be careful Andie. Your thoughts might go to my head," he teased.

"Never!" I giggled and walked to lean against the metal that lined the expansive balcony, looking out over the land that was now kissed with the light from the moon and the shooting stars that never stopped.

His arms wrapped around me from behind, his chin resting on my shoulder as he gazed out as well.

"I'm proud of you," he whispered in my ear. I leaned my head against his. "I know this is a lot to take on, but you've proven to me, through everything you have done, that you are growing, learning, and kind. That's what our people need."

I sighed and closed my eyes.

"You know I cherish how you feel about the job I'm doing, but I just worry that it's not enough for those people."

I stepped away, the anxiety kicking back in as I gestured inside. "They're waiting for me to fail. I just know it. Even with the display a while ago, I just can't help but worry about how they really feel."

He caught my hand and pulled me around back to him, tilting my chin up so his eyes pierced into mine.

"Don't second guess it. You won them over in there. Yes, you're going to have to prove yourself, but just the fact that they swore fealty to you tells me they're on board."

I shook my head to protest, but he put both of his hands on either side of my face, stopping my disagreement.

"Yes. It's true. Never in my life have I seen so many of the Fae groups in one room, actually getting along and enjoying themselves. *That* is a wonder. And you know who brought them together?" he asked.

"Yes, it was the destruction by Freya, the rise of Helios, and this evil that brought them together. Not me, Hunter."

He sighed and leaned in until our noses touched, and his soft breath whispered into mine.

"No Andie. It *was* you."

And I felt the truth of what he said run from him to me as he leaned in and kissed me.

Tingles raced across my arms as I succumbed to the heady feeling of his love. It was all-consuming, and my soul knew his like none other.

I knew that with him by my side, I would be able to conquer anything.

∞

"Wake up, wake up!" Emric bounced on the bed near my head while Charlie used his wings to tickle my nose.

I groaned and rolled over, knocking them both from the bed.

Thuds from either side sounded along with groans and a few growls. Star shot me a nasty look at being disturbed before nestling back into the crook of my arm.

"Was that really necessary?" Emric grouched as he jumped back up.

"No. I'd say that the two of you waking me up like that was definitely not necessary." I frowned at the two of them sitting near my feet.

"I tried to tell him you wouldn't like it, but he insisted it was the most efficient way to wake you," Charlie said, his eyes sliding to Emric who frowned back at him.

"And you my feathered friend, were all for it at the time. Now look at you, being all meek and subservient now that you're in trouble."

Arguing ensued as I rolled from the bed and strode over to the window to look out. The sun had barely risen, and today was the day that I would sit down with the dignitaries to map out a plan.

I certainly wasn't looking forward to it.

Below me in the courtyard the fairies flew in streaks of color, zipping around quicker than my eyes could follow. They worked hard to please Aine, and I'd never heard one complain. I'd long since deduced that the quickness with which they worked was actually intentional. The sooner they got their duties out of the way, the sooner they could relax and enjoy the fruits of their labors.

A few days ago I'd slipped out of my room after finding a secret passageway behind a painting of Scotland. Well, Aine might have alluded to it when she'd first shown me the room, but I hadn't had time to look for it until now. And it was a rare moment indeed.

Most of the time, there was always someone with me. Be it Emric and Charlie, Star, or the fairies that were assigned to take care of my every need.

That day, everyone had left me alone for a few hours when I complained of a headache and needing total silence. Sometimes being the leader and having everyone do as you say *is* a good thing. I hadn't really felt bad, but I had needed time alone.

And the time was well spent once I'd entered the hidden corridor.

I had no idea where I was going when I first entered. But I wasn't scared at all, only curious. It was lit with magical candles, and despite being worried about spiderwebs or bugs, it had been totally clean. I pictured the spelled brooms and dusters sweeping through it while everyone slept, none the wiser.

The hall that I traversed hadn't been awfully long and ended at an elevator. *Yes, an elevator.*

The contraption was made of glass. As I stepped inside, the doors shut, and it slowly descended into the bowels of the castle. Excitement ran through me. At that moment, I'd felt normal again. Like the teenage girl who was just exploring a fantastic place. A bit of nervousness at getting caught added to the excitement.

When the elevator stopped, a cavernous room was laid out before me, and I observed all of the fairies that filled the room. Some drank, some danced. Others lounged on lily pads that floated on a crystal blue pool shimmering in the middle of the room.

Everywhere I looked, there was some magical form of fun for the fairies to partake in. Slides, separate buildings peeking out from the stone walls, with storefronts and cafés. It was if they had their own little town separated from everything else.

It made sense. If I were much smaller than I was and had to be around all the gigantic things and people in the castle above, I'd want a place that was fit for me too.

None of the fairies had spied me yet, and I didn't want to interrupt their peace and fun, so I'd pushed the up button and the doors quietly slid shut as I was ushered back upstairs.

Turning away from the window now, I knew that I still had so much to learn about the different factions and groups. So much I wanted to know about where they lived, how they lived. I hoped that they would let me help them any way that I could to make their lives a little easier, a little more peaceful.

"And that, my dear, is why I have so much faith in you." Celeste rounded the corner from my sitting room, beautiful as always and holding the crown that I had gently taken off last night and sat on a satin pillow.

I eyed it as she brought it closer. It was something out of a fantasy.

Made from silver that had been twisted into shapes of magical creatures from near and far. Little diamonds twinkled between the figures and along the metal, light gleamed and traced, back and forth.

"Is the light really moonbeams?" I asked my guardian, the one lady whose opinions and advice meant the most to me.

She walked closer and lifted her arms, setting it upon my head gently before arranging my hair around it.

"Yes. The moonbeams are a part of me, that I have given to you and only you. As long as you wear the crown, a part of my magic is always with you and at your disposal."

I was blown away by her gesture. I knew that it wasn't something that could be taken lightly. To have a goddess share her powers with me... it was unheard of.

"Celeste... I-I don't know what to say," I stammered, my heart in my throat as I stared into eyes that knew every little thing about me.

She ran her hands down my arms and grasped my own. "You don't need to say anything. I wanted to share it with you, to help you, in even this small way. You are the closest I will ever have to a child. I am not quite sure how you did it, but you've woven yourself into my heart and soul as surely as if we shared the same blood. You mean so much to me, sweet girl. So much to *so* many people, and you haven't any idea. That is what makes you special. You live your life how you want, but at the same time worry about everyone else more than you do yourself. You're magnetic, full of life, and that is what draws everyone to you. And you are kind. So kind in such a hateful world."

A tear slid down her cheek as she pulled me in.

"Don't let hate and darkness change you."

She held me tighter than she ever had before, her words sending a chill down my spine despite the beautiful speech she'd just given me.

Did she know? Did she realize that there was something dark within me that I fought daily?

I wanted to share my fears with someone, but I just wasn't ready to voice it yet. It was like a part of me felt that if I did, it would make it rise. It scared the hell out of me.

"Let's go down to breakfast. Maybe we'll be able to get some sweet cakes before all the shifters gobble them up." She smiled at me and led the way.

∞

WE DID INDEED GET SWEET cakes. I made sure to pile some fruit and eggs onto my plate as well. It would be a busy day, and I'd need all the sustenance I could get.

Once we'd had our fill, everyone else filtered into the large dining area set up for the guests, many of them bleary-eyed from staying up too late and enjoying the festivities. *Good.* Maybe that would make them more agreeable to some of the plans I would lay out.

A white peony landed in front of me where my plate had previously been. I glanced up to see Killian standing beside me. His grin was infectious, and I wondered momentarily where he had been last night.

"What's this for?" I picked up the flower and brought it to my face, the soft petals gliding over my cheek.

"It's a peace offering," he said with an abashed grin. "To apologize for not being there last night." He ducked his head, and it reminded me of when our group had first come upon the shy boy. I wondered what had caused him to be so embarrassed. I would have never been mad at him for something so silly.

"Thank you for the flower, Killian. But no worries about last night. Everything okay?"

I wouldn't press him, but I hoped that he would share.

He glanced at Celeste, and she quirked her eyebrow. "I'll let you two chat for a few minutes, but then we really need to get busy working with the other groups on our plan."

I agreed, and when she got up and left, Killian slid into her vacated seat and the cheery guy I knew was gone.

I leaned forward, my voice low as I took his nervousness and depression in. "Tell me what I can do."

He fiddled with the napkin that lay on the surface in front of him before sighing and rubbing his hand over his eyes.

"It's Presley. I'd hoped she would be here. When she didn't show up yesterday, I called her. She doesn't sound right, Andie. Something is wrong, but she wouldn't tell me. When I pressed her, she told me to mind my own business and hung up. I spent the rest of the evening trying to call her back. I left her a million voicemails until it said it was full and I couldn't leave anymore. And she wouldn't return any texts."

This was troubling, but I knew Presley hadn't been the same since everything that happened with Teagan. Worry had me biting my lip as I thought about her. I felt terrible that with everything going on, I hadn't reached out.

Trela and Bea had been sent on a mission to scout all the different areas in the United States where rumors had popped up of strange happenings. I wondered if I could persuade them to go to Presley and check on her.

My thoughts were interrupted as the Titans surrounded our table, their large bodies throwing shadows over us.

Hunter stayed silent, his gaze bouncing from Killian to me. I leaned forward once again, grasping that beautiful white flower, and I tapped him on the nose with it.

"I'll find out for you. Everything will be okay. I promise."

Relief filled his eyes and he nodded.

I stood and looked down at him. "Come on, let's go. You're going to be my right-hand man in this." I heard a scoff behind me and turned around.

"Hush. You've got all of me. Don't be jealous," I remarked saucily, my lips pursed. "Lead the way!"

He gave me one of those piercing looks that made the air sizzle between us, before turning abruptly to walk in front of me. I didn't pay any attention to where we were going, my eyes squarely on the fine figure in front of me. I rarely saw him in anything but suits these days, but honestly, I didn't mind. If anyone could make a suit look good, it was him.

I was hustled around in the little bubble for a while before we came to a door I hadn't seen before. Granted, I still hadn't been able to explore Aine's castle fully. There just hadn't been time. But now as the doors opened and my guards stepped to the side, wonder filled me.

Why? I don't really know. I'd seen so many fantastic things over the last year, that nothing should surprise me now. But this did.

We were in a medieval room, the walls made of thick gray stone and candles lit in every available nook and cranny. In the middle was a large round table. Think Templar Knights. That's what it reminded me of. Around it sat the heads of the different factions. On one side of the table, there was an aqua blue body of water set into the stone floor. And wildly enough, a few people lounged in it.

"Leaders of the Merfolk, Nymphs, and Naiads." Hunter leaned in as I studied them.

Right.

I wondered how many other creatures were out there that we would eventually call on to help? Hopefully, we wouldn't need to.

He escorted me to an empty seat, and I was delighted to find Coeus sitting beside me as Hunter faded into the background.

He leaned in close. "Ready to wow them darling?"

His charm never ended. And for this I was glad. He was one of the few people who could instantly put me in a better mood.

Aine spoke up from the other side of the table, commencing the first part of the meeting. We'd agreed that she would be the mediator since she was much more used to things like this than I.

"We're here to discuss the threats that loom against us and the rest of the world. As you all have been briefed, we believe Helios is behind all the evil that has begun happening around us. That he sent Freya and even the Fomori to do his bidding. And we fear it will only get worse now that Freya has been stripped of her power and locked away."

She nodded at me. Her cue for me to take over.

I folded my arms on the table and leaned forward.

"As Aine said, we believe that Helios is behind all of this madness. It's our belief that he intends to destroy the magical realm so he may preside over it and the human world. While everyone thought he was long gone, he's been plotting and planning, and there's no telling what he will do to make it happen."

One of the Warlocks began to interrupt me, and I held up a hand. "Please give me one more moment and then we'll discuss. I look forward to hearing your thoughts." I took a sip of the water in front of me.

"If you have doubts about our foe being Helios, I will bring forward the evidence that we found at one of the last sites of destruction by Freya." I motioned to the side, and my dad walked forward wearing the gloves the Titans had spelled to keep him safe from the glowing stone.

A collective gasp ran through the room as they caught sight of it. Some just from the sheer beauty and power that emanated from it. Some because they knew exactly what it was.

"If you don't know already, this is a stone from Helios's crown. The one that was destroyed and sent flying in pieces across the world.

I can only imagine that right now, he is searching for the others, as well as the Keys. Yes, we have three of the Keys and they are safeguarded, but I have no doubt that he will do whatever it takes to secure them all. We can't let that happen."

I looked sternly at them, hoping they felt the magnitude of this.

Some still looked a bit skeptical; some of them had fear plainly written on their faces.

"So, with that, I propose we split into groups and get to know one another, come up with ideas to keep our communities and people safe, and I welcome any suggestions on how to take him down."

Small tables and chairs were placed around the room while Killian and dad split everyone up into groups of five.

I found myself ushered over to the pool of water. There were chairs situated around it facing the leader of the Naiads, Merfolk, and Nymphs. One of the chairs had a pillow on it, I assumed for my comfort. Without hesitation, I picked it up and placed it on the stone floor and then sat on it as gracefully as possible while Aine sat in the chair beside me, looking bewildered. The three guests in the pool had the same look grace their faces at my actions, but those looks soon turned into approval.

I had hoped that they would see this as a gesture that I did not hold myself above them. That we really were one.

Luckily, it seemed to have panned out well.

For an hour, we had lively conversation. I started it out asking all about where they lived, their people and traditions. They shared their fears about Helios and how they could effectively help when they had to spend much of their time in water.

It seemed simple to me, and I stated as much.

"We have communities along the water that need protection and that some of us are unable to get to effectively. You have magic and power within you to fight for these places should he attack them. We also need you to keep the humans safe who travel on the seas and by it." I nodded as I thought aloud. "Yes, you are very needed and a huge part of keeping our worlds safe."

To see their eyes light up at my suggestions gave me such a great feeling.

When it was time to switch groups, I met the new leaders with a much more enthusiastic approach. This was going well.

After a few more hours of planning, we broke off for lunch, and I could feel Hunter's approval of how I was doing before he even got close to collect me.

I turned to him just as he was reaching for me, and-protocol be blasted-I threw my arms around his neck and stood on my tiptoes, kissing his check before squeezing him to me.

He laughed and the sound bounced off the rock walls. In my peripheral vision, I saw the others staring at us, but did I care? Nope, not one wit.

I was happy, and he was happy. It was normal for two people to hug each other and show their love. I felt like this world needed more of it. If I was breaking protocol, why then, I say it's about time someone did it. Maybe it would help the lot of them loosen up, much as our conversations did, and lead them to show as much love to the world around them.

I'd listened to Coeus, Celeste, and Aine tell me over the last year to never lose my light. To be the light for others. Well, here I was. *Being a light.*

For once the blackness inside me hadn't risen for one minute, and I thought that maybe if I concentrated on the light, the love and happiness around me, I could keep it down forever.

Hunter sighed into my hair and pulled back away from me. He smiled, but I could see the worry crinkling his eyes.

"I wish I could take you away from all of your worries forever."

God. I wish you could too. But for now, we had to fight for our lives to make sure we got to the point where he could.

He nodded, knowing my thoughts and Dad came up to us bearing two plates of food while Killian carried drinks.

"Here you go, lovebirds." He smirked as I stuck my tongue out at him. He put his hands up in the air once we'd relieved him of the plates. "Hey, I didn't say I had a problem with it." He leaned in and kissed my cheek before walking off to visit with Celeste.

"Your dad is really cool, Andie," Killian remarked as he watched him go.

"Yes, he definitely is." I took a bite out of the turkey sandwich and chewed it slowly before remembering Presley.

"Can you do me a huge favor?" I turned to Hunter as he wiped a napkin over his lips and nodded.

"Of course. Anything."

I smiled and put my hand on Killian's shoulder. "Can you get ahold of Trela and Bea and see if they can check on Pres for us? We're worried about her, and I just want to make sure she is okay."

Hunter glanced at Killian, taking in the worry that emanated from him before nodding. "Of course." He sat his plate down on the table and walked the short distance to Coeus, who walked over to take his place as he left the room.

Well, he didn't waste any time. I loved how he never questioned me and only wanted to make me happy.

"Well, what's that lad up to now?" Coeus asked.

"Oh, just an errand for me, but he shouldn't be long," I answered, not wanting to get into it and have him question Killian about Presley. I could tell by the look on the poor guy's face that the more he thought about her, the worse his thoughts on her safety became.

Lunch was soon over, and our groups resumed. I felt my happiness slip a little as my current group didn't seem quite as enthusiastic as the others had been. It consisted of several heads from the Wereshifter clans from the West Coast.

One in particular from Oregon seemed to be overly negative about everyone's suggestions, effectively setting a sour mood in the conversations. I tuned them out a little as my mind wandered to Hunter. Where was he? I would've thought he would be back by now.

"Don't you agree?"

I realized the question was directed at me, and embarrassed, I asked that they repeat what I was supposed to agree to. We were interrupted by a door slamming open, and the Titans immediately surrounded me. It was Hunter's father. His eyes frantically searched the room until they fell on me.

"Take me over to him," I demanded, and the Titans hesitated. "Now!" I exclaimed, and they leapt into action, shuffling me across the large room until I stood in front of him. Something was wrong. My heart sped up and felt as though it would beat out of my chest.

"Please move aside." I tapped the large back in front of me, and he immediately moved a few inches. Sighing, I squeezed through. I wasn't about to be hidden from their own friend's father. He wasn't a threat.

"What's wrong? What happened?" I demanded. He rushed to soothe me, his hands gently grasping my arms.

"I'm so sorry to worry you. It's not Hunter. He's fine but he sent me for you. He was able to get in touch with Trela and Bea, and well, they had news." Anger shot from his eyes. "And it wasn't good."

That immediately raised the hairs on the back of my neck, and I turned to the Titan I had just shoved out of the way.

"Please gather Aine, Celeste, and Coeus and have them meet us upstairs." I turned back to Hunter's father. "Shall we?"

And so much like his son, the corner of his mouth tilted up, and he put his hand on my back to guide the way with my guards following close behind.

Chapter Four

WE ENTERED ONE OF THE small offices on the main floor, and Hunter swiftly came to me. I could tell he'd been running his hands through his hair repeatedly, and I grabbed them tightly.

"Tell me."

He pulled me over to a settee, and we settled on it together with our knees touching as his father looked on.

"I talked to Trela and Bea. They're in Tennessee now and happened upon a small town in the mountains that was full of tourists." He gulped. "Well, as they scouted outside in the woods around the town, they noticed something strange happen. They called them shadows. Black, inky darkness that slipped into the buildings, and then the screams began."

He wiped his face with his hands before sitting back, his fists clenched. "They had no idea what they were. *I* have no idea what they were. But I could hear the screams over the phone. They were *that* loud. I told the girls to stay back, that we had no idea what we were dealing with. They don't have the means to help with that kind of thing, anyway."

I stared at him in horror. What kind of beings were these shadow things?

Celeste, Aine, and Coeus rushed into the room then, with dread heavy in their expressions.

No one sat down, and Celeste wrung her hands with worry, but she kept her shoulders back and strength emanated from her.

I took a deep breath.

"Does anyone know what these shadow things are that the girls saw?"

Coeus and Celeste glanced at each other, and Star snuggled closer around my neck, softly purring against my skin. She was comforting herself just as much as she was me.

"Naiads up north have been gossiping that there is a rift in the mountains in Washington State. That there have been strange creatures sighted around it. Frankly, up until now, I'd just brushed it aside thinking nothing of it. But ... I can't help wonder if somehow Helios has opened a portal and demons are slowly escaping," Celeste finished with a deep sigh.

I stared at her in shock. I could only imagine the expression on my face as I took what she said in. Of course, I'd realized that there were nightmare creatures out there besides just the Fae. The fire demon who made the deal with Teagan for the hellfire was proof enough.

Why hadn't I questioned him about where the demon had come from then?

A million thoughts ran through my head at once, and an instant headache bloomed.

A warm hand rubbed my back, and I leaned closer to Hunter, feeling his strength seep into me.

I knew he felt my shock pouring into him, as well and I suppressed it as quickly as I could before glancing up at him sheepishly.

"Sorry," I whispered.

He only squeezed my waist before turning to Coeus.

"I'd like permission to visit the Hall of Thrones. There's a particular book there that I think might give me some insight into what these shadows are, and how we might stop them."

Coeus nodded. "Permission granted. Let me know what you find."

Hunter once again glanced down at me before kissing the top of my head.

"I'll be back soon. Please stay with your guards when you're not in your room."

As if I had a choice. I'd never be able to get away from them unless I used one of the hidden passageways. Truthfully, right now I didn't think I would want to be without them.

"I will," I promised, hugging him tightly and then feeling a little lost as I watched him slip out the door.

Anxiety crept into me, and the feeling that I needed to do something to help figure this mystery out was strong. But my hands were tied here in Fairy.

The oak tree flashed through my mind, and I immediately knew what I had to do. It was as if the magical tree was calling to me. Flashes of a book seared my mind. I'd never seen it before, and I couldn't recall the room it was in, but I had no doubt it was there. I needed to go to it.

I turned to Celeste.

"I need to go home. There's a book at the Oak that I need to find. Please don't ask me how I know, because I honestly can't tell you, but I need to find it," I pleaded with her.

I could see her mind going a mile a minute, her eyebrow arched in a silent question, and Coeus's eyes were resolute as he stared at me. I knew what he was going to say, and I rushed to argue before he did.

"I'll take the Titans with me, though Balwyn is sure to grumble, but I will."

A smirk lit his face, likely amused that I was now the one reading minds. Well not really-I just knew them well enough by now to know what they were most likely thinking.

"Yes, you will, and we will go with you too. We can't take a risk with you, and Hunter would never forgive me if I weren't personally there for you." His eyes danced merrily as he crooked out his arm to Celeste. "Shall we go tell Aine and the others?"

She nodded at him as she wound her arm with his and looked back at me when they stepped out the door.

"Go grab Killian, Emric, and Charlie, would you dear? Looks like we'll be leaving soon."

It wasn't long before Star and I rushed into my room to find Emric sprawled out on the bed, all four of his paws sticking straight up in the air, and Charlie flew circles above him, dipping low and swinging back up before Emric's paws could reach out to strike him.

"I'm going to get you this time, you feathered beast!" Emric growled before realizing they had company.

"What on earth are you two doing?" I asked as I ran to change into jeans and a T-shirt.

Charlie flew down to land on the dresser in front of me while Star hopped down and joined Emric on the bed.

"Emric was bored and thought it would be fun to play a game. He wagered he'd catch me on the first swoop down that I made. He didn't. And then he said the second time he'd get me. And guess what?"

"He didn't," I answered, pulling my jeans on and sliding my feet into my converse.

Emric rolled over onto his belly when he realized what I was doing.

"No, I didn't. But I would've if you hadn't interrupted. Now where are you going dressed like that?"

Grabbing a hair tie, I pulled my hair into a low ponytail.

"Home. And you're both going with us. Come on, I'll tell you on the way." They peppered me with questions as I flew down the stairs, and I quickly answered them as best I could.

At the foot of the stairwell, my Titan guards, Rhea, Celeste, and Coeus waited, along with Killian, who looked excited to be leaving.

I greeted them all, and they formed their usual circle around me as the fairies flew through the foyer in a titer, chattering and watching us, no doubt wondering what was going on.

Before we'd even made it to the door, I heard murmuring, and two of the guards parted. I was afforded a glimpse of Aine before she sidled in beside me.

She leaned in and spoke quietly, "You didn't think I wasn't going too, did you?" She smiled up at me.

I chuckled because I felt like I knew the real reason and he was standing on the other side of me.

She and Coeus seemed to be around each other all the time now, and I hadn't missed their smiles and dreamy eyes whenever they were. It was about time they explored a relationship, and just the thought of the two of them together made me giddy.

Love wasn't something to waste, especially now. With all of the turmoil and unknowns that we faced; it was high time that we all lived like each day was the last. To love like we might lose it the next hour. Heck, even the next minute.

I would never take anyone I cared about for granted ever again.

We were ushered out into the courtyard where butterflies swarmed the air, and a soft breeze kissed my cheek.

Everyone grabbed hands and before I knew it we were sifting through time to my favorite place.

Please don't let Balwyn be mad at me...

The sound of our feet meeting the wood floor inside the tree was loud, and Balwyn came running.

Here, the Titans didn't need to flank me at every turn and the entire group spread out, looking around since they'd never been here before.

My eyes were strictly on the Brownie who stood outside his hidey hole, glaring daggers at me. I would've felt slightly ashamed of the way we'd barged in had he not been wearing a new nightcap that was hot pink with a purple pompom at the end. It could only be the work of Eira. I swallowed a giggle and tried to right my face to look apologetic. He only scowled more.

Star wasn't amused and hissed at him before jumping down to run into my old room.

I knew she missed being here, and I was sure right this moment she was making a little burrow in the quilt on my bed.

Eira landed on my shoulder, looking around wide-eyed.

"I wondered what that noise was. It scared the daylights out of me!" Her eyes scanned the tall warriors scattered around the room. "But I can't complain. Look at all this eye candy you brought me!" She clapped her hands and bounced up and down, and Balwyn scowled at her before turning around to return to his room.

"Ain't no candy there for ya. Only sour pickles."

I laughed, and she paid him no mind, fluttering back into the air to swoop around them all.

Celeste and Aine found me as the Titans decided to settle into the various chairs around the room.

"So where is this book, Andie?" Aine looked up at the expanse of floors above us.

"I'm really not sure. I didn't recognize the room. I was hoping Eira would be able to help me, but it looks like she's a little busy at the moment." I nodded to where she sat on Lelantos' knee, chatting up a storm, and he raptly listened. The look on his face was filled with fascination.

Turning away, I headed toward the stairs with Celeste and Aine following. We went up flight after flight, and the higher we went, a tugging feeling inside of me built. Somehow, I knew that it would guide me.

When I reached the ninth floor, a vision clouded my eyes. I was lucky that I had a hand on the rail because it knocked me back a step.

Leif looked back at me, a smile on her pale face, her red hair a cloud around her head.

"You'll find what you need inside the room filled with flowers. It is tucked away behind the lavender. Use it wisely. Guard the information from anyone that could use it nefariously."

She blew a kiss, and then I was staring at the wall in front of me.

Both Aine and Celeste had a hand on my back to steady me, concern lined their eyes as I looked back at them.

"It's okay. I'm okay." I took a deep breath and swung my gaze around before it landed on a doorway to my left that had white roses growing around the door frame.

I'd been to this floor many times, and I'd never seen that doorway before. I *knew* I hadn't.

Nothing in this tree should surprise me, though. I'd sworn the hallway with the bedrooms hadn't been there before either, but when we all needed a place to stay, *Poof*, there they were.

"Uh... I think this is where it is," I gestured to the door and took a step toward it. Sweet fragrance wafted out, and as I peeked inside, a magical garden greeted me. I couldn't see any walls. There was no ceiling, only a blue sky. I truly felt as if I had stepped into a different place.

Flowers of all different species grew around me, but I focused on finding one particular kind.

Lavender.

Celeste and Aine were quiet as they looked around but stayed close by. I pushed through a group of peonies and walked by canna lilies, dianthus, and passionflower vines. Behind the thick foliage, there was a cluster of lavender. Some of the flowers were dark purple and the others a lighter version. They grew around large gray rocks and I kneeled down in front of them, slowly reaching through the blooms. I searched gently, so as not to crush the delicate flowers.

My hand landed on a smooth surface. *This has to be it.*

I grasped gently and pulled it back. In my hands, I held a book. An incredibly old book by the looks of it. Tan with cryptic looking symbols etched into every inch, with power pulsing from it.

There was a soft gasp behind me, but I didn't pay it any mind. My hands ran over the cover, and even though I was eager to pore over the contents right now, I felt like I needed to leave this room at the same time. That tugging pulled at me again, and I stood up, grasping the book to my chest.

"This is it," I told both of the women who stared at me. There was something akin to horror in both of their eyes, but I dismissed it, walking around them to leave the room.

I knew they'd follow.

Down the stairs we went in silence. Killian was laughing as he played a game of checkers with Rhea who turned with a curious look as I descended to the bottom floor.

Turning to Celeste and Aine, I felt slightly detached and not really myself, but the tugging pulled me toward my room.

"I'm going to study this and see what I can find. But I need to be alone."

The horror had left their faces, worry replacing it.

Celeste began to say something, and I only turned and walked away.

Closing the door to my room, the tugging finally stopped. Heat spread across my chest where the book was nestled, and I felt a lick of darkness rise.

Why did I feel like this? I knew the book had something to do with it. I didn't really feel like myself, and how I'd treated Celeste and Aine wasn't normal either, but the book was calling.

Chapter Five

STAR NESTLED IN THE blankets at the foot of my bed and only squinted one eye at me before tucking her head back under her paw. I crawled onto the bed slowly so as to not jostle her. Leaning back against the pillows that rested on the headboard I pulled the book away from my chest and stared down at it.

The warmth on my skin dissipated, but my hands tingled. The symbols on the book were ones I had never seen before. They were archaic, and as I studied them, they swirled. The power from the book pulsed in my hand, and somehow I knew it was urging me to open it.

The darkness rose as I turned the first page, and a giddiness that I hadn't felt before ran through me. I tried to push it down, but it was as if my hands and body had a life of their own. My mind was still the same, but there was something else controlling me.

I watched from inside myself as my fingers moved the pages with in-human speed. Words and pictures flew by like one of those books I'd made in elementary school. The faster you turned the pages, the drawings came to life like a movie.

It was like that, but not. I felt the knowledge from the book being soaked into my soul, and the darkness inside me lapped it up.

Shudders rippled my shoulders. I was trapped inside myself and knew that the harder I pushed, all it would do was drain me. I had to ride it out and hope that once this was over, I would still be me.

Seconds later my hands stopped flipping the pages, yet I still wasn't able to move.

Star sat up, staring at me. Her eyes squinted, and the hair on her back rose. A low growl began deep in her throat.

My mouth opened, and a hiss sounded from it.

That only led Star to screech. Over and over again.

The darkness coiled inside of me like a snake about to strike, and I was powerless to do anything about it even though I tried. I tried *so* hard.

Footsteps pounded outside, and as the door was flung open, whatever it was finally released me.

I slumped forward, and my breath whooshed out.

"What's happened?" cried Aine as she rounded the bed and picked up Star, who now shook violently.

Celeste eased onto the bed, turning my body toward her. I vaguely realized that Killian and the Titans had all filtered into the small room behind her. They were veritably squashed inside, their big bodies taking up all of the available space.

My hands still clutched the book as Emric hopped up beside me, sniffing.

I still hadn't met their eyes, preferring to gather my wits about me. My mind furiously tried to catch up to what had just happened.

"Who's been in her with you, Andie?" Emric sniffed the book before recoiling backwards. "Whoever it was stinks to high heaven."

I shook my head. "No one. It's just been me and Star."

My eyes raised up to meet Celeste's, and I knew she read me. I knew I had to come clean about the darkness. If what had just happened was any indication of the road I was headed down, I wanted *no* part. And I needed help.

Her eyes softened as they stared into mine, but the concern didn't leave.

She pulled me into her embrace, running her hands over my hair as she spoke directly into my mind.

I knew something was wrong the moment you came back with the third Key. This darkness, it won't win. We'll figure out something.

And then I cried.

I let out every emotion I had suppressed for the last few months. I cried for the fear that consumed me. I couldn't let the darkness win.

I don't know how I knew, but if I let my guard down for one minute, it would take over. Helios had found a way to set up a Trojan horse.

And that horse is me.

Once my tears were dried and I was certain I didn't feel a lick of the darkness inside, I sat up and pulled out of her arms.

Aine and Coeus had long since shooed the Titans out of the room, only leaving Killian, Emric, and Charlie inside with us.

They all just sat staring at me, and I felt insecurity rise.

I knew I needed to tell them everything, so I started from the moment I had taken away Freya's power, and how I'd fought this alien feeling ever since.

Nothing bad had happened with it yet, but after holding the book and being trapped inside myself, I wasn't sure how much longer that would last.

Lelantos stuck his head inside the door, interrupting me as I told them about how quickly my hands had turned the pages.

"Hunter is on his way."

Coeus nodded sharply, and I groaned. He was going to be so mad to find out I hadn't confessed to him first.

Knowing our bond, he more than likely knew something was wrong long before now.

"Do you think whatever got inside you is the same thing that drove Freya to do everything she did?" Killian asked.

I had that thought many times, and after today I was almost certain of it.

"I hope not, but seeing as how she no longer has power, that I drained it all and took it inside of myself, it's the only thing that makes sense." I sighed and stood up, handing the book to Celeste as I did.

"Somehow, Helios poisoned her with it long ago, and I can only believe that was the driving force behind all of her madness. He used her, and now he's trying to use me too. And what a perfect way to do it." I growled as my fury at the situation rose.

The oiliness rose, and I quickly took deep breaths, thinking about Hunter and my dad.

My dad. Where is he? If ever I needed him it's now.

"He is on his way now too," Celeste said quietly to my unspoken question. She was still reading me, and for once I wasn't upset about it. I needed that kind of accountability now. What if this thing inside of me took over and I wasn't able to stop it? I needed someone to read me every minute of every day, so they'd know if that happened.

"Shhh... quiet your mind. You're letting your anxiety take over," Celeste soothed. "We will find a way to get this out of you, or at least control it. Don't despair."

I knew she was right. We'd overcome many challenges. This wasn't any different.

I nodded and squared my shoulders just as the door was opened and Hunter rushed in with dad right behind him.

His arms engulfed me, squeezing tight, and Dad smoothed my hair as he stood beside me, staring into my eyes as I rested my head on Hunter's shoulder.

"You're okay?" he questioned, concern making wrinkles in his forehead.

"Yes. I'm okay."

Celeste walked over to the three of us, placing a hand on both of their shoulders.

"Rather than make Andie relive everything again, I'll show you."

Both of their eyes closed as she filtered the information to them. It didn't take long before their eyes opened and they both stared at me, Dad with concern and Hunter with resignation. He had known something from the beginning, I knew he had, but he'd kept it inside and hadn't pushed. Now he knew the extent of it.

I worried that he'd be angry with me for keeping it from him.

His fingers reached for mine, sliding gently over them before grasping tightly. His veins lit up, and his eyes swirled as they looked into mine.

"*Never*. I might get frustrated, but I would never be angry with you over something like this. I'm frustrated that you took Freya's power into yourself and the result was this, but you did it thinking you were helping rid the world of her evil. You couldn't have known that it wasn't hers to begin with. That it would only transfer to you."

He kissed my forehead and looked around at our group.

"I think I found something that will give us some insight." He pulled out another book before pointing to the one that I held earlier. "But first, we need to figure out what that is and why Leif felt it would give you the answers you sought. Why would an Oracle want to feed the darkness?"

It was a good question, one I intended to find out. At my first opportunity I planned to visit Leif again and ask just that. But right now, I had to figure out how to get this evil inside me under control.

We convened in the main room, where Eira hovered over me and Balwyn pressed cookies into my hands.

"Ya need sugar. Tat's what ya need," he grumbled, fairly running back to bring a hot mug of cocoa to me. "And something warm. Tat'll get you right."

I stared at him with wide eyes, biting my lip to keep from laughing. It never failed that he would try to pamper me when he was worried.

"She doesn't need cookies and cocoa. What she needs is a hot bath and an exorcism!" Eira shouted back at him, twisting her hands and scowling. The two of them never disappointed with their bickering. I tuned them out and wondered about the exorcism, and if that was a real possibility.

"Don't mind them dear. Let's hear what Hunter found out, and then we'll decide what to do from here. We won't delay," Aine said, cutting off my visions of an evil entity being pulled from my body while visions of The Exorcist and pea soup flittered through my mind.

My body involuntarily shuddered. I hoped it didn't come to that.

Hunter and I sat side by side on one of the couches. It happened to be the one that he had spent many days on when I'd first brought him back.

Warmth from his thigh seeped into mine where they pressed together, and his arm hung loose around my shoulders. He unknowingly lent me strength through our bond and I soaked it up. Being near him was like sitting on the beach and the sun's rays seeping into your very soul, making everything feel warm, happy and as if all were right with the world. I never wanted him to leave my side.

"So the book I found is ancient. I'd remembered seeing it during my training and it stuck out to me. As you've found, finding anything on Helios is pretty difficult. But this book," he held it up to show everyone, "tells all and is pretty enlightening."

He flipped through a few pages until he came to the one he was looking for. "I didn't get to read all of it, but what I did read might offer some insight into the shadows and even this darkness inside Andie."

Everyone waited silently, eager to know what he found.

"Helios had always wanted to be worshipped by the Romans. When his job was passed on to Apollo, he felt slighted and angry. He was angry with the Titans, and that only grew after Zeus killed Helios's son, Phaethon. His flaming body was found in the river Eridanos by Helios and his daughters, then Phaethon was placed among the stars as a constellation. Helios fell into a deep depression, only to come back stronger, yet not the same. His mind was broken over the death of his son, and he lashed out at everyone around him. He met out punishments that he felt revenged the death of his son unrelentingly. It was then that Persephone, who felt betrayed by her husband

Hades, had Helios kidnapped." He looked around at us to make sure we were following, a peculiar look in his eyes.

"I'm sure you're wondering why Persephone took him away. Well, at that time she decided that she wanted to take over the mortal realm and cast the gods into a deep slumber. Before she was able to make this plan come to fruition, Helios was saved by Kratos, who defeated Persephone and chained Atlas to the world in the Pillar's place. Atlas had tried to destroy Helios's power and the Pillar of the World, so Kratos served him with his own kind of justice. After Kratos and Helios weakened Persephone, Kratos fell off of Helios's Chariot. He nearly hit a cliff when he fell, but he was saved by the gods. For whatever reason, probably power. Kratos and Helios fought off and on after that, and Kratos tried to find ways to get rid of Helios. Maybe he wanted his power, maybe he was jealous, who knows. The gods were always fickle creatures."

He stopped and took a sip of his drink, shaking his head.

"Anyway, much later, Kratos came upon Helios, who happened to be crushed in Perses' hand and then thrown into the city of Olympus. Warriors converged on the wounded Helios using their shields to protect him from Kratos. They were no match for him, though. He used a cyclops to batter their defenses and then ripped out the cyclops's eye socket, killing it. Helios pleaded for his life, reminding Kratos of how he once saved him from Atlas. Kratos didn't care. He wanted the Flame of Olympus, to kill Zeus. They then fought, and Kratos ripped off Helios's head, severing it. As you know, Kratos would then use Helios's head to discover secrets, blind enemies and unlock new paths throughout Olympus as well as the underworld. Later, his body and head were found in Tartarus, where the Titans thought he remained. Until now."

Hunter flipped a few more pages, his finger lingering on a passage that was in bold lettering and stood out on the page.

"And this… this is what I found most interesting." He shook his head. "Here it states that while in Tartarus, he befriended Hades, the king of the underworld. He made a pact with him, that if Hades helped him escape and helped him take over and rise to power, he would help open up the underworld. He would provide a means for the creatures that Hades lorded over to run rampant through our world. To feast on the blood of magic and man alike."

He scoffed, closing the book while the passage's words clicked in the rest of our minds. Helios had help-he had an evil god with all of their powers combined, working to open up our world to creatures that had never before seen the light of day.

And the shadows? They had to be from the underworld. But where had they been let out from?

Dad mirrored my thoughts aloud. "There must be an opening somewhere, and those shadows that killed everyone in the town, are the first wave. There's no telling what else has been loosed in the world."

Shivers ran down my arms, and a sense of dread filled me.

Everyone in the room looked at me. I knew they were waiting. Just because I had issues of my own didn't mean that my title as their leader was taken away. I needed to delegate. They waited for me to do so.

Leaning forward, I grabbed a cookie off the plate that I had left untouched and chewed it slowly, thinking.

I could feel the collective breath that was held around me, but I needed to make sure we started with a strong front. That the orders I was about to give were what would be right for not only the magical world, but the human one as well.

I brushed crumbs off my shirt and watched as they fell to the floor where Star lapped them up eagerly.

It was now or never.

I sat up straight and looked each of them in the eye as I assigned the tasks.

"Celeste and Dad. I need you to gather with the covens and shifter packs. I want them to split their groups up. There always needs to be witches and warlocks interwoven with the packs and vice versa. The coven members need to put up spells around their communities and hold it. Even if they have to take turns to rest. A shield must be up all the time. Some of these groups are going to have to go out and do the same around cities and towns in the human communities. They must *all* be protected. If we don't have enough group members to spread out around the world, then they must plead with the others in the magical communities to help. Naiads, Merfolk, and anyone else. We need them all."

I turned to the Titans. "I need half of you to stay with me, and the other half to plead your case with your friends and check out the rumor that there's an opening in Washington State. I cannot stress enough how much we need you all. I've been apprised of the rules, but in this case, you must get together and decide which is more important. Staying out of this, potentially losing all that is around you, and maybe being cast into Tartarus yourself? Or putting it aside to work with us to keep our worlds from burning. *We. Need. You.*"

I grit my teeth as everything rebelled in me to ask this of them. Rhea had told me they felt physical pain by going against their rule of law. But surely somehow they could bypass it.

I couldn't worry about it now; I knew they'd figure it out.

Looking at Hunter, Killian, and Coeus, I took a strained breath. My throat felt like a ball was stuck in it, but I forced it away.

"You're with me. We're going to visit Leif, then plead our case with the trolls."

I gestured to Star and she ran up to curl around my neck.

"I'm getting dressed. Balwyn, please get our packs ready," I called as I walked toward my room.

I put on my suit, and while I'd come to hate it before finding the third Key, this time it felt like an old friend. Comforting and warm. I thought about the background information that Hunter had given us on Helios and it was then that I remembered the stone that we found from his crown.

The Titans had said that only someone with his power in them could touch it. Well, wasn't that now me since Freya's power was transferred? I knew without a doubt that the darkness inside of me was given from him to her and now to me.

I would be able to hold the stone in my hand. Maybe even harness its power to help destroy him.

As I walked back into the main room to a flurry of activity, the other stones that were still missing from the crown crossed my mind.

"We need to find the other stones."

Hunter's head lifted from the pack he held, curiosity lighting his dark eyes.

"Stones?"

I went on to explain to him what I had figured out about the green stone that we found, and how we needed to find the others before Helios did.

"I'm not sure having all the stones together right now is a good idea," he said, a frown pulling his gorgeous lips down.

"But that might just be how we can end all of this," I pressed. Coeus just shook his head. He wasn't convinced.

"And that *might* just be how he can take over you fully. Who knows what those blasted stones will do once you have them in your hands?" Emric scowled as he jumped to the table beside me.

"We don't even know yet what is inside of you. Let alone how it would react to the stones. Nope. Fat chance."

I couldn't believe it. No one seemed to think it was a sound idea. Yes, I understood their concern about the darkness, but I felt it in my bones that the key to ridding the world of Helios-and maybe even Hades, now that we knew he was involved-was the stones.

I decided to give in for now. But the argument wasn't over.

"Fine. For now, we'll get our plans in place, and depending on what Leif tells me, we will or will not find the stones. Does that satisfy you?" I asked the group with a huff.

Hunter just smiled with satisfaction.

I'd let him think he won this argument. But it was far from over.

"Right. Well, let's find Leif."

And with that we headed upstairs to the portal room.

We traveled one at a time through the same portal that Trela, Bea, and I took. Nothing had changed. The tropical oasis surrounded us, and I looked through the trees, waiting to see Leif perched high on a limb like last time.

She wasn't there.

It didn't surprise me. From my encounter with her before, it was always on her time. Not mine. She appeared where she wanted when she needed to impart some great knowledge to me.

Come on, Leif. I need that knowledge now!

I hoped that somehow putting that need out in my thoughts might call her to me, but unfortunately it didn't.

I wouldn't give up, though.

Hunter, Coeus, Emric, and Charlie stood with me in the green vegetation.

"I guess we're going to have to see if we can find her. I'm not sure where to go, but we might as well get started."

Hunter insisted on leading. He hadn't hung up his guard hat, and honestly, I wasn't upset. I got the best view in front of me as we walked.

He snorted.

"It's the truth!" I replied merrily.

We walked and walked. After a while, I just enjoyed the sights. Waterfalls and gentle running streams. Flowers of every shape and size nestled amongst the bottom of the tall trees. I imagined this is what the forest behind Celeste's home had been like when the Fae lived there and called it their home.

Peaceful and full of beauty.

A particular flower caught my eye. It looked like a bright orange balloon; the petals gently peeled back from the ball on the inside. I strayed from the path to inspect it, and just as I bent down, a hand shot out from above me, grabbing my shoulder.

"Argh!" I yelled, startled, before jumping backward as a body slid out of the tree.

Curly red hair blew in the wind, and those clear blue eyes stared unblinkingly into mine.

"You do not get near a crane flower. It is a carnivore, stinging its unsuspecting prey before consuming their flesh."

Yeah, I did not want my end coming from an innocuous flower.

"Leif! Where have you been?"

She tsked and frowned at me, waiting.

"Uh... thank you for saving me from the flower. Now, please... I need your help."

She smiled brightly and took my hand.

"Come, we will talk."

My group stared at the naked Oracle. I couldn't blame them. I'm certain I had done the same the first time I met her. She was ethereal and also completely oblivious to the reactions of those around her.

That or simply good at ignoring them.

She led me behind the large tree she had been in, and through the thick vegetation with the group following.

Not far from where we had been, we emerged into a clearing where a hut made out of twigs and branches sat. Vines grew up and over the top.

It wasn't what I imagined the Oracle would live in. Small and rather unimpressive.

"Why would I need anything other than this?" She lifted an eyebrow as she ushered us inside, where it was just as sparse and empty.

There were a few pillows on the floor, and plants grew in the corner, but there was nothing else.

She gestured to the pillows and I sat while the others elected to stand.

Sitting on the pillow in front of me, her long curly hair obscured her nakedness. Like before she leaned in and took both of my hands in hers.

"Ask your questions."

Her gaze bore into mine, and seriousness lined her face.

"Well, first, why did you want me to find that book if all it would do was bring up the darkness and feed it?"

She looked down at our hands where they were joined.

"The darkness must know what is in the book. You would not have been able to read the language without it. While it may have been the most unconventional method, that knowledge that it took in, is also inside you."

I began to protest but the look she gave me was fierce and shut me up.

"You will not be rid of the darkness until you rid the world of Helios and Hades. That is a fact, and one you must accept."

I heard shuffling behind me at her words but ignored it. I needed the truth if I was to be ready for all that was to come.

"You can fight the darkness, though it will be difficult. I cannot give you hope that there won't be times you fall prey to it. All you can do is lean on your friends to support you and work on keeping it suppressed as much as possible. But... there will come a time when you will be thankful for the black-as-night evil that resides in you. You can use it to your advantage."

Murmurs rose up in my group, but again I ignored them and so did Leif.

"What other questions do you have?"

"The stones from Helios's crown, I want to find them and unite them together. I believe that we can use them against him. Is that true?"

She nodded slightly, and her lip quirked up as her attention went behind me.

Her eyes did not move from whoever she looked at as she responded.

"It is true that they can be used against him, yes. But you also have to be careful, once they are united and in your hands, that the darkness doesn't feed off of the jewels. It will want them, and revel in their power. It can be done, but you must be strong."

She lifted her shoulder in a shrug as she let my hands go.

While she hadn't given me information that I was particularly happy with, she gave me information that would prepare me for the future.

A future of constantly fighting the evil inside.

I have to get rid of Helios. I just have to.

Hunter and Coeus were quiet as we left Leif in her hut. Emric and Charlie bickered nonstop about where they suspected the remaining stones from Helios's crown were.

The mood that surrounded us was thick with uncertainty.

"Who could've thought the nerdy girl from last year would be pegged to find the four Keys, become leader of the Fae, and filled with an ancient evil all at the same time?" I joked, trying to lighten the mood.

Hunter only gave me a stern look while Coeus ignored me.

Emric picked up on it, silly creature that he was. "Yes, and potentially holds the worlds future in her own hands. Crazy." He laughed, but his words hit home and settled like a pit in my stomach.

I held the future of the world in my hands.
I didn't think it could be any worse.

Chapter Six

WE SIFTED TO THE CAVE where the trolls resided. Though I'd been blindfolded the last time I was here, I felt certain I could find them.

We landed in the same big cavern as before, and I looked over at Hunter. "You're going to have to let me lead this time. The tunnels are small, and I think I know how to get there. Plus, Tinock trusts me. The rest of you? Probably not so much."

He didn't argue but was quick to tell me that if something happened, I should duck so he could jump over me and kill whatever threat lay ahead.

I loved his alpha tendencies.

The tunnels were dark. Twisting and turning, I followed the inner guidance and intuition of the path my feet had previously taken.

We rounded into a large cavern where guards stood at alert around the walls. At the sight of us, they jumped into action, their swords pointed dangerously at us.

I held up my hands.

"I'm Andie, and I'm here to see Tinock. I helped cure his wife from an illness not long ago. We are here in peace. Will you allow us access?"

The guards looked at each other skeptically before one of them went inside the door he guarded, shutting it behind him. The air around us was tense as the other guards kept their weapons trained on us.

Soon the guard came back and nodded to the others, who lowered their weapons.

"Come. He will see you."

We filed in behind him with another guard at our backs. The room inside had tunnels carved into rock that led in different directions. Trolls of various sizes and genders walked from one tunnel to another. It was like a town underground and these tunnels connected homes and who knew what else.

We were herded through the one directly in front of us, and a door was flung open halfway down the tunnel. Tinock emerged with happiness etched on his craggy face.

"Andie! Come, come. Wha a pleasant surprise. And yer friends are welcome ta enter too. Kalie is inside and excited ta meet ya under better circumstances."

I stopped in front of him, amazed at his change in attitude. *Where had the grumpy, rude troll gone? Had saving Kalie been the key to winning him over?*

He smiled again, his nasty teeth blaring in my face, and I realized that must be the case.

It still amazed me that he was married to her. She was so different than him.

My diplomatic training kicked in as I addressed him.

"Thanks, Tinock, for your warm welcome. I'm grateful for it and the chance to meet with Kalie again as well."

He waved us inside and the interior of his home was cozy, and somehow plants grew without sunlight. A strange feeling was in the air, but I ignored it and focused on the person in front of me that rested in a chair.

Kalie.

Her eyes lit up when I came into view, and she threw off the knitted blanket that rested on her legs, standing to greet me with a wide smile.

I stood before her and noted that she looked whole and well, much better than she had when I'd left her last.

Smiling, I gestured toward her body.

"Well, it seems that you've healed well and are doing much better than before. I hope you've not had any lingering side effects?"

She chuckled and reached for my hands, squeezing softly.

"Not a one, all thanks to you. I seriously imagined that I wasn't going to make it that day. But, thanks to you, I did. And I am much better for it."

She let my hands go and turned toward the sitting area.

"Dear, don't hover. I am sure you've got plenty to keep you busy. I'd like to have a chat with Andie, and I know it's nothing you'd be interested in. You know, girl talk. Why don't you take these guys and show them your war room?"

She smiled sweetly at her husband as we sat together on the surprisingly comfortable and beautiful hand-carved chairs.

He looked uncertain, but she shooed him and the others out the door with a flick of her hand. She had him wrapped around her fingers, it seemed. That in itself was an amazing feat.

"Now," she turned back toward me, with bright eyes, "we can talk freely. Not that I have anything to hide from Tinock. It's just there are some things he doesn't need to know."

Her eyes twinkled mischievously.

"Oh? And what is that?" I asked, hesitantly. I wasn't sure that it was something I wanted to know. Whenever a conversation started out like that, nothing good followed.

Her laugh tinkled through the air, and she shook her head.

"No, hun, I promise it's nothing bad. In fact, I think it's some information that will help."

I studied her face, not seeing any hint that she was lying.

"How do you know what I was thinking?"

Is she another person who can read my mind? I had to be careful who I let my walls down with these days.

"Oh no, not at all. The question was written all over your face. You really need to learn how to school your features."

She smiled gently as I tilted my head in acknowledgment.

"Yes, seems I *do* need to work on that." I grimaced.

"No need to worry about that here, Andie. I'm a friend, and I want you to know that you can confide in me. I actually knew your Mom once, a long time ago. We met when she and Celeste were traveling the world, and I have to say, we became fast friends."

Her eyes took on a distant and sad look, and my stomach clenched. There was so much I never had the chance to know about Mom. Any time I met someone who knew her, a feeling of sadness and regret always swept over me, along with excitement and eagerness to know more about her through them. It was a strange feeling.

"We won't have long before your friends and Tinock rejoin us, but I need to tell you about something Selene and I found once on our explorations. I've kept it hidden away for some time. Well, Selene actually told me to hide it, from anyone and everyone, and when the time was right, I would know."

Curiosity stirred within me. Somehow, my mom seemed to always have had the foresight of what might occur in the future, what I would need. I vaguely wondered if she had been a seer too. It made sense really.

I leaned forward eager to know more.

"What is it, Kalie?"

She stood and walked to a small bronze chest that sat against the wall with different colored quilts folded on top of it. Removing those, she drew out a key on a silver chain from inside her top and reached down to unlock the container.

The hinges squeaked as she pulled the lid up.

"Come here and see for yourself." She motioned for me.

I walked over and stared into the small box. There were beautiful fabrics folded inside, and a violet pouch lay on top with a silver string wrapped tightly around it.

"What am I looking at?" Bewilderment settled in. Surely she didn't think fabric and a pouch had any significance.

"The pouch there on top contains something that I've heard through the gossip vine is something that you need. Well, one of them anyway. You can take the contents out but be careful. I've got the stone wrapped thoroughly. You don't want to touch it."

The stone?

She had to be talking about one of the stones that had been lost from Helios's crown!

I clasped the pouch in my hand and walked back to the chair. Sitting down, I laid the pouch on my lap, gently pulling at the tiny silver string. It came away easily and gauzy fabric inside spilled out.

I pulled on it slowly, and Kalie was right, it had been wrapped well, but I could see the stone inside the fabric. It pulsed with purple light, much like the green one had. Its power sizzled and seeped into my veins. It wasn't an uncomfortable feeling. Warmth and a sense of acknowledgment came from the stone. As if it recognized me.

I knew then that I would be able to touch it. That I could handle it and it wouldn't hurt me.

Because I had Helios's power inside me.

Because I'd taken it from Freya into myself.

I shuddered at the realization. Even though I had long suspected the darkness was from him, I couldn't hide from it any longer.

Shaking off the slimy feelings that rose within, I unwrapped the package to reveal the stone. It was beautiful, and as I reached out and ran my finger over it, Kalie gasped.

"Don't worry. It won't hurt me," I soothed, but never took my eyes from it.

She quieted, and I could feel her gaze on me.

The stone pulled me to it. It soothed me. But I knew I needed to explain to her before she ran out and got the others.

It was hard to pull my gaze from it, and with great difficulty I turned my face to look at her, while still touching the stone.

Her eyes held worry and disbelief. Her lip trembled.

"Somehow, when I took Freya's power, which you've no doubt also heard about, I gained some of Helios's power. That's the only way I can touch it."

Her eyes widened, but she didn't say a word.

"I didn't realize Freya had been carrying around his power all this time. That it was him working through her to do so much evil. But it wasn't long after that I began to feel this darkness inside of me."

I bit my lip and looked back at the stone. Sympathy and fear warred in her eyes, and I couldn't handle seeing it as I told my story.

"I tried to ignore it at first, hoping beyond hope that it was a bad dream, or a side effect from her nastiness... But it wasn't."

I hesitated. I hadn't even described all of this in so much detail to Hunter or Celeste. I just felt a need to get it all out now. Kalie seemed so genuine. She seemed liked someone I could pour everything out to. So, I did.

"It's a slimy, oily darkness. It's everything evil and horrible. And it's stuck inside of me. When I get upset or angry, it rises up like an alien, taking over my body and my mind."

I turned back to her.

"And it scares me."

Sometime when I was speaking, she had settled her shoulders and back ramrod straight. Her mouth was set in a thin line, but her eyes told me that she was taking in everything that I said.

She reached for my hand and grasped it tightly. "Go on. I know there's more. I promise, I'm here for you just like you were for me."

Strength oozed from her into me.

I swallowed thickly and continued.

"I'm so worried that something will happen, and I won't be able to control it. That Helios will find a way to use me to do something awful. I couldn't handle that. I *have* to find a way to get rid of this power. But honestly, I have no idea how, and so far no one else has figured it out either."

I quickly wrapped the stone back up and shoved it into the pouch, tying the string tightly.

"Maybe you should look at the bright side," Kalie said, and I snapped my gaze back to hers.

She held her hands up. "Hear me out."

She stood and began pacing in front of me, her hands stuffed into her pockets as she marched back and forth.

"Obviously, the stones recognize his power inside of you. And you need the stones to help defeat him, correct?"

I nodded.

"You felt something when you entered this chamber- I could see it in your eyes. What if you're able to feel the other stones that you need? What if they call to you? Without this darkness inside you, you'd never know where they were. You wouldn't be able to handle them to use in taking him out."

She stopped and looked down at me. "That is why this could be a positive thing."

What she said made sense, and hope bloomed inside of me.

"And, when this is all over, I may know someone who just might be able to take the power from you and get rid of it once and for all."

I sat up straighter, focused on her even more.

"Who could take this from me?" I breathed deeply and my heart sped up.

"Let's just say it's someone who owes me a favor and leave it at that for now."

She winked and turned toward the door just as Tinock and my group walked in.

Disappointment filled me. I wanted to know who it was, but obviously our conversation was over.

Kalie and Tinock led us to their dining room, where everyone sat at a large table, and Tinock's servants placed a rich soup in front of us for dinner. I barely tasted it.

The conversation around me flowed freely. They all discussed what was happening with Helios, the Fomori, and possibly Hades. Tinock agreed to help anyway that he could, even if it were a bit reluctantly.

I hardly touched my food and stayed silent as my thoughts were on the stones. *Who could this mystery person be that Kalie spoke of? And how could they rid me of this evil when no one else could?*

Once everyone had their fill, and the talk had all dwindled, we sifted back to the Oak.

Eira and Balwyn waited for us as if they knew we would arrive at any moment.

While the guys told them about our visit with Tinock and Leif, I went to my room with Star snuggled around my neck. The quiet of my space soothed me, but still I put my earbuds in and turned up my music as I laid down. I needed to get the rambling thoughts out of my head, and the only way I knew how to do that was to go to sleep.

Mountains were on fire around me, and red glowed from cracks that had opened. If anywhere could look like hell, this place fit the bill.

Ungodly sounds met my ears from above and around me. The sky was dark and the glow from fire lit up the night and the creatures that soared above.

Pterodactyl-like things, with webbed wings and sharp beaks, soared through the clouds, blocking out the stars that twinkled behind them.

A shiver ran over my spine as a crashing noise came from the surrounding trees. Demons with red and gold eyes stumbled out, their bodies roped with chains that dragged behind them. There were thousands of them. And they all had their sights on me.

"Andie. Andie, wake up, sweet girl."

A soft hand brushed my cheek over and over, and I felt sweat soaking through my clothes.

I hadn't had a nightmare like that in a while, and I shuddered as I remembered it.

Squeezing my eyes tight, I willed the visions still stuck in my head to go away and prayed that it wasn't something that would come to pass.

"You had a vision, didn't you?" Celeste's soothing voice matched her hand as I felt warmth enter me.

I grasped her hand and held it to my cheek, my eyes still closed, just basking in the love that I had for her. I'd only known her a little over a year, but she showed me love, strength and resiliency.

"If I haven't told you before. Thank you."

I sighed and opened my eyes as she leaned down and kissed my forehead.

"Whatever for?" She laughed as she moved back so that I could sit up.

I shrugged. "For being here whenever I need you. For showing me how to be strong and giving me the love that I needed. For being tough on me, and hanging in there with me, even when I was a brat."

A tear leaked out the side of my eye and down my cheek, and I swiped it away.

She smiled at me, cupping my cheek, her brilliant eyes sparkling.

"It is one of the greatest pleasures this life has given me. I knew this day would come when you would be here with me, but I had never imagined the joy you would bring. So really, it is I that should be thanking you. It proves that this universe can still surprise us all with goodness. Even an age-old goddess like me."

Her lips tilted up in amusement.

"Since you're awake now, how about we have a cup of tea?"

Chapter Seven

WE SETTLED AT THE TABLE where two cups of steaming green tea sat waiting. Rhea and the Titans were already up and reclined on the couches and chairs around us, some of them with curious stares as we sat down. Though Rhea gave me a gentle smile before turning to study one of the fairy paintings on the wall.

Hunter wasn't among them, and I didn't feel his presence in the tree.

"Where's Hunter?" I asked, taking a deep breath to quell the anxiety at his absence that seemed to rise lately.

Celeste smiled, taking a sip of her tea. "Since Trela and Bea hadn't yet had a chance to go to Presley like you wanted, he took it upon himself. He knew that you were worried and felt the need to take one less thing off of your plate."

Warmth curled inside me. Who would have thought a year ago that he would be such a softie?

Celeste nodded toward the fireplace, where Killian stood talking to Lelantos. "Plus, he cares for that one, though he'd never let it show. He hopes to get information that will ease his mind as well."

I hoped he did too. Presley and Killian were my friends, and I hated to see them hurting. I only hoped that Pres wasn't hurting because of Teagan. Because that would not help Killian feel better at all.

Balwyn trudged out of his space in the wall, holding a tray bigger than he was. It was filled with plates bearing eggs, sausage, and pancakes. The smell made my stomach growl, and in the quiet, he must have heard it because he made sure to serve me first.

He set the plate down with a disdain that was just so Balwyn.

Staring at my stomach and then back into my eyes he grimaced when another loud rumble sounded.

"If ya don start eatin' more, I's gonna have to make Eira put a fattinin' up spell on ya. Now eat!"

He trudged across the room and fairly shoved the other plates at the Titans and Killian, grumbling the entire time.

He was still salty about me bringing them here.

"So, tell me about your vision."

Celeste's voice pulled me from watching the others, and I shivered at the remembrance of the dream.

"It was just awful." I ran my hand over my face and sat my fork down. I'd eat, but not until I didn't have to think about the awful creatures I'd seen.

"I was somewhere in the mountains, and everything was red. Like a volcano had erupted, but it wasn't that. There were huge cracks in the ground and mountains around me. And there were these things... flying in the air and making horrible noises. They looked like pterodactyls, and then other creatures came from the forests all around me, with chains wrapped around them."

I described the creatures in detail because it was burned into my brain. By that time, the conversations around us had stopped and I knew everyone was listening intently, and Coeus had come to stand behind Celeste with his hand on her shoulder.

Neither of them showed fear, but their bodies were tense, and that was enough to let me know that they were on edge from what I told them.

"Well now. That is a horrible vision, one that we'll work extremely hard to not let come to pass." Celeste tried to school her voice in a positive light, but there was an edge to it too.

Coeus was quiet but quickly smiled down at me, his eyes mischievous and I knew he was up to something.

"I know just the thing to perk up this sobering talk!" he said jovially.

I quirked my eyebrow up at him as I shoved some of the pancake I'd smothered with syrup into my mouth.

His smile grew wider, and he threw out his arms, exclaiming to the room, "Aine and I are going on a date!"

I choked on the bite I had been in the process of swallowing, and Killian hurried to pound on my back as I sputtered and spewed.

Coeus looked on, and I was happy to see embarrassment color his cheeks pink. I'd never seen him embarrassed the entire time I had known him. It was nice to see that he was human. Well, showed human emotion anyway.

I was so happy for him and Aine. Even though I'd known something was going on, they'd always kept it hidden. The fact that he was willing to announce it to us all-and the timing of it-wasn't beyond my notice.

He'd chosen this moment to get my mind off of the vision. And I was grateful. Even if he'd made me almost die from choking.

I jumped up and threw my arms around him, hugging him tightly.

"Thank you," I whispered to him. "I needed that news."

I pulled back and looked into his eyes, teasingly. "Can I plan the date for you?"

His eyes flashed uncertainty, and I could see his mind going a mile a minute.

"Uh... I'm not sure how Aine will feel about that, but I'll take it into consideration." He cleared his throat, his cheeks turning pink again.

"She doesn't know you were going to tell us, does she?" I laughed, quickly catching on.

His cheeks turned even duskier, and I was reminded of a much more fit Santa Claus.

I looked around the room, and everyone bit their lips to keep from laughing at his predicament. I wouldn't want to be on the receiving end of Aine's wrath if she got upset that he told us.

I took pity on him and looked at everyone sternly, trying ridiculously hard not to smile.

"This is not to leave this room. It's a secret that Coeus told us all in confidence, and when and only when, he gives us the okay, will we acknowledge their relationship."

I looked at Coeus and saw relief flow across his face. "Will that work?"

He nodded quickly, sheepishly smiling.

"I, uh... may have jumped the gun a bit. Thanks for your discretion."

His demeanor amused me, and I only nodded. It was the least I could do after everything he had done for me.

Speaking of dates, it was high time Hunter and I went on one. Just when, in all this madness, was the question.

He had hinted at it several times, but there was always something that came up. We'd have to steal moments in the craziness that surrounded us to have one.

There was still so much to learn about each other. Our relationship was far from normal, that was for sure. The events of the past year had pulled us together so much quicker than even I could expect. Emotions ran high, and if it taught me anything, it was to not waste time. Life is fragile, and we could lose each other at any moment. I wanted to make those moments count.

My heart ached a little, and I rubbed my fist over it as Celeste gave me a knowing look.

"He'll be back before you know it. And hopefully with good news."

I sure hoped so. I didn't think I'd ever get used to this feeling of loss when he was away.

While we waited, Rhea challenged me to a game of checkers. I hadn't played that in forever, and as we moved the pieces across the board, my mind settled and focused on the challenge. She beat me the first two games, but I whooped loudly when I finally won the last game.

She smiled, her brow raised, and I couldn't decide if she'd let me, or if I'd genuinely won.

I didn't have long to think on it as a breeze blew my hair around my face, and I looked up to see Hunter and Presley sifting in.

Shock ran through my veins at the girl who stood beside him. Her blonde hair hung limply, and dark shadows lined the skin under her eyes.

I ran to them immediately. My eyes skimmed over Hunter, taking stock that he was fine.

My hands landed on Presley's shoulders, and I squeezed softly before pulling her body into mine. I hadn't missed the haunted look in her eyes or the whimper as she trembled in my arms.

"Pres, it's okay. It's going to be okay."

I didn't know what happened, or why she seemed to be just a shell of my friend, but I'd get to the bottom of it. I'd make it better if I could.

Killian hovered behind her. Uncertainty and longing made his eyes dark as he stared at the back of her head. His fists clenched and it was clear that he was physically holding himself back from rushing to her.

I pulled back from her slowly and her chin raised, her eyes meeting mine.

"I'm sorry. I'm so sorry," her lip trembled as she spoke.

I smoothed an errant piece of hair that stuck out above her ear.

"Shhh. There's absolutely nothing to be sorry for."

Grabbing her hand, I ignored the stares of everyone around us and pulled her to the sofa. I pulled the blanket that rested on the back around her shoulders, and she held it tight.

Balwyn quietly brought her a cup of tea, his usually grumpy demeanor was gone, and instead he softly patted her knee before disappearing back inside his hidey hole.

I angled myself where my knee touched hers, hoping to lend her some warmth and strength.

I could feel the others focused on us, but I ignored them and spoke to her as if we were the only ones in the room.

"Can you tell me what happened, Pres? I want to help," I asked her.

Her eyes met mind before skittering off to the side where Hunter stood.

"Hunter can tell you. I don't think I can repeat it all again."

The mug in her hand shook and hot tea slopped out to land on her skin, but she didn't even wince.

I wouldn't give Hunter a moment to speak. She needed to tell me. If she didn't, I felt that she would continue to pull into this shell that she'd built around herself. This wasn't the Pres I knew. Not at all.

I made sure to put some extra strength into my voice, she needed that more now that she did softness.

"Pres, you can tell me. I don't want Hunter to. I *need* to hear it from you. Go on now."

I reached for her hands, but she continued to grip the blanket, so I just laid my warm ones over hers.

I held my breath, as did everyone else in the room as she stared down at our hands.

It seemed like forever before she finally spoke, her voice like a knife in the quiet.

"I tried to help him. I thought I could make him better. He would talk to the walls, and his face would change. Like he was fighting some monster inside of him. I could tell he was physically hurting."

She took a deep breath and looked up at me.

"I'm afraid Teagan is lost to us. Whatever it is that's taken him over is evil, Andie. Plain evil. For the longest time he fought it, I could tell he did. His parents didn't know-he didn't let them in his room-but he had me secure him to the chair or bed. He was afraid of what he might do."

Her lip trembled, and she bit it hard.

"Last week..." She stopped, and I saw that she fought to keep from breaking down. "Last week, he let it take over. It wasn't him anymore. He broke through the restraints and went crazy. He tore apart every piece of furniture in his room, before turning on me. I tried to talk him down, tried to reason with him, but his eyes glowed blue and the way he looked at me..." Her voice cracked. "It was as if he hated me to his core. He came after me then, wrapping his hands around my neck so hard that I was afraid he would break me. I had no choice but to shift and defend myself. I didn't hurt him bad, but after I lashed out, he'd broken through his door and was gone. His parents didn't even see him leave, only the destruction he left in his wake."

Her body trembled violently, and she pulled the blanket tighter.

"I couldn't save him. I don't think anyone can."

A chill ran through me at her words, and the room was deathly silent.

Warmth seeped into me as Hunter moved closer. I didn't know what to say to Pres, to anyone really. I'd known it was bad, but I still had hope that Teagan was in there somewhere, that we could pull him from the clutches of evil that had hold of him. And there was no doubt, just as Helios and Hades had planted a Trojan horse in me, they had in Teagan as well. Declan had to have been made a spy by one of them, and in the early days of this war-because that's what it was-Teagan had been none the wiser.

He had thought taking on the hellfire would help our fight. He didn't know that he played right into their hands.

I had no idea what we were going to do, how we would get him back. But just as always, I was determined. One way or the other we'd save the world and save him too.

Presley was worn out, so I led her to my room and tucked her into my bed. Star must have taken pity on her. That or she just wanted a warm body to snuggle. She'd hopped down from around my neck and scurried under the covers Pres had pulled up to her neck.

I leaned over and pressed a kiss to Presley's forehead. "Sleep well, friend. Everything will work out. I promise."

She gave me a small smile, and my heart clenched to see it.

"If anyone can make it okay, it's you, Andie."

Her eyes closed, and I tiptoed out of the room, shutting the door softly behind me.

Leaning back against it, I closed my eyes. The weight of the world never felt heavier.

"Hey," whispered Hunter as he walked toward me, before grabbing my hand and pulling me to him.

"It's going to be just fine." He smoothed my hair as he held me tight. "You know if I could take all the burdens from you, I would. You aren't alone. I'm here to help, and so is everyone in the other room."

I knew he was right, but I couldn't help but feel at times that it was, and would be, all up to me.

The next morning, I woke up on the couch, my head tucked into Hunter's neck. He snored softly beside me, and I wondered when we'd fallen asleep. The last thing I remembered was discussing our options to find Teagan.

I slid out from under Hunter's arm, stretching, my stiff body as I stood. I spied Celeste at the table, sipping a cup of tea and chatting quietly with Eira. Balwyn brought out a tray of pancakes and laid them in the middle of the table.

My stomach growled and they all looked over with raised eyebrows.

I joined them at the table as Eira laughed low.

"You'd never be able to sneak up on anyone when you're hungry."

That was no joke. My stomach always rumbled louder than a boar when it needed food.

I was surprised it hadn't woken Hunter.

"Did I miss anything last night after I fell asleep?" I asked them, and Celeste only shook her head.

"Not really, dear. But we did decide that it would be a good idea to go back to Fairy. If only to meet with Aine before we head to Washington. She needs to know about all of the new developments."

I agreed, we needed to get going. I felt an itch deep down inside of me. I wanted to end all of this once and for all.

Chapter Eight

As we talked in low tones, I felt a warmth approach from behind, and Hunter softly brushed my hair to the side and placed a gentle kiss on my neck.

"Good morning, sunshine."

His voice was raspy with sleep, and my eyes closed as his arms wrapped me in a hug from behind.

"We were just talking about going for a visit to Fairy." I squeezed his hand, and Celeste's eyes sparkled as she watched us together.

He slipped into the chair beside me with thoughtful eyes and nodded.

"We do need to go soon, but I think it might be a good idea to stay here one more day. Let Presley acclimate a little more and get her mind right before we throw her back into all of the craziness. Plus," his lips quirked, "we have a date."

I stared at him in shock. I mean, a date? Excitement and hesitancy warred within me as I stared into his sweet eyes.

"A... a date?" I stammered, and a chuckle sounded behind us.

"You know, where a guy takes a girl out to do something fun, or to eat. Usually ends with a kiss." Killian laughed as he poured a cup of tea, wiggling his eyebrows at me.

"I know what it is, doofus." I pretended to scowl at him. "It just surprised me, that's all."

I'd actually never been on a date before, and a little thrill ran up my spine at the thought of doing something so normal.

I looked back at Hunter to see uncertainty lining his face and immediately felt bad.

"Of course! I'd love to go on a date with you. I'm sorry, it just surprised me, and I guess I just hadn't thought we had time to do normal stuff like that." I sighed and grabbed his hand so he could feel what I was feeling. It was the easiest way to explain the confused feeling that warred within. Between being a teenager yet also a leader with so much on my shoulders.

His eyes softened as they looked into mine.

"And that's exactly why we need to have some time just to be ourselves and have fun. The world can wait for a few hours."

Celeste stood just as Emric and Charlie pranced into the room, and the rest of our group stirred, waking up with the sunrise that filtered through the small windows.

"I, for one, think that is a grand idea. We'll stay with Presley. I have an idea that I think will help perk her up and pull her out of this funk. I'm going to get her to help me with some online Christmas shopping."

Killian snorted, and Emric chuckled as he hopped onto the couch. "You best pull out your best credit card then. She's a shopper, that one, and you're likely to spend all your money and then wonder later what happened."

He wasn't wrong. Shopping was one of Pres's favorite things, and she'd have Celeste buying *all* kinds of things. But wait, she'd said Christmas presents? I groaned as I realized that I'd completely forgotten about it with all that was going on.

Hunter pulled me to my feet, twirling me fast and then pulling me back into his arms. With a quick squeeze, he kissed the top of my head and then let me go.

"How about you go get ready?"

"Now?" I stared at him and he nodded.

"Yep, our date starts now."

I hurried to get ready in my dark room, trying to tiptoe and be quiet enough not to wake up Pres and Star, who both snoozed deeply in my bed.

I wasn't sure where we were going, but opted to wear jeans, a soft purple sweater and a pair of boots. I'd rather be in a T-shirt and my Converse shoes, but this was a date, and I wanted to look nice for it.

My head swirled with the possibilities of what we'd be doing. I mean, it was only seven in the morning. Not exactly a normal time for a date, but I'd take it whenever I could get it.

Star peeked up at me from under the covers with one eye open, before yawning and snuggling even deeper in the blanket.

I loved her but was I was relieved she wouldn't be coming with me. Sometimes I needed a break from her constant presence. From everyone's constant presence, really. Over the last few months, I'd hardly had any time just for me.

Shutting the door softly behind me I fairly skipped back out into the main room where Hunter stood waiting. He had changed too and wore jeans and a long-sleeved green shirt that hugged his broad shoulders and the muscles of his arms.

I loved how he looked in his suits, but I think I loved this look on him even more. He made anything look good really.

"Eh, pick your tongue up off the floor, missy, and get going," Emric teased, making Hunter chuckle.

I pretended not to hear him as Hunter grabbed my hand in his and looked toward where the Titans now sat eating breakfast while Eira flittered over them.

"We'll be back later this afternoon. Keep your phones handy just in case I need to reach you. I don't expect any trouble though."

A tingle of dread rushed through me, but I quickly pushed it aside. It really would be just the two of us. No bodyguards. I was going to enjoy every minute of it, and I wasn't going to let anything ruin it.

Celeste handed him her keys before hugging me tight.

"Don't worry about a thing. Just go have fun."

I squeezed her back. "I'll see you in a while."

And with that Hunter and I sifted to her house where her car was parked outside. Hunter opened the passenger door for me, and I slid in. He then shut the door and rounded in front of the car to the driver's side. As he settled in beside me, his dark eyes slid over me. "You look gorgeous, by the way."

My heart squeezed, and my cheeks heated. "You do too." My voice squeaked, and in my embarrassment my cheeks got even hotter. He just winked at me before starting the car. "Buckle up, baby."

And right then and there, with that single endearment, I melted into a literal pile of teenage infatuation for him all over again.

We drove out of Junction, and I realized that all the homes we passed were decorated for the holiday. Lights dangled from rooftops, Santa and reindeer sat on lawns, while wreaths graced every front door.

The giddiness I used to feel every year at this time rose within, and I realized then that I couldn't let my new responsibilities, no matter what they were, dampen my wonder and excitement for the normal things.

"Hey, we're here. Where'd you go?" Hunter sat looking at me, and I realized that we'd stopped.

"Sorry, I was just thinking about how easily I'd forgotten about normal things, like the holidays and celebrating. Just taking a ride in a car. You know? I never thought I'd ever feel so good just doing this again."

He nodded, and I felt his understanding. "I do. And we both need this." He smiled. "What do you say we find a Christmas tree?" He swept his arm out, and I finally looked away from him to see where we were.

What I saw made my heart squeeze and joy radiate through my bones. Acre upon acre of Christmas trees sat in front of us, with one huge one in the middle all decked out with lights and ornaments, a huge star sitting on top. People milled around with steaming cups in their hands, and kids ran through the trees laughing, their eyes bright and happy. He'd brought me to a tree farm.

I opened the door, and he hurried around to my side and reached a hand down to pull me up.

I just stood there in wonder, taking it all in.

"I thought we could pick out a tree to take back to the Oak to decorate. Maybe put some Christmas carols on and hang up some stockings?" I pulled my gaze away from the farm to look up at him. He looked down at his feet before finding my eyes again, and I realized that he was feeling uncertain about bringing me here.

"This is perfect. *So* perfect, Hunter." I smiled big and jumped at him, wrapping my arms around his neck before squealing. "Let's go get a tree!"

For the next few hours, we argued playfully over which tree we thought would be perfect. He was adamant about a big perfect tree, but I fell in love with one that was smaller, a little on the scraggly side. I don't know why I felt like that one in particular was the perfect one, but it called to me. I could dress it up with decorations and make it beautiful. It was a little like me. Different but not less. Ragged around the edges but still strong and fighting to live.

In the end, Hunter suggested that we get both. We could put the bigger one in Celeste's house and take the smaller one to the Oak.

I thought that was a wonderful idea, so we had one of the workers get them pulled and ready to go. While they got the trees ready, we found a small store situated in the middle of the farm. Inside was a smorgasbord of ornaments and decorations, along with a small café. My stomach rumbled at the smell of cinnamon rolls and coffee that permeated the small building.

"Hungry?" Hunter's eyebrow rose, and his mouth tilted up in a smirk.

"Ugh. I don't know why my stomach is so loud." I laughed.

He pulled me over to the counter, where all kinds of yummy confections sat inside the display shelf and a grandmotherly lady stood behind ready to serve.

"We'll take two of those," he pointed at the huge rolls of cinnamon perfection, "and two cups of coffee, please."

The woman nodded with a smile and filled his order.

"It's a lovely day for tree shopping isn't it?" she smiled, handing us each our coffees.

"It sure is," I breathed out.

She smiled and turned to help the next people in line, and we found a small table in the back to sit at.

I sighed as I bit into the sweet roll. "This has been the best morning. I'd forgotten how much fun just being normal is."

Hunter chuckled but agreed with me.

"One day, we'll have this all the time. I promise. But for now, we'll just have to carve out time in all that's going on to have more normalcy. I have a few things planned." His eyes were mischievous as I looked at him.

Leaning forward, he kissed my lips tenderly. Then with his finger, he gently swiped at the corner of my mouth before raising it to his own.

"You had a little frosting there."

I saw a small bit of white on his fingertip before he licked it off, and I immediately thought that maybe I should be messier when eating if he'd do that every time.

He looked pointedly at me with smoldering eyes, all signs of teasing gone.

"If I did that every time, I'd prefer to kiss it off. And I'd never stop."

Chills ran through me, and had we not been in a public place, I might have put him to the test right then and there. I could tell he felt the same, as the heat that radiated between us raised a notch.

A little voice beside us pulled us from the bubble of intensity, thankfully, and I turned to see a small girl standing by our table.

"Hi," she said with a wide smile, her dark hair braided with ribbons winding through it.

"Whatcha doin?" she asked.

Hunter grinned down at her. "Hi. We were just having some cinnamon rolls. Would you like one?"

The girl's eyes grew big and hopeful as she stared at him. "My mama said I already ate and didn't need one."

Right then the lady in question came up behind the little girl, looking flustered.

"Gina, I told you to not leave my side! I've been looking all over for you."

The woman looked up at the two of us. "I'm sorry if she was bothering you. I just turned for a second and she was gone."

I smiled gently at her. I could tell that she had been worried sick.

"She wasn't bothering us at all. We were just talking about these yummy cinnamon rolls."

The little girl nodded quickly, her eyes never leaving the food on our table.

"They asked if I wanted one, Mama. Can I have one? Please!"

Her mom shook her head, scolding her. "You've already eaten, and I don't have the extra money for sweets. I already told you that. We saved our money for a tree, and we can't have both."

My heart broke at her words and the little girl's face fell, but she quickly nodded to her mom.

I could tell that Hunter felt the same sympathy for them. It was Christmas, and all little kids should feel the magic of it, and not have to decide between treats and a tree.

The mom turned her daughter away from the table and the little girl sadly waved at us before she was ushered outside.

Hunter stood quickly and went to the counter. I watched as the woman handed him two cinnamon rolls and he walked back over to the table.

"Wait here, okay? I'll be right back."

My heart squeezed as I watched him rush out of the store. I had thought he'd go to the woman and little girl, but instead he found one of the workers who helped load up trees. They spoke for a minute, and Hunter pointed at the woman and girl as they walked through the trees. He handed the man the rolls and some money before turning to come back inside. I watched as the man hurried after the mom and disappeared from sight.

Hunter settled back into the chair beside me, satisfaction written all over his face.

"You are something else, Hunter. How'd I get so lucky?"

He looked embarrassed and dug into his own cinnamon roll, not saying a thing.

"You just made that little girl's day, and you paid for their tree too, didn't you?"

He just shrugged. "It was the right thing to do."

And it was. But not many people would do that for someone else. That was just Hunter. He seemed tough and no-nonsense on the outside, but inside? He was a softie who wanted to make others happy. Brighten up their day and give them something that may not seem like a lot to some, but to others would mean the world.

Just this small act of kindness, could set off a chain reaction. I had a feeling that mom and daughter wouldn't forget his thoughtful deed anytime soon.

After we finished eating, we found a ton of ornaments and decorations. I had never had so much fun! Apparently the Titans had an infinite credit card limit. Even though I balked at the amount of things Hunter urged me to get, he wouldn't take no for an answer.

"This makes you happy, and we're going to get everything that you want to make it the perfect Christmas."

When we got done loading up the car with all our purchases and the workers had the two trees strapped to the top of the car, I felt a little like I was in the National Lampoon's Christmas Vacation movie. We just weren't driving a station wagon.

"How on earth are we going to get this all back to the Oak?" I asked as we drove home.

He laughed and turned the radio to a station playing Christmas carols before saying, "Don't worry. I have my ways."

And boy did he.

When we got to Celeste's house, we unloaded everything into her living room. It was quiet here with just the two of us, and a little eerie.

I glanced at the bookshelf that held the Keys and felt reassured to see the old book still discreetly tucked away.

We sorted what we'd take to the Oak and put it aside, and Hunter got busy putting up his big perfect tree in the corner by the fireplace. While he did that, I made us some sandwiches and turned on some music.

I had never had so much fun decorating as I did then. We took turns placing ornaments here and there, hung the stockings on the hearth and in between Hunter would grab me up and dance me around the room, kissing me until I was breathless before letting me go again to decorate more.

Hours later, we stood back and looked at our handiwork, satisfied and happy.

"It looks so beautiful." I clasped my hands to my heart as I stared at the tree lit with white lights and decorated with red and white ornaments, a huge bow topping it.

Hunters' arms circled my waist, and he rested his chin on my shoulder.

"It is. But not half as beautiful as you."

Heat emanated between us, and I didn't want this day to end. I could stay in his arms forever.

He made a noise of agreement before reluctantly letting me go.

"The day isn't over yet, baby. We still have one more tree to decorate." He eyed my scraggly one with fake distaste.

I shoved him a little, laughing. "Hey, don't look at it like that. All it needs is a little love."

He raised his eyebrow, nodding slowly.

"I'll remember that." His eyes once again burned into mine.

Clearing my throat, I broke the stare. "So how do you propose we get this all there? We can't possibly hold it all while we sift, and I really don't want to have to trudge through the woods with it."

He nodded and went to stand beside it, gesturing for me to do the same.

"I told you I have my ways. Hold my hand," he said.

I grabbed ahold, and with his free hand he made a circular motion and a lasso of light shot out encompassing the packages and tree.

Shock coursed through me, though I wasn't sure why. He was a Titan, after all, and obviously he had more power that he hadn't shown before.

Once the lasso had made its way around the two of us as well, he spoke in a strange language and we sifted in the blink of an eye.

"What tha tarnation?" Balwyn exclaimed as our packages tumbled to the floor beside him.

Eira swirled to them, her wings fluttering in excitement and she clapped her little hands together as she peeked into a bag full of ornaments.

"Oh, we are going to have so much fun!" she squealed.

Emric sniffed the tree and then promptly sneezed.

"Why do we need a tree inside a tree?" He gave me a look of disdain, and Charlie landed on one of the branches.

"It's tradition, you old fuddy-duddy," he said as he looked down at the Phooka. "People put up evergreen trees and decorate them to celebrate the Christmas season. I myself think it will give this old tree a festive air."

He smiled over at me with his birdie smile.

Celeste wrapped her arm around my waist, and I hugged her to me. "We just put one up at your house too and got it all decorated. I think you'll love it."

She smiled back at me, her eyes bright with happiness. "Thank you both. I'll have to venture over there later and see it."

Rustling of bags got our attention, and I looked over to see Eira flying out of one of them, a trail of lights flying through the air behind her.

"Get the tree up, and let's get to decorating!" she called out as she flew like a maniac through the air.

The Titans obliged, and within a few minutes the tree was set up and everyone just stared at the sparse limbs and squat size.

I felt a bit defensive, but Hunter came to the rescue before I even had to say a thing.

"It's beautiful, isn't it? Let's get these lights on there."

Everyone but Eira and Celeste looked at him like he'd lost his mind, but he just winked at me and then got busy.

With so many of us decorating, the tree was done in no time, and laughter sounded throughout the room. This was what we all needed. Not just me.

I stood back a little way from everyone and saw the happiness that lined their faces. Even Presley had come out of the room and joined in with a lightness that hadn't been there the day before. Star batted a red ornament around the floor, and Balwyn brought out cocoa and sugar cookies in the shape of a Christmas tree and decorated perfectly. How he'd whipped these up so fast, I had no idea, but it had to be a Brownie thing.

Before long, the Oak looked like something out of the North Pole. Eira had brought out fairy lights, and they bobbed through the air, while red ribbon and greenery ran around the banister on the stairs.

I wanted this feeling to last forever.

Hunter joined me then, pulling me to him. Wordlessly, he pointed up above us, and I looked and saw a ball of mistletoe hanging there.

He leaned down, and as his lips touched mine, the noise around us faded away and I was consumed by him. It was a kiss that took my breath away. When he finally pulled back, it took a while for my lungs to fill back up.

"Wow," was all I said, and he chuckled.

"Wow is right. I think I need to put these all over, anywhere we go," he teased.

I secretly agreed.

That night, I cuddled with Pres and Star. It was like old times. We laughed and talked about our day, and she teased me about Hunter. We stayed far from the subject of Teagan. And I was hesitant to mention Killian, though I'd caught them laughing together earlier. I could tell things weren't the same between them, and they may never be again, but I knew that they'd always be friends.

After we'd turned out the light, I sighed, happy and content and ready to take on the day ahead of us.

As I drifted off to sleep, I felt my stomach roll, and that familiar inky blackness that hadn't risen in a while roared to life. My body didn't feel like my own, and I couldn't move a muscle, no matter how hard I tried.

Images of fire seared my vision, and a pain lanced through my brain. Darkness clouded everything out, and fear held me tight as everything faded.

Chapter Nine

"Hey, sleepyhead." Pres nudged my shoulder. "It's time to get up. Everyone's waiting to leave."

I groaned and rolled over, every muscle aching, and I immediately remembered what happened. I shot straight up in bed and grabbed her arm, causing alarm to light her face.

I bit my lip and loosened my grip, but the darkness was still there. I felt it waiting.

"I need you to get Hunter, please," I ground out, pushing back at the blackness. He would ground me. I knew he would.

She nodded quickly, worry heavy on her brows as she backed out of the room.

Star looked up at me curiously and growled low in her throat.

"I know. I know," I replied.

Hunter rushed in and sat beside me, his hands taking hold of mine.

"Just breath." He squeezed my hands and I felt warmth radiate into me. "Close your eyes for me, baby. Think about yesterday, all the fun we had." His deep voice grounded me, and I did as he said.

I felt Celeste come up beside me.

Funny how I'd never noticed before how I could feel her presence too.

Her hand rested on my head, and that peacefulness that always came from her soaked in. Between the two of them, the darkness backed down, and after several minutes of deep breathing and visions of everyone's happiness last night, it disappeared altogether.

"There. It's better now, right?" Hunter soothed, smoothing his hand down my arm.

I bit back a sob and nodded.

"Yes. Better," I gasped, my shoulders slumping and the tension in them released.

"Thank you. I'm... I'm sorry. I don't know why that happened. Last night when I was falling asleep, it did too. I couldn't control my body and I just remember hurting and passing out."

Hunter and Celeste shared a look before helping me off the bed.

"Why don't you get a shower in? We'll get things ready to go." He nudged me in the direction of the bathroom. "Celeste, will you stay in her room in case she needs you?"

"Of course. I'll be right here, dear." She sat on the end of the bed and Star hopped into her lap. "Take all the time you need."

I opted to take a long bath instead. I lit some candles and added my favorite jasmine bubble bath. I hoped that the warmth from the water would ease the achiness of my body, and I knew the others wouldn't mind waiting.

After the water began to turn cold, I dragged myself up and out and started getting ready. I found myself staring at the clothes in my closet. I reached for a pair of black skinny jeans and a black top that Pres had once bought me, but I'd thought the neckline was too low so I'd never worn it. I'd only pushed it to the back of the closet, figuring that maybe one day I would.

I can't say why I decided to wear it, other than the feeling that I needed to be fiercer than I felt.

And so, I decided to take it a little further. Instead of putting my hair up into a ponytail or braiding it like I normally did, I found the curling iron and put it to use. The end result was long shiny waves with a little bounce to them.

Hmmm... I looked a lot older with my hair like this.

My eyes spied the makeup in the corner of the counter, and I immediately began putting it on. When I was done, I looked into the mirror and liked what I saw.

I looked older with the dark eyeliner and mascara. The red lipstick I had run over my lips made them look much fuller and somehow made my gray eyes stand out more.

I don't know what got into me, but I felt like now I was ready to take on the world. I dared anything to make this day bad.

It must have been a shock to everyone in the room, for their mouths hung open and shock colored their faces when I walked in. I stared right back, challenging them all. Hunter especially, as his eyes pierced mine trying to get through my armor.

Their eyes all fell, and they resumed their conversations, though there were a few awkward glances in my direction. Celeste only looked concerned for a second before she left me alone with Hunter who had come to stand in front of me.

"This is new." He gestured down my body and tugged on a wave of my hair. I liked how he didn't say it at all judgmentally.

I nodded and smiled up at him. "I felt like I needed the strong Andie to make an appearance. It's different, but strangely I like it. A lot."

Heat lit his eyes, and he leaned down to whisper beside my ear. "You've always been strong, and I love you the way you are. But this is nice too. I like fierce Andie."

His lips trailed up the side of my cheek before he sighed.

"I'd love to stay here and take you on another date. Right this minute in fact, but we've really got to get going."

I knew he was right, and as much as I'd like to have another normal day, I itched for the craziness that our life was most of the time.

"Well, let's get this party started then."

I turned around and in a most un-Andie-like way, I ratcheted up my voice to be heard over everyone else.

"I don't know about y'all, but I'm ready to go kick some Helios's butt!"

Again, they all stared at me until Killian began laughing out loud and clapping his hands.

Pres walked to my side and grasped my hand. "Let's do it!" She smiled tentatively at me before raising her free hand in the air and yipping loudly.

There's my girl.

∞

We landed with a clap of our shoes on the stone patio outside Aine's castle. The fairies were momentarily stunned at our appearance before they went on their way again, flying through the air and going about their duties. Aine and Coeus had gone ahead of us and now greeted us at the door. Once again, I got the look-over with raised brows.

I just snickered.

"Go with it," Killian murmured to them as he walked into the castle, Emric and Charlie hot on his heels.

"Say, anyone hungry? I'm famished. You don't happen to have any chocolate cake, do you?" I heard Emric question as they went.

He never stopped thinking about his stomach. And chocolate cake? That was a first for him. Usually, he was more of a meat eater. Huh. I guess there's a first for all of us.

"Well...uh-huh...you look rather dark, Andie," Aine stumbled, still trying to work out my new look in her mind.

"Yes, well, I thought I'd try something new, and it turns out I rather like looking like this."

"It certainly is different. But you do look stunning." Coeus offered, his smile as jolly as ever. They knew all about the darkness, and I realized that every single one of my friends questioned this change in me. Maybe it was the blackness inside that liked this look more than I did. I really didn't care as long as it didn't take me over like it

87

did before. This was much better than that. Plus, I liked the strength it lent my soul. I despised the fear. I'd take this any day.

We were ushered into a drawing room where Amarie and some of the other Elves waited. I ignored their reactions to me and walked to one of the chairs up front and sat down, everyone else following suit.

"I hope you are all doing well," I said to the room. "Today, we will make plans to go to Washington State where there have been rumors of a rift in the mountains. We need to see exactly what's going on and assess the threat from there." Many of them nodded in assent.

"I looked toward Killian and Hunter. "We need Trela and Bea with us. Can you please make sure they head back here today?"

Killian perked up and nodded, looking at my Titan.

"I'll get them, if that's okay? Probably a good idea for you to not leave Andie, anyway."

I grit my teeth. He was probably right; Hunter grounded me. But it still stung to acknowledge the fact that I didn't have full control.

They ironed out the details, and Killian left the room to hunt them down. Presley's eyes followed him as he did.

It hurt my heart to see her so lost. I didn't think that she really knew what she wanted. But somehow, I knew it wasn't Killian. Amarie cleared her throat. "There's been news on Teagan."

Presley's eyes snapped to her and she sat on the edge of her seat waiting to hear. I think all of us did.

"Go ahead. Please tell us," I said.

"Well, he actually reached out to us. Kitt received a phone call from him."

This surprised me. First that he had Kitt's phone number, and second that he even had a phone. It must have been a burner phone because he'd left his at his parents' house.

"It was an unknown number, but Kitt's been answering all of his calls whether they're known numbers or not, for this reason alone. You see, he had gone to visit Teagan soon after the accident and gave it to him in case he ever needed us. And I guess now he's decided he does."

I had so many questions, and the normal Andie wanted to belt them all out, but I sat on my hands now and quietly nodded for her to continue. Presley bit her lip, and I could see a war inside of her.

Amarie nodded at Kitt to tell us what he'd learned.

"I'm not going to lie- he sounded rough. He sounded really desperate and wanted help. He mentioned something was inside of him that he couldn't control."

My gut twisted at his words because I knew that feeling all too well. It was the worst of the worst.

"He knew he'd done terrible things, but he said he'd tried to fight it, that it was too strong. He mentioned Declan and how he'd messed up ever making a deal with him." Kitt rubbed a hand over his face and sighed.

"He rambled on a lot, and I could tell that his mind is really messed up right now. I mean, it's not good. I tried to get him to tell me where he was, but he wouldn't. He only said that Declan wants to talk to Andie. He was adamant about it, which I don't get because he had just told me he wished he hadn't made the deal with Declan. I think somehow that Declan's controlling Teagan. He is a fire demon after all. Who knows what he can do?"

Hearing that monster wanted to talk to me sent the inky tide inside of me rising. Presley gasped as she witnessed my eyes turning black and the Elves flinched.

I put my hands up in the air and took a deep breath in.

"It's okay. Really. I've got this." I told them, feeling Hunter's hand on my shoulder. Looking at Aine and Celeste, I inclined my head and they proceeded to fill everyone in on my predicament. I'd told them earlier before we left that I wanted everyone who would be working with us to know. It was their right, and I wanted to be stopped by whoever could stop me if the darkness got out of hand.

Leif's words came back to me, and I realized she knew this would all happen. That's why she'd told me to fight it.

I knew my eyes were still dark by the way that Pres stared at me. It was disconcerting. I imagined I looked like a demon to them. But I was still me. Just a little *extra*.

Once everyone heard the tale of the darkness inside me, they seemed more at ease. Well, I suppose as much as they could be. A dark laugh sounded off inside my brain. It startled me at first, but then I relaxed into it. Deep down, I knew that my fear would feed it, so for now I might as well just go along for the ride.

"Okay, now that everyone knows what's going on, I need you to also know what I expect from you." They watched me raptly.

"If I should take a turn. If the darkness takes over and you can't bring me back, you must stop me."

-Pres hiccupped loudly.

I looked at her, then Hunter and held his eyes. "By any means necessary."

I stared at him, and I felt his resistance to my words, but I wouldn't back down. "I mean it." He began to argue, as did some of the others, and I shouted to be heard.

"No! You don't know what I can do. This thing is not to be messed with, and I wouldn't be able to live with myself if I did any-thing to one of you, let alone unleash this into the world. Who knows what could happen?" I spit out. "No. You will do that if need-ed. Or I'll do it myself if I have to. There will be no arguments about it. Okay?" I stared at them all, and they reluctantly nodded-except Hunter. He fumed. I felt it rolling off of him. And I understood it, but I could not do anything about it.

I raised my eyebrows at him, and he curtly nodded before turning on his heel and leaving the room.

I got up to follow him. I didn't want him mad at me, and my heart twisted at causing him any kind of pain.

Celeste's hand caught mine as I went to leave too.

"Give him just a little bit. He'll come around. He's just dealing with this in his own way."

I knew he was. But one thing that I knew that he'd forgotten was our bond. He'd *never* let me get to the point of anything needing to be done to stop me. And if he couldn't do anything to prevent it, he'd follow me down. Our bond demanded it. Should anything happen to me, or vice versa, we'd both die.

This whole speech was for the darkness. It was for its benefit. I wanted it to think I was scared, even if it didn't feel it. I wanted it to know that I was aware of what it was capable of.

That was the only arsenal I had against it. Tricks and misdirection. I knew Hunter would understand that the next time we touched.

It would be okay.

I felt my eyes returning to normal, and discreetly slipped out hoping to find a little time to myself. No one even saw me go. The thought that Declan wanted to meet with me sat heavy in the back of my mind. *Should I?* Part of me knew it was a bad idea, and the other part thought that maybe if I did meet him, I'd somehow be able to get Teagan back, *and* learn more about what we were up against.

Up the stairs I went, admiring all the beauty that surrounded me. A silver orb floated by, and I reached out, running my fingers over it, making it bob through the air. Before long I found myself in a hallway I'd not been in before. Instead of bright skies projected on the ceiling, this one had darkness with lightening streaking through it, and I found myself fascinated.

"It's amazing isn't it?" a voice called from a nearby doorway that was cracked open. I could see someone reclined on a bed, watching me. Silver hair reflected in the flashes from the streaks of light.

"Come in. Let's have a chat, Andie," the female voice called again.

I slowly made my way to the door and opened it further. I recognized Freya's mother instantly from the photo's I'd seen of her.

Aine had told me she was doing much better, but the woman watching me seemed of completely sound mind and looked healthy.

She pointed to the chair beside the bedside. "Sit here, dear. I've been hoping you'd come. I've some things to tell you."

I was intrigued and sat slowly beside her as she scooted up against the headboard to better be able to see me.

She smiled gently. "I am sure you expected a crazy old lady, right?" I started to protest but she interrupted me. "No, it's okay. I was crazy, but only because I'd been alone so long with my pain from not being able to protect my daughter. Had I, she might never have had her soul stolen and wrecked so many people's lives. Well, really it wasn't her who did it. Her body was just a vessel. Helios has been using her since childhood. I can't say how they came to meet, but make no mistake, he took advantage of a sweet young girl and turned her into what she is today." She scowled. "And now I imagine you know what she went through to some extent."

I stared at her, dumbfounded.

"Oh, yes, I'd heard you took her power into yourself, and that can only mean that his darkness transferred to you. While I should be happy that it is gone from Freya, I know that it now will plague you. Only I think you have a much greater chance of defeating it than an incredibly young girl did, or at least learning how to control it."

She sighed and picked at the cover that lay over her lap.

"I tried to help her-I really did. I tried everything that I could, but nothing worked. Its tentacles held on tight to her and wouldn't let go. Then she began taking my powers when the darkness realized what I was doing. I think deep inside it knew I'd find a way at some point, and the only way to keep me from helping her was to drain me. That of course made it even stronger." Her voice cracked a bit. "I wish I'd fought harder."

My heart ached for her and all that she had been through. For years, her life had been nothing but pain and regret while she wilted away in that hidden tunnel underground.

"Aine says you're getting much better," I offered. "I'm hopeful that you'll lend us all your wisdom for the trials to come." I smiled at her.

"Oh, I plan to, child. Starting now." Her face took on hard lines. "You need to know that Helios has always planned on opening a rift here. And now I think he has done it. He's trying to widen the chasm to let Hades' demons run amok. To destroy the human world. That's his first target. Next the magical world. These demons are like that fire demon I've heard Aine talking about, and some much worse. You have no idea the carnage that will occur if you don't somehow find a way to stop him."

She reached toward me. "Give me your hand please."

I hesitated, but something inside me knew I could trust her. I reached out, and she clasped my hand gently, her eyes becoming vacant.

"You've got a hold on the darkness for now, child," she smiled and continued, "and you also have untapped power just waiting for you to discover." Her eyes focused back on me and were alight with merriment.

"Will you let me try something?" she asked.

"Of course."

"I want you to think of something and direct it at me, willing me to hear it."

"What?" I stared at her incredulously. She laughed and nodded.

"Yes. Please just try."

I wasn't sure if this was the power she had been talking about, but I was curious and closed my eyes.

Can you hear me? I want you to hear me.

She clapped loudly and bounced slightly in her bed when I opened my eyes.

Her eyes twinkled. "Yes, I heard you loud and clear. You can speak telepathically with someone, Andie. That'll come in right handy during these tricky times."

Seriously? I knew Hunter could hear me, but I thought it was just because of our bond, and Celeste because she was the Moon Goddess.

I'd never expected I would be able to do it too.

I laughed with her, and we tried it a few times, and she responded back to me in my thoughts. Man, this was cool, and I couldn't wait to tell Hunter.

We talked for a while longer, and she asked me to check on Freya and stop by again when I could. I promised her I would, and then took my leave.

Chapter Ten

As I retraced my steps back downstairs, haunting music reached me. It floated on the air and I felt myself following the melody. It wasn't that long ago that I'd taken the same hallway and heard the same music. This time, the sadness of it didn't get to me because I knew at the end of the day we'd always be together. I pushed open the tall door to see the guy who always took my breath away. His fingers flew over the keys on the piano, and his emotions flowed freely on his face as he concentrated. I vowed right then that wherever we stayed must have a piano for him to play.

I leaned against the doorway and just let myself float on the music. It relaxed me and seemed to somehow soothe the darkness.

A kiss to my cheek had my eyes flowing open to see Hunter in front of me, yet the music still flowed, the keys moving up and down on the floating piano.

"What..."

He placed a finger on my lips and grinned. "Magic." He twirled his finger in the air and then the next moment he had me twirling around the floor. With a flick of his wrist, the lights dimmed and fairy lights high above us came on, lighting the room and turning it into a breathtaking sight. The music changed to a more romantic ballad, and as he slowed our steps to match, he twirled his hand again and tightened his hold on my waist. Our feet left the floor and we rose into the air.

Shocked, I squeaked and he just laughed.

"How in the world are you doing all of this?" I cried with elation at the feeling of literally dancing on air.

"Oh, I've learned a thing or two over the last few months about my powers. Seems there's quite a lot I can do," he winked. "And I can't wait to share it all with you."

As the music came to an end, he leaned in and kissed me so sweetly that I wished it wouldn't end. He smelled like cedarwood and tasted like oranges. I wanted to burrow into his arms forever.

"Mmm... you've got to stop tempting me like that, Andie." He pulled back and looked into my eyes. "If I had my way, I'd lock you up and keep you all to myself forever." He smiled, and I knew he was teasing, but the thought was pretty appealing.

"Maybe one day." I sighed as our feet touched the floor again. "I could get used to all of this."

"Hey." He tilted my chin up to look into my eyes. "We're going to have a lot more moments like this. A lifetime of them. We've just got to get through a few storms first, and then it's all rainbows."

God, I hoped that was true. I wanted that more than anything. And as corny as it sounded, they were the sweetest words I'd ever heard. It amazed me every day that this was the same cocky guy who I'd met that first day at school, the one who I thought hated me.

"Hey, I wasn't that cocky," he said cheekily to me, laughing. "But I'll take the other stuff."

I laughed with him and remembered the new power I'd found.

I love you more than I ever thought I could love someone.

His eyes widened.

"Did you just speak telepathically to me?"

"Yep! Isn't it great? Now you say something back to me," I urged.

And I love and cherish you, baby. I will protect you with my life and always try to make you happy.

My eyes teared up, and I laughed in happiness. "I feel like we're reciting vows or something."

His eyes bored into mine, and his expression turned serious. "It *was* a vow, Andie. And I'll make many more through this lifetime. We may not be married, but you are mine, and I am yours. Forever."

If I could've swooned, I would have. My toes curled, and my heart sang. Even with the darkness inside me and surrounding us, nothing could dampen this moment.

Well, except the fact that we had to leave soon. I sighed as he wrapped his arms around me.

"So how did you figure this new trick out?" he asked.

I told him about Freya's mom and everything that she had told me. It strengthened our conviction that we might find what we dreaded in Washington, and the mention of Hades also heightened the danger.

If both of the gods were working together, our job to find and get rid of them would be that much more difficult. Just the name Hades sent shivers down my spine. I didn't want to think about how on earth we were supposed to even get rid of Helios, let alone Hades.

"We'll figure it out. Come on. Let's go see if Killian is back with the girls yet."

As we walked hand in hand to the foyer, voices greeted us, and I broke away to run toward the two girls who looked around the castle in awe. Killian and Trela stood close together, and I didn't miss the way Trela constantly looked at Killian from the corner of her eye, or the way he looked at her when she was busy perusing everything.

"Hey!" I ran to the girls and they both converged on me, and we hugged tightly.

"Aww, group hug!" Killian yelled and threw his arms around the three of us. The girls giggled, and I just rolled my eyes at Hunter over their shoulders.

He chuckled and shook his head, walking closer.

"Ladies. So glad you made it back okay and weren't hurt," he said smoothly.

They pulled away from me, and with another giggle they both leaped at him and wrapped him in a hug. His arms hung loosely beside him as he recovered from the onslaught. He quickly hugged them and stepped back.

We were joined then by Celeste, Aine, and Presley, who looked a little out of sorts. She'd met Trela and Bea before, but they didn't really know each other well. I hoped to change that soon.

The dragon shifters went around the room, doling out their fierce hugs, and when they got to her, they waited to see how she'd react.

"Oh, what the heck-come here." And she threw her arms around both of them. "You girls kept my girl safe when I wasn't around, and I can't thank you enough. I hope we can get to know each other and be friends too." She smiled at them, and I knew my Pres was back. She had just needed to be around those who cared for her and be reminded of who she was.

The three of them then went on to chat up a storm, and I turned to Celeste. Aine and Coeus stood on either side of her, waiting as if they knew I would need something.

"When do we plan to head out?" I asked.

Coeus spoke up first.

"We leave tomorrow. I've contacted the coven and the packs, and the leaders will all meet us there. We need to be prepared for anything, and the more of us there, the better."

I agreed and relayed again what Freya's mother had told me. Their faces were grim and set with determination as we talked.

"I also need to start my search soon for the other stones. I think it's imperative. If anything, we need to find them before he does, even if for some reason they are no help to us."

There were only two more, and I just knew if I got close to where they might be, I'd feel them.

We moved our conversation to the dining hall, where the magic plates were being delivered. After being seated, a full meal of steak and baked potatoes were flown out from the kitchen, along with salad and rolls. I was really digging the hometown food that Aine had been serving us lately. Give me comfort food any day over fancy food, and I was a happy girl.

Dinner was a lively affair-well anytime Bea and Trela were around, it was. There's just something electric about them. Their personalities were larger than life, and add Pres to the mix? Explosive.

It was a fun and lighthearted dinner. We had plenty of time for the heavy stuff later.

When we all had our fill, Aine stood up, and two bottles of wine landed on the table. She took her spoon and tapped it to her glass.

"I want to make a toast, please." Her voice rang out and all conversation stopped. She smiled around at all of us.

"I know these are trying times, and I want to acknowledge how much you all have done. Most of you are still so young, but yet you've thrown yourself into this fight whole heartedly and without fear. You have been selfless and bold. Strong and sure. You are the future of the magic world, and I can assure you we are extremely blessed that we have you for future leaders, and a leader now," she turned toward me. "And you, my dear girl. I've watched you grow so much over the last year. I must admit, I had my doubts when I brought you to Junction, but you've defied those doubts at every turn and surprised even this old girl. I am-well we all are-eternally grateful for you. Not just for the journeys you've accomplished, or the leadership that you give us, but for the beautiful soul within you that you share with us all. You've shown us how to be selfless and daring." She motioned to my getup. "How to take chances and bet on love over everything else. All the while you've thought we've been teaching you, and it's been the other way around."

My eyes had teared up at her words, and I swiped them away as my heart swelled anew.

The bottles went around the room, filling glasses with the sparkling wine, and Aine raised her glass as everyone else stood up and did the same.

"To Andie, our Queen."

A round of "here, here" was shouted and I felt a little embarrassed by the attention, but the darkness inside soaked it up, and I let it.

Standing, I made my way to Aine and hugged her fiercely. "Thank you. You mean so much to me."

She rubbed my back gently and pushed me back a little. "You mean everything to me, darling. And I meant every word. Now, let's have a good time. We'll deal with the rest tomorrow."

That evening, the girls and I decided that a sleepover was in order. Even though we were still full from dinner, we had the kitchen send up popcorn, sodas, and cookies.

After changing into pajamas, we piled on my bed and put a scary movie on the laptop.

Emric and Charlie had long sense vacated the room, grumbling about squealing girls. We'd offered to paint their toenails for them, but they weren't having any of it. I'd thought Emric would look fantastic with a turquoise polish. Him, not so much.

By midnight, we were all yawning and I switched off the bedside lamp.

A round of goodnights and I was falling fast asleep.

∞

It was probably the best sleep I'd had in a while. No dreams, no darkness dragging me under.

I woke up to bodies curled all around me and stared at their relaxed faces as they slept. Here I was, a girl who used to not think good friends were so important, and now I couldn't imagine life without them.

I tried to crawl over without disturbing them as best I could. Trela mumbled a little and turned away into my empty spot, snuggling down into the pillow.

It was still early, and I wanted to get to the food hall before everyone else. Slipping out the door, I closed it softly behind me and tiptoed down the hall. I really hoped I didn't run into anyone since I was still in my pajamas with rainbows all over it, and I'm sure my hair was a mess.

Oh well, I've looked worse.

The fairies were up and busy as always, and I chatted with a few as I made my way down the stairs. I hoped that one day, when everything wasn't as hectic, I could get to know all of them better. It was still hard to think that they were, or anyone for that matter, my subjects. But I guess they kind of were.

A quick glance at the sand timer that floated in the air showed that it was around six in the morning. No, I couldn't read the sands; it had a digital clock projected on it.

101

The smell of bacon and maple syrup floated in the air, and my stomach rumbled loudly.

"We should tame that beast."

I jumped a foot in the air, startled by Hunter as he fell into step beside me. "Jeez, you scared the daylights out of me."

He laughed and grabbed my hand, squeezing it, and like always the fire that danced through his veins was fascinating.

"Sorry. I woke up early and thought I'd head down for breakfast before anyone else. Imagine my surprise when I saw you sneaking down the hall. And in your jammies, no less." His eyes twinkled and I bumped my hip into his.

"Yeah, well, now we're sort of even. Don't forget I've seen you in far less," I teased.

His eyebrows shot up, and I saw that he'd forgotten up until now. Neither one of us at the time it happened had been concerned even one iota about his nakedness. The only thing at that time that had consumed me was keeping him with me.

"Yeah, I don't think that's even close to being even. You might have to rectify that at some point."

My jaw dropped, and he wiggled his eyebrows before grabbing two plates and promptly filling them up as I still stared.

"Here you go, let's go sit by the window and we can watch the sun rise."

He'd completely turned the subject, and honestly it probably was a good idea. The darkness inside me liked to retort back with more scandalous things than I'd normally say.

We ate without talking much, just enjoying the company and watching the sun rise over the trees. Butterflies danced right outside over the flower garden by our window, and as Hunter waited for me to finish eating, he ran his finger over the glass. One by one, the butterflies flew to where it traced, their little bodies aglow with his magic, reminding me of the time in the butterfly house.

I wondered if they had magic of their own that spoke to his.

"We all have some amount of magic in us. Even humans," he said as he focused on a large blue butterfly that seemed to hog the space on the window. "It's just that humans have no idea it lies dormant in them, so they don't feed it to make it grow."

Interesting. I'd never heard about this before.

He nodded to my thoughts and said, "All humans were once Fae. They've just forgotten, and we don't remind them. It's just too late for them to know about us now."

I made a mental note to study up on this later.

A commotion came from down the hall, and around the corner came a group singing at the top of their lungs, led by none other than Emric.

They sang some bawdy Irish song that I'd never heard before. Some of the wording made even *me* blush.

Emric bounced to each beat of the song, and Charlie, who sat on his back bobbing up and down with each step, rolled his birdie eyes.

Trela, Killian, Pres, and Bea skipped behind him, their arms all linked together. By the time their song ended they were at our table and I looked at them amused.

"You all seem to be in a great mood."

Trela let go of Killian and spread her arms out, her look incredulous.

"How can you not be when you're in a place like this? Man, look around you. Magic and beauty are everywhere. Food in abundance? This is the life! Oooh, bacon!"

She hurried off toward the food. The others laughed and followed her to fill their plates too.

It was so great to see them all so happy. I wished with everything that I didn't have to basically toss them in the fire, but I couldn't do this alone.

I stretched my arms above my head and stood, with Hunter following suit. "I should go get ready. What time are we leaving?"

"I'll come with you," he grabbed my hand again. "And we're leaving just as soon as you're ready."

I looked over at him as we walked, a little annoyed that he didn't think I could get ready alone.

He chuckled and shook his head before stopping and pulling my hair.

"It's not that I don't think you can get ready alone, it's that I don't want you to. Don't worry I'll hang out in your room while you shower. No peeking. Promise." He held up his hand in promise.

"Okay, but this calls for a pinky promise, not whatever that is." I waved at his hand and stuck my pinky out. He stared at it for a minute before grinning and linking his large one with mine.

"Promise. Now," he bent down and gestured to his back, "hop on."

Well, this was a playful side of him I'd never seen before. He actually wanted to give me a piggyback ride, and one up the stairs?

I shrugged and hopped on. He easily caught my legs, and I wrapped my arms around his neck.

He took the stairs two at a time, and I marveled at his strength and agility. Then I tried to see if I could distract him. I kissed the ear that sat right by my mouth, with little pecks here and there. He shook his head gently.

"What's wrong? Ticklish?" I asked gleefully and did it again.

"Yes, that tickles a lot, and I can't do anything about it unless I drop you. And that is not an option." He blew out his breath, grimacing.

"Yeah, I wouldn't do that if I were you. I guess you're just going to-" I kissed him. "deal" I kissed him again "with it."

He fairly ran to my room, kicked the door all the way open, and deposited me on the bed as fast as he could.

It was hilarious, and it took me a few minutes to stop laughing as he tried to glare down at me, but eventually he sat and laughed with me.

"Just wait. When you least expect it, I'm going to get you back for that." He poked me in the ribs, and I screeched before hopping off the bed and running to the bathroom. I slammed the door and locked it behind me.

There was a small knock on the door, and I lay my head against it, catching my breath.

"Yes?"

"Andie, keep the door unlocked. I need to be able to get to you if I have to."

Uh-huh, sure. That's why he wanted me to unlock it? Unlikely!

"Andie," he growled. "Don't test me. I'm still your bodyguard, and if I have to, I'll knock the door down. I promise it's not for any sleazy reason. If I wanted to see you in the shower, I'd ask. I mean, not that I don't want to, but now isn't the time." He stumbled.

I chuckled and figured I'd put him out of his misery.

"Okay, okay. Unlocking now. But only because I trust you."

A sigh sounded through the door, but that was it and I turned to get ready with a smile stretched across my face.

I took my time, following the same routine I'd gone through yesterday, though this time I decided to straighten my hair. It amazed me how one tool could make your hair look sleek and longer. Even the brown of my hair looked darker somehow.

Looking through the closet, I pushed my T-shirts and jeans aside and opted for a dress. *Yes, a dress.* A slight thrill ran through me as it was totally out of my comfort zone, but today, it just felt right.

I slipped it on and ran my fingers over the soft red fabric. It was a knee length sundress with small black buttons on the bodice and thin straps that hugged over my shoulders. The hemline was loose, and I twirled in front of the mirror and watched it flare out into the air.

It was a strange feeling wearing a dress. I almost felt naked after always swallowing myself in big T-shirts and hoodies. Now, I actually had a figure and looked like how Pres always wished I'd dress. It was kind of a freeing feeling.

I searched the bottom of the closet for shoes that would go with it and settled on a pair of black sandals with a slight heel that added a small amount of height to my 5'6" frame.

Once I felt like I was all put-together, I walked outside into my room expecting to find Hunter patiently waiting.

Instead, he paced the floor, his eyes full of storm clouds.

"Sorry it took me so long. I didn't mean to make you upset."

He stopped pacing and stared at me, shaking his head. As I got closer to him, I felt worry radiating off, and I knew it wasn't me who had him upset.

"Wow. You look absolutely stunning." He breathed out. His shock at the sight of me warred with whatever had him upset.

"Thank you, but tell me what's wrong." I grabbed his hand and pulled him to the end of the bed.

We sat down, and he grasped both of my hands and solemnly looked into my eyes.

"Kitt just got a call from Teagan. He's in Junction and wants to see you."

My heart stuttered in my chest, and I felt a little lightheaded. But this was what I'd hoped for. Teagan must be doing better if he was in Junction.

I bolted up. "Let's go now. If he wants to talk to me, I need to go."

He grimaced and pulled me back down.

"What are you doing, Hunter? You know we need to go to him. He's our friend, and not only that, but we also need him in this fight too. This might be our only chance to help him."

He looked at the floor, gathering his thoughts before steeling his jaw and looking back at me with serious eyes.

"Okay, we'll go. But I need to speak with everyone else first and delay the trip to Washington," he sighed. "I don't want you getting your hopes up either, okay? He might not be the same Teagan you expect. Kitt said he still sounds bad."

I knew that Teagan probably would never be the same again, but he was family. We had to try.

"I know," I told him quietly.

He stood and leaned down to kiss my head before turning to leave the room. "I'll be right back, and then we'll go."

I was lost in my thoughts as I waited and didn't hear Charlie enter the room until he settled his feathers around him on the dresser across from me.

"So you're going to Junction, eh?"

I nodded and just watched him. I knew he had something to say. Charlie wasn't a big talker most of the time, so when he did speak, I knew it would be important.

"Well, Emric and I are going with you and Hunter then. I have a bad feeling about this visit, Andie."

I did too, but I certainly wasn't going to voice it. Teagan needed me, and I'd been through far worse scenarios before.

He went on, "I've always gotten feelings, you see, but this one I can't get a good handle on, and I'd feel better if you have us there with you for backup."

A shiver ran down my spine, and the hairs on my arms stood up. I still didn't know exactly what Charlie was, but I knew that if he said he was uneasy, I should be too.

Hunter came back into the room then, followed by Emric.

"Are you ready?" he asked me, and I took a deep breath.

"Let's go get Teagan."

We held hands, and Emric wrapped himself around my leg, his fur tickling the bare skin of it, while Charlie tucked himself into Hunter's suit jacket.

And we were off.

We landed at the site of the old high school, the crater in the ground from when it had exploded unchanged.

Main Street looked deserted except for the employees' cars who worked at the stores that still happened to be open. It hurt my heart to know that the damage Freya and the Fomori caused still lingered here, and fear ran high.

"Where are we supposed to find him?" I looked up and down the street, hoping to see his lanky frame somewhere.

"Kitt said that Teagan would find us, so I guess we wait."

I spotted a bench under a tree on the outskirts of the crater. It was untouched by the explosion and likely had seen many teachers sit on it while they watched kids play on the nearby playground.

Without a word, I walked to it and sat down, Emric and Charlie right behind me, while Hunter still scanned the street.

As soon as I sat down, I felt the air shift, and a breeze sent my hair into my face.

And in front of me stood Teagan.

His eyes were wide and frantic, his hair a mess. I scanned the rest of him and noticed his clothes were torn and dirty in many places. And over his prosthetic leg, he'd torn the jeans completely off at the knee.

I wanted to jump up and hug him. I wanted to never let him go. But I knew that wasn't an option. Madness filled his eyes as he darted his head to Hunter when he ran up to stand off to the side of him.

Teagan jerked back from us, as if scared of Hunter and what he might do. Emric and Charlie stayed silent, their gazes penetrating him as if they could see his soul.

I stood but didn't move from my spot.

"It's okay, Teagan. I'm here now, just like you wanted. No one is going to hurt you, I promise. It's just us." I waved to my companions and spread out my arms.

His eyes bounced around the group and then back to me, piercing into mine.

"I need you to come with me, Andie," he said urgently, desperation littering every word.

"Where do I need to go? Please tell me what is going on and I'll see if I can help. I want to help you, Teagan. You've been my best friend, and you know I'd do anything I can to help you."

I heard a grunt from Hunter, but I didn't look his way. I kept my eyes trained on Teagan. Right now, he needed steadiness, and I'd try to give it to him if I could.

"Declan wants to talk to you."

Hunter began to interrupt.

Wait... let me see what he has to say.

I sent the message to him telepathically, and he immediately responded.

Okay, but if he tries anything-and I mean anything, Andie-I won't hesitate.

I know.

Teagan fidgeted, and I could tell that some part of him rebelled against what he was going to say, but I held still and quiet. I was determined to hear him out.

"He said he's got a deal for you. You need to talk to him, Andie. This might be the only way."

His lip trembled, and my heart hurt for him. This was a shell of him, he was so broken. I'd never imagined I'd see him like this, and I wanted to take it all away, make it better.

My mind was made up then. I knew I'd have a fight on my hands with Hunter, but he likely already knew.

"Okay, I'll go with you. But Hunter has to come with me."

I peeked quickly at him to see his reaction. His eyes were like molten fire as he stared at me in anger. He didn't want me to do this. But this might be my only chance to free Teagan.

I looked away before my resolve crumbled only to see Teagan shaking his head emphatically.

"No, absolutely not. He can't come with you. Declan made that clear. No Titans."

My heart fell, and I scrambled to think of some way to convince him it would be for the best.

"No deal. Come on Andie. Let's go," Hunter's voice rang out, furious.

Teagan didn't look at him but pleaded with me. "I promise I'll protect you. With my life. You'll be safe. I'd never let him harm you." His eyes beseeched me.

"That's why I left, because I couldn't *stand* the thought of anything happening to you because of me. Don't you see that?"

I stared into his eyes, and I knew what he was saying was true.

"Give me a minute with Hunter." I said and turned away from him, leaving Emric and Charlie to keep an eye on Teagan, before grabbing Hunter's arm and pulling him away.

He refused to turn his back on Teagan and backed up instead.

"I'm not letting you go alone. Something isn't right if he doesn't want a Titan there. This Declan is bad news, really bad news. I just can't let this happen," He whispered furiously at me.

I understood his fear. I felt it too, and I had to struggle to contain it as I felt the darkness rise. I closed my eyes and breathed deeply, thinking and weighing my options.

As I opened them and stared into his eyes, I felt a weight settle on my shoulder.

"I'll go with her," Charlie spoke quietly but with strength in his tone.

"I think this is something she needs to do for all of us, not just for Teagan. I feel it deeply. And I promise to protect our Queen with my life from him or any other threat there may be."

Hunter stared at him and still wasn't convinced.

But I thought it was a wonderful idea. Charlie somehow knew things. How? I didn't know. But he was intuitive in a way that sometimes creeped me out, plus the fact that he could shift into any kind of animal possible seemed helpful.

He can defend me if needed.

But he's not me. I can't lose you.

You won't lose me. I promise. I'll take no chances.

I saw the moment when he relented, by the change in his eyes. Defeat and fear shone bright. "If you are determined, I won't hold you back, but here's the deal. If you aren't back in one hour, I will hunt Teagan down and I will destroy him."

The anger returned as he cast his gaze behind me, making sure to say it loud enough so that Teagan heard him.

Hunter looked at Charlie, "And you as well. You'd better not let one hair on her head be touched."

Charlie looked down his nose at Hunter, if that was even possible before jumping down to the ground and changing into his black panther form.

"Nothing will happen to my Queen. She will be protected."

With a sharp nod, Hunter walked around me, and I turned to see him stop in front of Teagan, so close that their noses almost touched.

"We may have been friends once, but if you let one thing happen to Andie, if you have anything nefarious planned, it will be the last thing you do. I'll send you to hell, and then I'll follow you and make sure I torture you for the rest of your existence there."

Teagan winced but nodded vigorously, and I could see relief loosen his shoulders as they slumped.

Hunter stalked back to me, grabbing me quickly in a fierce hug and then swept his mouth over mine, sending me off with a kiss I wouldn't soon forget.

"One hour," he said, his forehead against mine.

"One hour. I promise."

Charlie and I went to stand beside Teagan, who reached down and clasped my hand in his clammy one.

"I'll see you soon," I called to Hunter and Emric as the vision of them wavered and then disappeared altogether.

Chapter Eleven

We landed in a valley between two tall mountains. Trees surrounded us and the tall peaks disappeared into the clouds.

"Where are we?" I asked Teagan as he stepped away.

"Oregon," he said quietly, moving off abruptly, his prosthetic not slowing him down one bit. I was actually quite impressed with how well he had adapted to it.

"Come on! This way," he called as he trudged down a well-worn path in the trees.

"Stay close to me," Charlie growled as we followed. He sniffed the air, his nose scrunching.

"What is it? Do you smell something?"

He nodded his feline head and scowled. "Sulfur and smoke. I don't think the chasm is in Washington after all. I think it's *here*."

I swallowed a groan. Hunter would kill me when he learned that we were at the place where Helios was literally causing hell to escape.

As we passed through the dense brush and trees and out into an open space, chaos greeted us.

A huge split in the side of the mountain spit fire, and lava ran out and into a small stream where it smoldered and bubbled. I couldn't see anything else, but strange noises filtered from the crack and set me on edge.

Teagan stopped walking. His eyes were trained up a small hill off to the side of the mountain. I followed his gaze up and saw that a cabin was nestled in the trees, lights glowing softly from the window.

"He's there. Let's go." His voice was reluctant, and he sounded so defeated. I would get him away from this somehow. If not today, very soon.

I steeled my shoulders and straightened my back. Time to be fierce, I thought as I trudged up the incline.

The cabin was old and rickety, boards on the porch caved in, and I had to step over a few broken ones carefully. Teagan opened the door and turned with his hand ushering us in.

The interior of the cabin was sparse, and Declan sat at a small table, the light from the fireplace and several candles lending an eerie look to his already devious expression.

He laughed as soon as he saw us and stood.

"Ah, so you actually came. I'd begun to wonder if you'd rather see the world burn than make a deal with me." He gestured to the other chairs. "Sit, sit. Time to talk."

He rubbed his hands together. Evil seemed to emanate from him, and it made my skin crawl.

I sat down, keeping my eyes trained on him while Charlie stood beside me, his gaze focused on Declan as well and a fierce look in his feline eyes.

"I never said I'd make a deal with you. I came to hear you out, so let's get on with it. I don't have a lot of time."

His brows lowered as he looked at me, anger flashing through his eyes.

"I want the Keys. Plain and simple. And if you're smart, you'll get them for me."

I scoffed. I'd never give him the Keys. He must really think I'm stupid. "That's not an option. Now, tell me what else I can do."

He clenched his jaw and leaned forward, the scent of sulfur wafting off his breath.

"You. Will. Get. Me. The. Keys. I want nothing else. And if you don't? Well, you can expect towns and cities throughout the country to go up in flames. One by one. The screams of those being burned alive will haunt you forever before I find you again and do the same to you and your friends. You have no idea who you're dealing with."

He growled, veins standing out in his forehead.

I leaned forward and tried to not breathe in his stench as best I could. Staring him directly in the eyes I stated firmly, "You will never have the Keys, and you will never cause the destruction you seek. I will not allow it. You may think you're dealing with just a stupid teenager, but think again. You have no idea what I'm capable of. I don't think you want to find out."

Charlie growled low beside me, backing me up. Teagan fidgeted in his chair, tense and on edge. But he didn't take his eyes from Declan. Even though I could almost smell his fear, his eyes were stony as he watched the demon in human form.

Declan sat staring at me, his evil smile back in place and a mischievous look in his eyes.

"Well, it looks like we're at an impasse. If you're not going to give the Keys to me... then I guess I'll just have to make you."

He lunged for me then, grabbing my arm and his touch seared me to the bone. I screamed out in pain and anger. Charlie lunged for Declan over the table, knocking him back away and I scrambled to my feet, clutching my arm to my chest.

I tried to get a clear shot at Declan, but Charlie was in the way between us both and I didn't want to risk hurting him too.

Declan laughed from where he stood by the wall, looking around Charlie at me.

"You can't even fight for yourself you have to have your pet defend you. What kind of Queen are you? Fight! Show me what you're made of!" he screamed, spittle flying in his fury.

Teagan stood, and I realized that he knew Declan wouldn't stop. Angling his body positioned toward the demon, he was ready to take him on if needed.

The maniacal laughing continued, and I watched in horror as he leaped with inhuman strength up into the air and over Charlie's head, landing with a boom on the floor in front of me.

"You can't stop me. No one is going to stop me." As he reached his hand toward me, his eyes lighting with flame, Teagan's prosthetic shot out kicking him away.

He turned immediately to me as Charlie raced to my side. "Go! *Now*! I'll hold him off."

I stared at him, wanting to grab him and take him with us. "Come with me, Teagan. Please!"

He shook his head and looked at me with sad eyes. "I can't. This is what happens when I'm around those I love. I'm sorry."

I saw Declan coming up behind him and screamed. Teagan turned quickly, and hellfire shot from his fingers at the approaching demon.

"Go right now!" Teagan screamed at me as Declan threw fire right back at him, their magic clashing in the air.

"Let's go, Andie," Charlie growled, setting his paw on my hip.

And the horror before me spun away while I cried out Teagan's name.

I fell to the ground as soon as we landed, and Hunter rushed over to us, scooping me up.

"What happened?" he demanded, looking me over and feeling all my bones to determine I was in one piece. I whimpered as his hand ran over the raised spot on my arm where Declan had grabbed me.

He sat down on the ground with me and untucked his shirt, tearing a piece of it off and quickly wrapping it around the burn. I hissed, but I'd had worse injuries. Right now, what hurt the most was leaving Teagan behind.

Charlie explained everything to Hunter, and I followed up with the chasm we'd seen.

"I don't know what's in Washington, but it isn't the opening. Maybe it's a decoy, trying to throw us off of the real one, but Oregon is where it is."

Hunter ran his fingers through his hair and blew out a breath in frustration. "How could he think you'd just give up the Keys? That makes absolutely no sense."

I agreed. It made no sense at all. "I don't know. But I'm sure we'll figure it all out."

My mind drifted back to Teagan. "Hunter, we've got to find a way to save Teagan. He saved me back there. He fought for me. I think he believes that if he comes home, it'll will be to the detriment of us all. But I just don't think that's true. He's broken, his mind is weak right now, and I'm sure that Declan has somewhat brainwashed him. Not enough to not protect us, though. I think in his own way he thinks staying away is doing that."

He nodded. "It does appear that way. And I am grateful that he put himself in the line of fire to give you time to get away. That alone speaks volumes."

He stood up easily with me in his arms, brushing his lips over my cheek. "Let's get you back to the castle and get this burn taken care of."

He whisked me back off to Fairy, and we were greeted promptly by the entire gang. Celeste had Hunter take me to my room, where she applied a salve that Aine's alchemist whipped up. Immediately, the burning stopped, and I could see the skin bubble where the medicine worked to regenerate new skin.

It was amazing. I thought about all the good it would do in the human world with all the burn patients who endured skin graft after skin graft. And I wondered why we couldn't integrate some of the magical healing into their lives without them knowing.

Thoughts for later.

Hunter was beside himself, even though I wasn't seriously injured. He paced back and forth again, and I knew it was only because he hadn't been able to be there with me. He felt helpless.

Once again, Charlie and I relayed all that had gone down with the rest of the team who'd piled into my room.

Star cuddled up on my lap, and I felt some of her magical energy seeping into me. I guessed it was her way of apologizing for not being with me either.

"It sounds as if we need to take a different tactic if this is happening in Oregon. And from the sound of it, the area is not one that we can easily sneak up on with large amounts of people," Coeus said thoughtfully.

Trela handed me an orange juice and a plate with a turkey sandwich on it. I smiled gratefully at her as the conversation went on around me.

"He wants the Keys badly, and I can only assume that Helios is growing desperate," Charlie said roughly, laying his head on his black paws while Emric snuggled into his side.

"Personally, I think he's realized that Andie is more powerful than even he imagined. More than any of us imagined, and this is just the beginning of her power. We have no idea what she can do with his power inside of her mixing with her own," Emric said lazily.

I stopped chewing and took a quick drink.

"That's it!" I exclaimed. I remembered the book and Leif telling me that the darkness inside had needed to find out all of the information from it to use later. Even if her words hadn't made sense to me then, I was beginning to think I now knew what I had to do.

"What if, the knowledge from the book that the darkness inside of me took in was information that will ultimately help me in defeating him? Or even finding the last two stones to his crown and the last Key? I mean, in a strange way, it kind of makes sense. Maybe I have to tap into the darkness somehow. Learn how to use it to my advantage."

They all stared at me skeptically. All except Hunter, to my surprise.

His expression was thoughtful, and he sat down beside me on the bed and looked around.

"You know, I've heard the servants who take care of Freya talking about how she mumbles all the time. They say she speaks nonsense about Helios and her power. But what if... what if she might have some knowledge in her messed-up mind, of how Andie can control it?"

Killian began to argue, and Hunter stopped him.

"Hear me out. Yes, Freya couldn't control it, but that had to be because the power took her over as a young child. Her mind was too weak and fragile then. She didn't have a chance. But if it's at all close to how it was when I was trapped inside myself, you're still there, you hear everything going on around you. You're just powerless to stop it. So, what if she knows?"

His gaze slid to mine, and he grabbed the other half of my sandwich and took a bite.

"You up for it?"

Wonder filled me at how calm he was now and this idea that Freya could help us. It was worth a shot and made so much sense after he put it like that.

I smiled sweetly up at him.

"I'm ready for just about anything if it will help us win this war."

"Good." He kissed the tip of my nose. "Finish up and then we'll pay her a visit."

Chapter Twelve

We walked down another dark hall with storms raging on the ceiling. I wondered why these were dark like that, and the rest of them always had clear, beautiful skies.

Aine does that to help visitors know which halls contain prisoners, or guests who can potentially be a danger. It's a warning to stay away.

I guess that makes sense if you know about it. Me? I had no idea and had just been meandering through them all without a clue.

He chuckled and led me to the door at the end of the hall.

"Aine had Freya brought here. It's her interrogation room. It'll just be you inside with her. We felt that's best so she wouldn't be intimidated. But there's a wall with a huge tapestry of Fairy hanging on it. That's where we'll be watching from. It's like a two-way mirror. So if anything happens and we need to get you out, we'll only be seconds away.

He smiled and backed toward the door to the left. "Go ahead. We'll be right here."

I hesitated with my hand on the door handle. I could do this. She wasn't a threat at all anymore, just a shell of the evil she'd once been. Part of me pitied her now that I knew what the root cause of that evil was and experienced it myself.

I pushed the door open and closed it quietly behind me. The room wasn't too big, and it had a table situated in the middle of it. On one side sat a woman I wouldn't have recognized as Freya had

I not known. Her once beautiful black hair was streaked with gray, and her eyes were dull, her mouth slack.

Her arms were shackled behind the chair, though I wasn't sure from the look of her that I would've even needed her bound.

I sat in front of her and relaxed my posture. I tried to be confident, yet not intimidating. I needed her to talk to me.

As I settled, her eyes met mine, and a multitude of expressions passed over them.

Fear, pity, hate, and then finally acceptance.

She blew out a breath, causing the bangs that hung to one side to shift back. "You know what it feels like, don't you?" she whispered.

I nodded slowly. "I do. And it's terrible. Although I feel that you got the worst out of it, and for that, I am sorry. It must have been excruciating living the life you did, with no control over it."

She looked down and her lips trembled. "I tried once to tell my father. He didn't believe me. He said I needed to quit telling stories. My mother tried to help me, but by then it was just too strong, even for her."

She shifted in her seat, the chains rattling behind her.

"Would you like to try and make things right now? To undo some of the pain that your actions caused so many?" I asked softly, my eyes never leaving hers. I wanted to be sure that anything she told me was truthful. I'd know if she was lying. She couldn't hide her true feelings from me anymore.

"What can I do?" she scoffed. "I have no magical ability anymore, nothing."

"You don't. But you have your memories. I need you to think hard and tell me if you have any knowledge on how to get this dark power inside of me to cooperate and be used to my advantage. Things are happening now that you're not aware of. Helios has opened a chasm in the mountains, and one by one demons are escaping. So now not only do we have to worry about him, but there's also the threat of hell being unleashed to take out all of humanity, magical or otherwise. We need an edge on it, and I think that if I can harness the darkness and mesh it with my own powers, along with finding the last Key, we just might stand a chance."

Her eyes widened, and I could see the point in my speech where the information clicked, and that lightbulb came on. She scrunched her brows as her eyes unfocused, and I knew she was searching for any memory she could find that might give me the answers I needed.

We sat quietly for some time until her shoulders slumped in defeat.

"I can't remember!" she cried out and stomped her foot on the ground. "Why can't I remember?"

I sighed and glanced at the tapestry on the wall, gently inclining my head. The next moment, Celeste entered.

I looked back at Freya again. "Celeste can help you remember. Will you consent to let her?"

She stared at Celeste who remained standing regally by my side with a peaceful air. "Will it hurt?" she asked.

"No dear, it won't hurt a bit. It might be a little uncomfortable as you uncover things that your mind has kept hidden, but that is all," Celeste advised.

Freya thought for a moment and then consented with a nod of her head.

Celeste glided around the table to stand behind her, and she gently placed her graceful fingers on Freya's head.

"Close your eyes and just relax. You don't need to say anything or do anything. I'll see your memories as if they were my own."

Freya did as she was told, breathing evenly as Celeste got to work.

Fascinated, I watched as Celeste's eyes moved behind her own closed eyelids. Every now and then she grimaced, and I knew some things she was seeing were difficult and not pleasant at all. This went on for a good twenty minutes, and I worried about all of the energy she must have been using.

Her body sagged some as she removed her hands, and Freya's eyes opened back up.

She just smoothed her hand over the woman's dark hair and walked back around the table. "You poor child. I hope you find peace in your new life. Thank you for letting me see your memories."

She inclined her head at me as she walked out the door, letting me know she had what she needed.

I leaned toward Freya. "Thank you for this. In all sincerity, I second what she said. Giving us your memories might just be the nail in Helios's coffin and the end to all of this madness."

Her eyes were the clearest I'd seen them since I walked in as she looked at me fiercely. "I hope it is. And when you do get rid of him, I hope you'll allow me to watch that monster be put down."

I studied her, pleased with her reaction, and smiled a bit. The darkness liked it too. "I'll save you a front row seat."

I hurried out to find Celeste and make sure she was okay. Aine and Coeus hovered over her in the next room, where she sat on a sofa sipping a cup of green tea.

Disgusted, she waved them away. "I'm not an old woman. Well, I guess I am, but I can take more than that."

I chuckled as I sat down beside her. "You know they're just worried about you. I was too, but I see that you're fine."

I smiled and hugged her close.

She smiled at me and patted my cheek. "See? You get me, my dear." Setting down her mug, she leaned back again and looked around the room.

"There was a lot going on in Freya's memories. As you can imagine, they were painful to see, and what she went through was horrendous. She tried to fight it, so very hard, but she just wasn't strong enough." She looked at me with pride in her eyes.

"You have more strength than you know. I was inside her memories and felt what she did. I felt how hard she tried. All in vain. For you to hold the darkness down like you have is actually a wonder. It is immensely powerful. There were several memories I was able to lift where the darkness spoke to her. Or rather, it spoke to itself and she listened."

She grasped her hands in front of her, her face turning serious.

"There is a way for you to use it, but it's going to be difficult. I worry that somehow it might take over if you let it."

Giddiness that I could actually harness this thing ran through me. I'd deal with whatever worries she had as we went.

"You're going to have to stop pushing it away so much. Let it rise a bit and get the feel of it. We already know you can control it before it gets too big, but now you will have to let it rise higher each time, learning to put that brick wall up that you so often do, just in a different way. It's part of you right now, and you need to make it comfortable with your control."

Commotion surrounded us as I looked into her eyes. It was a risk, a huge one. I didn't want to let it out and risk it doing something to someone I loved, but if I did as she said and let it out to play little, by little I might be able to tease it into thinking it was safe with me. And really, it had to be, at least until we figured out a way to get rid of it. Hopefully, that would be by ending Helios.

I stood and hollered over the din. "Okay, okay, settle down. Listen, I don't like it either, but it makes sense, and it might be our best bet right now. You all know as well as I do that the threat against us is more powerful than most of us combined. We need this, whatever it is, to help us."

I walked over to Hunter and grabbed his arm, pulling him to me. "And you my love, are going to help me."

He smoothed my hair back, nodding. "Anything."

∞

I decided to begin working on controlling the darkness the next day. I wanted to enjoy the rest of today. At dinner, I learned that Teagan's parents were alerted to what went down in Oregon and were currently on their way there to see if they could get him away from Declan and get him to go home with them. Their coven was traveling with them to provide backup if needed.

I worried about Toni and Logan. They were certainly no match for Declan. Yet I knew that with him being their only child, they'd die trying.

They were supposed to report back to Coeus once they got back. I sure hoped it was soon, or we'd all be worried sick. Presley bit her lip at the news, and I knew I'd need to talk to her soon about Teagan. She'd avoided me quite a bit after I returned.

Whether she denied it or not, I knew that she had strong feelings for him, on top of the fact that they'd been friends for far longer than he and I.

Throughout dinner I felt restless, and I think Hunter knew it.

As soon as he was finished eating, he stood, grabbing my hand and excused us from the table, pulling me behind him.

"Where are we going?" I asked as we ran out the front door into the courtyard.

The moon hung high in the sky yet looked so close to us. Fairy lights lit up the trees, and the golden and silver orbs bounced gently on the breeze, while the trickle from the fountain seemed so loud.

"I think we need another date night after all that happened today." He grinned widely. "Come on, I want to show you something."

He pulled me around the back of the castle, and I saw a path lit up ahead of us. I had never ventured out anywhere other than the fighting grounds.

The scent of night jasmine wafted around us, and the further we went, the darker the path got.

"Just hang onto me. It'll be brighter soon," Hunter called ahead of me.

And it did as soon as we stumbled from the path and onto a sandy beach. Ahead of us, water shone in the moonlight, and there was no one around.

It reminded me of a little cove I'd visited once with Nan long ago. Quiet and peaceful. Beautiful.

"Wow. How did I not know this was here?" I gasped.

"Well, you haven't exactly had time to explore all that Fairy has to offer. I found this place when I was here training with the Titans the first time. It became my place to escape, and I wanted to share it with you. I felt you needed a little escape at this moment."

He was right, I did. But I also felt the need to use up some of the pent-up energy inside of me.

Grinning coyly at him, I backed toward the water. "Wanna race?" I nudged my chin behind me before grabbing the hem of my dress and yanking it over my head. I watched his eyes widen, and laughter rippled through his chest as he began stripping down to his boxers. I knew there'd be no way to beat him if I didn't get a head start, though. I turned and ran in my underwear down to the water, diving in and pushing my muscles as fast as they would go.

I heard a splash behind me, and I knew he was already gaining on me. My heart sped up with adrenaline, and I kicked harder and faster.

To no avail, though.

Soon his hand grabbed ahold of my ankle and dragged me back to him, stopping all of my momentum.

He swirled me around to face him, and I splashed water into his face, laughing.

"You'll never outrun me."

I laughed and felt so free out here in the night air. The water was cool, but not cold and the heat from Hunters body kept me warm.

"No, I'll never run from you, but I sure do like it when you chase me." I grinned playfully.

He swirled in a circle, holding me tight, and stared into my eyes with so much tenderness that I felt it to my core.

"I'll follow you anywhere and everywhere, to the ends of the earth if I have to." He kissed me then.

We were so lost in the kiss that I didn't even realize it had begun raining until the steady beat of drops hitting the water reached my ears, and I looked up at the sky, water running into my eyes.

There was one cloud above us. Just one, while the rest of the sky was clear, and stars sparkled around the moon.

"What in the world?" I laughed in wonder and looked back at him.

He held me tighter, smiling. "You ever read *The Notebook?*"

Had I? Of course I had.

"Yes..."

"Well, so have I." He carried me out of the water with my legs wrapped around him to stand on the bank.

"My favorite scene in the book is when Noah and Allie kiss in the rain. In the book it signifies that they both realize that their relationship isn't over, that it's just beginning." He smiled down at me. "I wanted to have our own rain scene. But for us, this signifies the washing away of our fears, and the start of our epic romance. Next time rain falls, I want you to think of me, and all the new beginnings we're going to have throughout our long lifetime."

I don't know how long we were out there kissing and just holding onto one another, but it was late by the time we'd dried and come back inside. The castle was quiet, and it seemed everyone had already retired to bed.

Hunter carried my sandals and walked me to my room, stopping at the door to lean down and kiss me goodnight.

"Get a good rest, baby. I'll see you in the morning." And with that he turned away, whistling as he went down the hall.

I slid through the door and tried to be quiet as I went to change into my pajamas, but a voice spoke up, startling me.

"Where've you been, young lady?"

Charlie snickered at Emric's version of a mad parent, while Star growled when I flicked on the light, stirring her from a deep sleep.

"None of your business, Emric, though I'm sure you already know. Nothing gets past you," I muttered as I walked to the bathroom.

"Nope! And it never will! You best be glad that I know Hunter is a gentleman!" he hollered as I shut the door.

I changed and then jumped into bed, yawning. Emric kept chattering away, so I put in my earbuds, turned the music up and passed out.

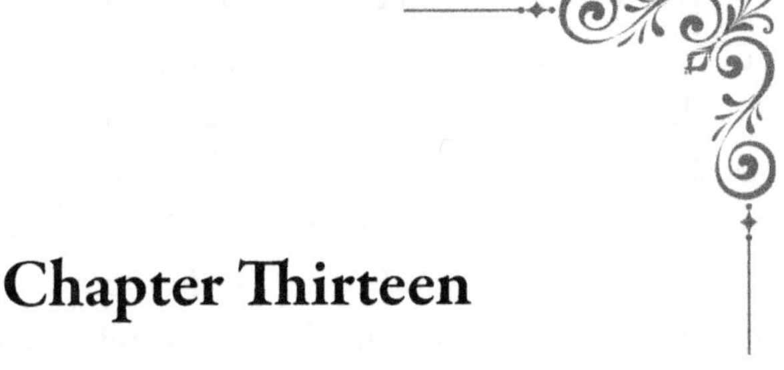

Chapter Thirteen

I was woken the next morning by Trela and Bea sweeping into the room and jumping on my bed. Emric squealed and hopped down while Star just gave them a dirty look and snuggled back up under my chin.

"Why are you still in bed, sleepyhead?" Bea asked, pulling back the covers. "Come on. Aine said she'd show us the Snowflies today."

I'd forgotten about the Snowflies and their ability to soar over Fairy. It sounded like a fun and carefree day. One I wasn't going to be able to participate in.

"I'm sorry, Bea, I can't today. But you guys should go have fun. Oh! And have them take you to the town, I can't remember its name, where all the shifters are. Who knows? Maybe there will be a dragon shifter there too," I said, excited for them.

Their eyes lit up, and they had all kinds of questions which I tried to answer as best as I could.

Soon after, I shooed them out the door and got ready to begin my first test with the power inside me.

But first I'd need to find Hunter.

I searched all over the castle but couldn't find him. I even asked several of the fairies, who said they hadn't seen him.

I couldn't feel him either, and I began to worry.

As I rounded the corner back into the foyer, I ran into Rhea. It'd been a while since I last saw her. She steadied me and laughed. "In a hurry?" She cocked a brow.

"Sorry! Yes, I was just trying to find Hunter, but it's almost as if he disappeared. I'm um, kinda worried."

She looked at me sympathetically before smiling. "I'm sure the bond can be difficult at times. I've heard that you can't be far from each other for long periods, or it can drive you mad."

Is that what this feeling is? I didn't know anymore. I just knew that dread filled me up when I didn't know where he was.

"Don't worry, honey. He's downstairs in the basement where the gym is. You probably can't feel him because that floor is spelled against magic." She leaned in and whispered, "It's where the dungeon is too."

Relief ran through my veins, and I quickly thanked her before hurrying to the stairs that led down.

I'd never been down here before, and this floor was much less stunning than the rest of the castle.

Concrete walls greeted me as I stepped off the stairs and into a long hallway. Light filtered from glass walls along the length of it, and a barred door stood at the very end. That must have been the dungeon.

I hurried along and looked through the glass.

There he is!

My heart settled as I watched him hit a large bag that hung from the ceiling. He wore nothing but gym shorts and tape around his hands as he landed hit after hit on the bag.

Power rippled through the muscles in his shoulder blades and biceps, and sweat trickled down the line of his back.

I couldn't help but admire the picture that he made.

I could have watched him forever, but the show was cut short when he abruptly dropped his hands and turned his head to the side as if listening for something.

I know you're out there, Andie. Quit gawking and come in.

I giggled a little and opened the door, peaking around to see if anyone else was in here with us.

"It's just us, baby. Come here."

I walked toward him, watching as he ran his hand through his sweaty hair, pushing it out of his eyes, his chest flexing as he did.

The darkness inside of me purred. And if I was being honest, I did right alongside it.

When I stood in front of him finally, I hoped he'd kiss me silly again. The darkness hoped for more.

He shook his head at me and winked. "That sounds awfully nice. Maybe later. Right now, we're going to train."

He picked up some gloves that he'd set off to the side and handed them to me. "Put those on. You're going to try and let a little of that darkness rise as you punch this punching bag." He thumped the bag in question. "Just a little at a time. You aren't going to let it go completely."

I strapped the gloves on and looked at him questioningly.

"Okay, so what you're going to do is let just a little out. When you feel like it is pushing more, you're going to punch the bag as hard as you can at the same time pushing down on it. Got it?"

"Yes, I think so. But I'm not really sure how punching this is going to do anything. I'd think it would help it rise quicker because of the aggression?"

He smiled. "Trust me?"

I nodded. "Of course!"

"Good. Now begin and remember I'm here to ground you. I won't let anything happen."

I shook my arms out and bounced on my toes a little. Then I forced myself to be still and concentrate on the inky black inside.

I let go just a smidge of my control on it, and it slithered up. My stomach rolled a bit as it went higher, and I swung back and punched the bag as hard as I could.

I felt the slither stop, as if it wasn't sure, so I punched again and pushed it down. I could feel the resistance as I did. It wanted up, and it wanted up *now*.

I hit the bag in quick succession. *One. Two. Three.* My arms burned, and so did my stomach.

But I felt the darkness retreat, and I slammed those invisible bricks down.

Even though I hadn't exerted myself much by punching, the energy I put into keeping the power at bay had me gasping for breath.

Hunter's hand steadied me, and I felt a bottle of cold water placed in mine. "That was good baby. Take a drink."

I slid to the floor and gulped the water down. Acid from stomach had my throat burning, and the cool liquid soothed it.

"You okay?" he asked as he squatted so we were eye level.

I looked into his dark eyes and nodded. "I'm good. Let's do it again."

And so, I did. Over and over until I'd mastered letting it out about halfway and then pushing it back down.

My stomach felt as if I'd done a thousand crunches, and I pleaded no more.

"Let's get you upstairs and into a bath to soothe you," Hunter said quietly, scooping me up off the floor. I felt like a pile of jelly.

Still, I smiled at him, holding on tight as he carried me up and out into the first floor.

In my room, he walked past Emric, Star, and Charlie, who all just watched without a care. In the bathroom, he flicked his wrist while still holding me and the water began to pour into the tub. Gently, he slid me down his body until my feet touched the ground.

"Do you think you can manage on your own?" he asked.

I expected to see a mischievous light in his eyes, but all that was there was worry and seriousness. "I'll be fine Hunter. I promise. If you want to wait outside, I'll call if I need you."

He nodded and backed out of the bathroom, closing the door quietly behind him.

After pouring some bubble bath into the water, I slipped in, sighing as the warmth permeated my sore body. Sliding further in, I dunked my head back and closed my eyes.

I really wish I hadn't done that.

In my weakened and relaxed state, I'd let my defenses down. The bricks crumbled, and the darkness rushed up. I heard a laugh in my mind, low and cruel, and the oiliness spread around in my chest. A growl sounded deep in my throat. I didn't have time to think, I just knew I couldn't let it out.

Pushing with all my might, I slammed my body back into the water, submerging my face.

Invisible hands tried to pull me up, but I wedged my hands and feet inside the tub, not letting it get its way. My lungs burned, and my eyes ached as I stared up at the swirling sky above me through the water.

Just as I felt like I would explode and my vision darkened at the edges, I felt it let go.

That's right. You're not winning today. Not ever, I thought to myself, just as strong hands snatched me out of the tub and worried eyes were the last thing I saw.

∞

Gentle hands rubbed my back, over and over, and someone else smoothed my hair.

I was on my side, naked under the covers of my bed, and everything hurt.

I coughed and cracked open my swollen eyes to see Presley in front of me. She was the one smoothing my hair. "Shhh... don't try to talk just yet. Breathe. Aine has a rush on some medicine to soothe your throat coming right up."

By now I knew that the hands rubbing my back were Hunter's. The warmth that only he gave me began spreading throughout my cold body.

He didn't say a word, but I felt the worry and guilt running through him. He felt like he'd pushed me too hard yesterday.

You didn't. I pushed myself. At least now we know that I can't wear myself down so much.

I should have never left you alone in there.

Hunter, you didn't know. I didn't know.

Elation flew through me as I realized that even though I had been close to death, I'd managed to defeat it even when it snuck up on me and my body was depleted.

I conveyed that to Hunter, and his hands paused in their rubbing before starting up again. I could feel the relief rush through him at knowing what went down in there.

Aine came through the door then, all no-nonsense, scooting Pres out of the way and taking her spot. She lifted me up some and held a small glass bottle to my lips. "Drink. It'll help," she said softly.

I did as I was told, and instantly the tightness in my throat and lungs eased, my muscles relaxed, and my eyes felt normal again.

I cleared my throat. "Thank you, Aine. It feels much better now." I smiled up at her and she leaned down to kiss my forehead.

"Child, you keep giving us scares like this and I don't know how much longer my immortal heart can take it." She laughed a little and stood up.

"I'll let these two take care of you." And with that, she was gone again.

I rolled over onto my back and looked at both Hunter and Pres on either side of me, grasping for their hands. "Thank you both for taking care of me."

I squeezed their hands tight, and Pres laughed. "You'd do the same for all of us, and really, I didn't do a thing other than come in here when I heard Hunter yelling at the top of his lungs."

She leaned in and stage-whispered to me, "He's a keeper, this one."

I smiled back at her. "Yes, he definitely is."

Emric, Charlie, and Star all pranced in then, and took in the scene.

"You trying to get yourself killed once again, my girl?" Emric asked with dry humor.

"Yep. Can't seem to stay away from it." I rolled my eyes and stuck out my tongue.

"I think you'll be fine." He rolled his eyes back and hopped onto the window seat to stare outside.

"Looks like we have company." He turned back to me with serious eyes. "Teagan's parents are here."

"What?" I squeaked and tried to get out of bed.

"Hey, take it easy." Hunter eased me back, and Presley looked ill at ease. "We'll see what is going on and let you know."

Standing, he walked from the bed. As he did, I swung my legs over and stood. "Listen, I'm fine! And I'm coming with you." I argued, letting my temper get ahold of me.

He turned and looked at me sternly before sighing and walking to my side.

"Fine. But if you're going, I'm carrying you. You just went through a traumatic incident and I'm not going to take the chance of you falling down the stairs." He huffed.

I curled into him and smiled, content and happy to have gotten my way. "I'm getting pretty used to this." I kissed his neck and he groaned as we headed down the stairs, Presley following close behind us.

We found them in one of the sitting rooms with Coeus, Celeste, and Aine. Lelantos and Rhea stood outside the door looking somber but didn't say a word as we passed them.

Toni and Logan looked up as we entered, and confusion lit Celeste's eyes as she saw Hunter carrying me. I guess Aine hadn't had a chance yet to fill her in on what happened.

"I'm fine. He's just overprotective." I smiled as he put me down. He didn't argue with me for once, and I turned to Teagan's parents.

"Logan, Toni." I put my arms around them both and pulled them in for a hug. Toni's shaky arms hugged me tightly in return, and when I pulled away and studied her, I could tell she'd been crying.

"Please sit. Tell me what happened."

They went on to tell me how they and the coven had traveled to Oregon, to the exact spot we had gone to and confronted Declan. At first, he wouldn't let them see Teagan, only shouted at them from the cabin above, ordering demands for things that weren't theirs to give.

They would have attacked the cabin had Teagan not been inside, but they couldn't take the chance. Finally, after a while of Declan gloating about all he would do, he led Teagan outside. He had a collar around his neck, and Declan told them that he was his slave now. If only Teagan had done what he asked and killed me while I'd been there, he wouldn't have been put in this position. But Teagan refused.

The coven and his parents had no idea how to get Teagan free, and Toni was beside herself after seeing the shape her son was in.

I leaned forward in my seat and grasped her hands, looking deep into her gray eyes that were so much like mine. "I promise you. I'll get him back, one way or another. I swear." I said it with conviction because I knew that I would, just like I had Hunter. I just wasn't sure how I would do it yet. But I would. And I knew everyone else would help me.

Presley requested some time alone with the two of them, and the rest of us left the room to give her the privacy she needed. She'd been through a lot with them when we weren't around. And I knew that between the three of them they could find some solace.

I turned to Rhea and Lelantos as we walked out, and the doors shut behind us.

"Can you and the other Titans do me a huge favor please?" I asked them. Their eyebrows both rose at the same time, but they nodded.

"Can you all brainstorm and see if you can come up with a scenario where we get Declan to come here, or anywhere really, away from the epicenter of evil that he's opened? If we can deceive him and set up a trap, then we might just be able to get Teagan from his clutches. It doesn't have to happen right away, of course, but the sooner the better."

They looked at each other, and then back at me. I could see the wheels already turning in their minds, and Rhea nodded stiffly.

"We'll see what we and the others can come up with and let you know."

"Thank you. There's just so much going on that I need some extra brains working on this."

She smiled at me. "I bet Perses and Phoebe will have some grand ideas." She winked.

Yeah, I bet they did too. Those two always seemed to be pranking the others or coming up with devious plots. I always thought it was mainly because they were bored. But they would definitely come up with some good ideas.

"I can't wait." I turned to Hunter and asked him to call for my dad. I wanted to see him.

He was there within the hour, and I rushed up to him, hugging him like my life depended on it.

"Hi, sweetie. You doing okay?" He brushed my hair back and looked me over, assessing.

"I'm fine, Dad. I just needed to see you and talk some things over with you." I smiled up at him.

"Of course. I'm here for you anytime you need me, just a call away."

He had been off visiting all the different factions, helping to secure their defenses and set up protection for the surrounding towns and cities. It was a huge job, but he had been the best choice for it.

"How's everything going?" I asked. "Any trouble?"

He shook his head as we walked to the nearest sitting room and settled in together on the couch. Hunter had stopped outside, giving us privacy but also guarding the door. From what, who knew? But he had the best intentions.

"It's going well. We had a little trouble with some of the Merfolk, but that's smoothed out now and they're cooperating immensely. So far we've gotten the entire eastern seaboard protected, and there's a team working overseas in the UK and Asia. We still need to get some teams over to the other countries, but the packs and covens there are doing what they can."

I nodded. It sounded like things were coming along just as they should.

"So, what's up, honey? What can I do?" Worry lined his eyes. He knew I was pretty self-sufficient and always had been. So, when I needed him, I'm sure it struck as something being wrong.

"Everything's okay," I laughed. "Well, as good as it can be with what all is going on." I filled him in on the training to control the darkness, what we'd learned from Freya, the visit to Declan and Teagan.

He listened without saying a word, and just getting everything out to him seemed almost soothing to me. I knew he wouldn't judge any of my decisions, and most likely would back me up in whatever I wanted to do.

I rubbed the necklace he had left me, now empty of the feather, but with his and Mom's picture snug inside.

"I know I've got a lot going on right now, and it's only going to get busier, but Christmas is next week. I want to have Christmas at home. Maybe Celeste's house? Or the Oak, I don't care which, but I think it's really important for us to celebrate it. Together." I reached for his hand. "We haven't had a chance to celebrate a holiday together before, and I don't know, it would really mean a lot to me. Especially with all the uncertainty around us."

He smiled gently and pulled me to him. I rested my head against his chest, and my soul just felt calm and satisfied to have my dad wrap his love around me.

"Of course we can have Christmas together. You don't know how happy it makes me that you want that." He whispered into my hair. "All those years without being able to do it, I had dreamed of the time we could be a family. Nothing would stop me from being there now."

I sat back up, happy, and pictured what it would be like, my mind already running through what meal we'd have, and what presents I would get.

"Great! I better get to planning then. Although I might need your help with a special present."

His eyes glittered as he looked to where my eyes had landed on Hunter as he was turned away from us.

Reaching into his pocket, Dad pulled out a piece of paper and a pen.

"Write it down, or else you might spoil the surprise." He chuckled, knowing about our bond and us being able to hear each other's thoughts.

So I wrote it down, and as he looked at what I'd written, his eyes teared up, and he swiped quickly at them before looking at me. "You sure?"

"Surer than I've ever been about anything in my life." I smiled, swiping at my own tears. There was just something about seeing a parent cry that got to you every time.

"I'll make it happen, sweetheart." And he pulled me in for another hug.

He left shortly after with my note safely tucked away in his pocket and a big hug for Hunter, who looked at me with raised eyebrows over Dad's shoulder.

I just shrugged and smiled. I was looking at two of the most important men in my life, and my heart squeezed tightly.

After he departed, Hunter took me to the dining hall, and I spotted Killian and Trela at one of the tables. Their eyes didn't leave each other's, and I could literally see the sparks flying between them.

Good.

They both needed happiness and deserved each other. I looked around for Bea and saw her talking to a girl I hadn't seen around here before. She saw us and waved us over, excitement evident in her facial expressions.

"Hunter, Andie, I want you to meet Shay. She's a dragon shifter." Bea beamed at me, and Shay did the same, sticking her hand out.

"Nice to meet you." Her face quickly paled, and before I knew it she'd dropped into a curtsy.

I laughed and pulled her up. "That's not needed."

Her cheeks stained red like her hair, the freckles that covered her nose standing out even more. She was cute, and I could see by the way that Bea looked at her that she thought so too.

Love seems to be blooming all around us, I thought as I looked up into Hunters smiling face and he gave a gentle nod.

"Welcome, Shay. I couldn't be happier that you're here. And I know I speak for Aine and all of us when I say you should stay as long as you like. I'm so happy to see that you found each other." I looked again at Bea, and she bounced on her toes and squeezed Shay to her.

Giggling they said goodbye and headed out of the room.

"Well, that certainly is something," Hunter mused.

"Yes! I had mentioned that maybe she'd find another dragon shifter at Talisia, but I wasn't counting on it. They've looked so long." My breath caught on emotion, and he squeezed my hand.

"I think this is just the news we needed today. And I have another idea. Let's not get food here tonight. Give me just a minute." He stepped away and pulled out his cell phone.

He looked so in command of himself as he spoke into it, pulling the black suit jacket back as he stuffed his hand into his back pocket.

Have I said how much I like his suit before?

Gah. What a hottie.

His eyes flicked to mine, heat pouring from them as he finished up his call and put his phone away before strolling over to me.

He bent down, his mouth close to my ear, his breath tickling. "I warned you before about those kinds of thoughts, Andie. Don't play with fire."

Mmm... a sultry voice filtered through my mind, and I let go a little of the darkness. "But our fire is my favorite. Don't worry. I won't get burned." I winked at him this time and turned away.

Looking back over my shoulder, I saw his smoldering gaze before he shook himself out of it and raced to catch up. "Come on. It's time for another date night."

Laughing I let him pull me out of the castle again, anxious to see what he had planned this time.

We ended up on Main Street in Junction, and I looked around. The only light on was at Sari's Café. "What are we doing here?"

He smiled and ushered me towards the café, his hand on my back.

"We're having dinner." He smiled, opening the door.

Inside, Sari stood beside the counter. Flowers littered every available surface, while fairy lights danced near the ceiling. Candles were lit on a table situated in the middle of the room, while the rest of them had been pushed back against the walls.

Sari walked forward, her hair was still the bright purple it had always been, though she'd shaved one side off while the other side was long.

Her arms surrounded me, and she rubbed her hands up and down my back.

Stepping back, she looked at Hunter, who nodded. "I'll go and get your dinner. Have a seat you two."

When she disappeared into the kitchen, the main lights lowered leaving us in the soft glow of the fairy lights and candles. Then music began playing.

It was a beautiful acoustic rendition of "Can't Help Falling in Love with You" and instantly gave me all the feels.

Hunter sat across from me, his eyes soft as we listened. About halfway through the melody, I gasped.

"Is this you playing?"

A blush rose to his cheeks as he looked down at the table and nodded.

"Oh my God, Hunter. It's beautiful! But who's playing the violin? The two instruments sound just lovely together."

He just smiled at me.

"Wait, you play the violin too? How did I not know that?"

He was a man of many talents I was coming to find out.

He shrugged, "I taught myself both when I was younger. I just don't have as much time to play lately. It was always an outlet for my rage and anger at my dad when I was younger. Now it's an outlet for stress and emotions I don't know how to express fully. It's soothing."

"I'd love for you to record all that you play for me. You know music helps me too. And if I knew it was yours, well, I can only imagine the effect. But how did you mesh the two instruments if you were playing both?" I asked curiously.

"I played them separately and then went into Aine's studio and spliced them together to create this. It's not a big deal." The corner of his mouth lifted into a half-smile. "But to answer your question, yes I'll record whatever you want. Tell me your favorite songs, and I'll make it happen."

"Deal." I smiled at him softly.

Sari came out then, just as the song was ending, and placed our plates in front of us. "I hope you enjoy, darlings. If you need anything at all, I'll be in the kitchen."

And she hurried back to leave us alone.

I dug into my meal, and my eyes rolled back. Sari had outdone herself this time. Grilled chicken with a side of asparagus and mashed potatoes that tasted like nothing I'd ever had before. I wanted her to go back to the castle and cook for us all the time.

I noticed that it didn't seem to have the same effect on Hunter and asked him why.

"Sari's magic doesn't work on Titans. We're immune, though I must say it is delicious even without it." He grinned and chewed slowly. "But the company is what makes this date so special."

It occurred to me that he had been planning a lot of dates lately, and it slightly alarmed me that maybe it was because he was afraid of what the future would bring us.

"Stop it," he said sternly. "I'm not afraid at all. I have all the confidence in the world that things will turn out in our favor. I just want to show you how much you mean to me. Give you a taste of what normalcy is in this crazy time. This is how your teenage years should be, Andie. Not out fighting wars, suppressing evil power, or leading millions of people." Anger flashed in his eyes before he got a handle on it.

"You deserve to have everything. I'm only trying to give you what I can right now. That's all."

And that right there was why he was the one.

My person. My love.

∞

We danced after we ate, and it truly was a magical night. We hugged Sari goodbye after she promised to come visit us soon.

I spied Hunter slipping some bills into her hand, much larger than I'm sure she expected by the look in her eye, but that was Hunter for you. He went big and he knew that the café was struggling with all the turmoil that was going on.

As he led me out into the night, I was high on life and love. Yeah, I realize how corny that sounds, but it's the truth.

He twirled me around on the sidewalk and out of the corner of my eye, I noticed someone ducking back behind one of the buildings.

Stopping him from twirling me again, a question lit his eyes, and I nodded in that direction.

Someone was there. I think they were watching us, but I didn't get a good look at them before they ran.

Any other night I'd go after them, but I can't take the chance with you, baby. Let's go.

His eyes scanned the area as he held me tight, and he shifted us back to the castle.

He pulled out his phone as soon as we touched ground, quickly calling Sari to warn her of what I saw.

She had already locked up and set the magical barrier that the coven had put around her café. I breathed a sigh of relief knowing that she was as safe as she could be.

Once again, Hunter walked me to my room. Stopping at my door, he lifted my hand to his lips and placed a kiss on the back of my hand while his eyes never left mine.

"Goodnight sweetheart."

I entered my room to find Trela and Pres waiting. They lounged on my bed together, petting Star, and I could tell Pres had been crying.

I immediately went to her, ignoring Emric, who teased me about my date.

"What's wrong, Pres?" I asked as she scooted over to make room.

Sniffling she wiped her eyes and hiccupped.

"I'm just so worried about Teagan. His parents are too, and I know they're desperate. I can't imagine what he is going through at the hands of that monster, and it makes me sick."

"I know, sweetie. Me too. I promised his parents that I'd find a way to get him out of there. And I'll make you the same promise, okay? We're going to figure this out and save him. From Declan, and from himself. You care for him, don't you?" I asked.

She looked me in the eye all tears gone. "Yes, I do. I didn't realize it until he'd left. I think a part of me always has, but we were always such good friends, then he had a crush on you, and well, things just never went any further. I don't know how he feels about me, but I do care for him. So much."

I nodded. I understood the feeling she spoke about. I knew it well.

"We'll get him. And then you guys can explore this relationship fully." I smiled bravely at her, willing her to feel my strength and conviction.

I hoped the Titans came up with an idea soon. If they didn't, I wasn't sure if there'd be anything left of Teagan to save.

Chapter Fourteen

The next week was a flurry of activity. Between meeting after meeting with the faction leaders and the mounting danger around the world, I was barely able to find time to work on controlling the darkness, let alone plan for our Christmas get together the week after.

Every day I fell into bed exhausted, and rarely did Hunter and I have any time alone together.

Several times the darkness reared its ugly head, and with the stress that I was under, it became harder to control my anger each time it did. Which in fact only fueled it more.

I let it slip out a little at times, and whoever was on the receiving end of my harsh words would always give me an incredulous stare and flinch slightly.

Sometimes I immediately apologized, and other times, I'd just smirk and walk away. The thing inside of me purring and a satisfied feeling would take over my body.

I learned to pick my battles with it, but I refused to participate in the destructive thoughts that it would sometimes push into my brain.

When it came to more mundane things, like makeup, clothes, and hair, I gave it a pass, so each day this week it had me wearing black outfits. And it appeared to really appreciate leather.

Today, I wore a tight black corset top with leather pants. My hair tumbled down my back, and red heels that were surprisingly comfortable graced my feet.

As I stared at myself in the mirror, darkly painted eyes stared back. I thought about Sari's nose ring and how it would make this look perfect.

Yes...

The voice inside my head slithered into my thoughts, and warmth spread over me like a hug.

Without a thought, I called the horde of fairies that insisted on attending to me daily. I outlined what I wanted, and their eyes darted back and forth to each other in uncertainty.

"I wasn't asking," I said briskly and thought to add a *please* as they hurried out.

Within minutes, they were back and gathered around me as I sat still in my chair. I watched as one of them held a sharp needle while another hung in the air beside her.

It was over faster than I could blink, and there had hardly been any pain.

I rose to look in the mirror and absently thanked them as they rushed out the door. Most likely worried about what Aine might do when she found out.

I stared at the tiny diamond that sparkled where it sat in my left nostril, and it amazed me how one tiny decoration could alter your appearance and give you a certain type of confidence that you had lacked.

I smirked as I thought about what everyone would say, their reactions when I walked into the room would surely be hilarious to see.

I didn't care. I was my own person and even if I was the leader of the Fae, I wasn't going to worry about what they thought of my appearance. They only needed to judge me on the things I *did*, not how I looked.

When I stepped out of the bathroom and into my room, Emric whistled low.

"The dark witch has arrived. Look out, world."

I frowned at him and tossed my hair back. "I'm not dark. Don't say that."

He just chuckled. "Whatever you say, my dear. I suppose that rock in your nose lends you a little brightness."

I ignored him as Star hopped up onto my shoulder and he and Charlie followed behind. I could hear Charlie whispering something to him, but only the words *darkness* and *control* reached my ears. I hoped he was admonishing Emric and supporting the fact that I had this under control.

Downstairs, the castle was complete chaos.

I found Killian and Trela in the middle of it, with Bea and Shay watching on. Pushing through the crowd of frenzied fairies and Titans, I rushed to them.

"What's going on?" I demanded with my hands in fists on my hips. Total silence ensued as all eyes turned to me.

Surprise. Shock. Uncertainty.

All of those emotions ran over the faces of the crowd around me. I cringed a little, but the darkness smirked.

"Is someone going to tell me what the commotion is about?" I asked, my eyebrows raised.

"Presley is gone. No one has seen her since last night, and we've searched and searched and she's not in Fairy any longer." Killian ran his hands through his hair, worry wrinkled his forehead.

"What do you mean she's gone? She didn't say anything to anyone?"

How could she have left without saying anything? Dread filled me as my intuition kicked in. We'd just found out about Teagan being used as Declan's slave.

Killian shook his head and Shay stepped forward. "I may be able to help with that." She frowned, and I could feel anxiety rippling off the poor girl.

"Yesterday, I heard her talking with one of the fairies about sifting somewhere. I didn't catch the location, only that she needed to leave early in the morning. Something about needing hiking boots too, though not sure why she'd want to leave here to go hiking." Shay's face was lined with confusion. "I'm sorry. That's really all I heard. I wish I could help more."

I placed my hand on her shoulder. "Thank you. You've helped more than you know." I turned to Lelantos and Perses, who had come to flank both of my sides.

"Would you please round up everyone? The Titans, Aine, and Celeste."

They nodded and left me in Killian's care, with Rhea watching on. I was about to go hunting. Good thing I'd dressed for it. Though the heels would have to go.

Turning, I headed toward the closest meeting room, seating myself at the head of the table as everyone else filtered in. Hunter came to stand before me, his eyes taking in every bit of my outfit, then lingering on the tiny stud in my nose.

His eyes sparkled with mischief, and his thoughts filtered into me as he leaned forward, both hands planted on the table.

Feeling a little bad today?

I smirked and ran my finger down his arm before smoothly grabbing his shirt and pulling him closer and rubbing my nose against his.

"Maybe a little. But I have a feeling I'm going to need it today."

He cleared his throat and stood back up, rounding behind my chair and laid his hands on my shoulder, grounding me as the reckless darkness began to rise.

His presence helped balance the constant discord between myself and the alien inside of me.

Once everyone sat around the table, all eyes were on me. I ignored any of the new looks I received and got right down to business.

"Presley left and I know where she went. We have no time to lose because I'm afraid that Declan will end up with two slaves instead of just one. She's on a mission, a reckless and stupid one, to save Teagan."

I filled them in on her feelings for him, and how lately she'd been depressed.

I lined out how Bea and Trela would carry me, Killian and Hunter to look for her. I only hoped we could intercept her before she got to close to the rift in the mountains, and before she happened upon any stray demons roaming the area. Who knew what they would do to her? She had no magical abilities except shifting.

And while her white tiger could certainly do enough damage, she was no match for demons from hell, let alone Declan.

Once again, there was a flurry of activity as we got ready to depart. I ran up to change into boots and then back down to find my group waiting and ready.

All four of them were decked out in their suits. Trela and Bea had their specially made ones on for when they shifted, and I noticed that Killian wore a brand spanking new one that was dark blue with silver accents.

"Fancy," I said as I passed by and he straightened his posture a little, defensive.

"Trela had it made for me. I think it looks pretty sharp." He put his hand around her waist.

"Oh, it looks really sharp. And," I turned back to him, "definitely fitting for you. You needed something a little more than the plain one you wore before. You're part Titan. Time to start dressing like it." I winked at him, and his cheeks bloomed red.

"Time to go!" I hollered as Star clung to my neck, wincing at my yell.

In the courtyard, we sifted to a place not far from the mountains but desolate enough that no one would witness Trela and Bea shift.

The guys both turned their backs as they transformed, and I stuffed their suits into the packs that I hung around their necks.

Dipping their necks down we climbed on. Hunter and I together atop Bea, with my body leaning against his broad chest, while Killian scrambled to seat himself on Trela's back.

Their blue scales glinted in the sunlight and I ran my hand gently over Bea's head admiring the beautiful sight that they made. It'd been too long since we flew together.

With immense strength their wings beat against the air and their powerful legs pushed off.

Before long we were gliding through the crisp air, and I was glad for the sun as it was much colder here than in Texas. I hadn't really thought it out well when I'd just changed into boots. Should have thrown on a jacket too. I shivered a bit, and Hunter hugged me to him to share his warmth.

"While I love everything about this outfit you're wearing, I really wish you had changed into something warmer." His whisper in my ear started the shivers all over again.

I just shrugged and studied the land below, my eyes searching for Pres. I really hoped she was in her tiger form. The white would be much easier to spot from above.

We did several fly-bys around the outskirts of where the chasm lay. Smoke filtered into the clouds from that area, and we made sure to hang far away from it until we were sure she wasn't anywhere in the surrounding woods.

There wasn't a trace of her. Killian even used his thermal imaging magic that he'd recently learned to master, and still nada.

Disappointment and fear coursed through me as I pictured her and Teagan both wearing collars and being subjected to who knew what by the fire demon.

A cackle sounded inside of me, and I pushed the oiliness down.

No, she's fine. She has to be.

I nodded across to Killian and Trela, who saw my motion to go forward.

The dragons' bodies shot across the sky as we moved to fly directly over the rift.

Sulfur rose to greet us, and I choked on the horrible stench. The air was hazy and as we got closer, shrieks and hideous noises rose from below.

My eyes strained to see through the smoke, and dark figures moved steadily below us.

The shadows...

My eyes went to the cabin on the hill and alarm coursed through me as I spied Declan standing outside, a rope in his hand tethered to a person standing in front of him.

Teagan.

He looked so much worse than before. Even from here, I could see how much weight he'd lost and the dark circles under his eyes.

His gaze was trained on us as we flew over, but there was no emotion there. It was as if all the fight had left him.

The sight twisted my heart, and I didn't even realize I'd cried out, until Hunter murmured to me that it would all be okay.

I lost sight of him, but not before I'd seen Declan wave and his maniacal laugh filtered through the air to us.

A lead weight settled in my stomach as I realized that Pres wasn't out here. I'd been wrong.

It just made no sense. I felt certain that this was where she'd come. Trela and Bea circled back to where we'd taken off and with as soft a landing as they could manage, their large feet touched down and we slid off of their backs.

They made quick work of shifting back and dressing. We had no idea if any of those shadows we'd seen were now hunting us.

Sifting back to the castle, I felt frustration rise.

Where is she?

"Killian. I need you and the girls to get on the phone, call everyone you know in the shifter and warlock communities. See if they've seen her. I'll get a hold of Teagan's parents. Maybe they know where she is."

They quickly dispersed to do what I asked, leaving Hunter and me standing in the courtyard, activity buzzing all around us.

"Hey. Take a deep breath. We'll find her," Hunter soothed, his hand steady on my lower back.

Even with his touch grounding me, I felt the trickle of darkness licking its way up inside.

"We need to train." Hunter steered me in the direction of the entrance, and I found myself in the gym without remembering walking there.

"Punch the bag now, Andie." His voice was strained as his eyes stared into mine. "*Now*," he said more forcefully as I hadn't moved.

My arms felt like weights were attached to them as I strained to pull them up, all the while pushing the cancer inside of me down. Sweat beaded on my forehead, and I swung as hard as I could at the mass in front of me, my fist connecting but the bag barely moved.

"Harder!" Hunter shouted. "Put all your anger into it. Show the power inside of you who is in control."

Swinging again, this time the bag swung wildly, and I concentrated again when I felt the flames of darkness hesitate.

You will not control me.

With each hit, I contracted my stomach muscles, pushing down the essence that wanted up. Brick by invisible brick slammed down on it until there was not even a whisper able to penetrate.

By the time it was done, I was spent, and my arms screamed.

Hunter gathered me to him, slicking back my hair that was wet with perspiration. "You did it." He hugged me tight. "You've mastered it for now. Just remember that. You have control over it. Not the other way around."

I nodded into his chest, breathing deeply.

"I have control over it. For now. It's just so exhausting, Hunter."

He pushed me back so that he could look at me, and his eyes swam with gold fire.

"I know it's tiresome. I know there's so much on your plate right now, but I've never doubted that you can overcome anything you set your mind to." He pointed at the Unalome on my arm. "This is your journey. It's going to be filled with lessons, pain and won't always be perfect. But in the end, you're going to come out of this. There will be a time when things will be boring, and you'll miss all the craziness." He teased with the last, his mouth turned up in a smirk.

"I won't ever let you give up or give in to this power inside of you. It will get better. I promise. We just have to get through some hurdles, and then life will really begin."

His words resonated within me. I was ready for that day, and I'd do whatever was needed to reach it, with as many of my family and friends that I could have by my side.

My fingers traced the intricate tattoo that Aine had placed on me all those months ago. And I was grateful for the reminder.

After Hunter escorted me back to my room, he left to make some calls and I took a long hot shower.

I dressed in some comfortable leggings and one of my favorite T-shirts. Feeling more myself, I cuddled on the bed with Star and pulled out my phone to call Toni and Logan.

The phone only rang a few times before Toni's voice came on the line.

"Andie? Is everything okay?" Her voice was shaky, and I knew that she expected news on Teagan. I gritted my teeth and shook my head, even though I knew she couldn't see me.

"I was hoping that you might know where Presley is? She left and no one knows where she went."

A sigh filtered through the phone, and I imagined her face was full of relief that I didn't have terrible news about her son.

"I haven't heard from her since we left Fairy. Do you think she went to Declan?"

I explained to her how that had been my thought as well, but that we hadn't found her. We spoke for a few more minutes and I promised to update her with any news going forward.

I settled into the bed, my mind full of chaos, and hoped tomorrow we'd get some answers.

Smoke and stench surrounded me as I turned in circles. The air was so heavy with fumes that I had a hard time seeing through it.

"You didn't think I'd let you get away so easily, did you?" a deep voice resonated through the fog.

A darkness moved closer, and I squinted to see better.

"This has always been the plan. You fell right into my hands, and none of you- not one-had any idea." The voice laughed and goosebumps trailed my arms.

I couldn't move now. My feet were glued to the ground and I felt the evil inside me swell up.

"You're mine to do with as I please. Your body is no longer yours. You will burn cities and murder thousands. And there will be nothing you can do about it."

Terror filled me up and my head shook back and forth in denial, a scream stuck in my throat as I stared into the eyes of pure evil. And I felt it deep inside of m, that what he said was true.

Chapter Fifteen

I woke to Star purring beside me and patting me with her paw fretfully. Her eyes looked into mine with knowledge that no normal animal could have. The remains of the dream or vision left me cold. As I struggled with which one it was and the fright that consumed me, Charlie flew from his perch near the window to land on my lap. He too stared at me with knowing.

And where Star was non-verbal, he was.

"Do not let your dreams get the best of you. Remember that Helios's power inside of you could also cause these. You've come so far, and you must not let anything deter you from your path." His eyes glowed, much like Hunter's, and different colors seemed to radiate from his wings that I'd not noticed before.

His aura.

"Remember what the sea witches told you, Andie," he whispered, his eyes mesmerizing me, and I flashed back to that moment where Frost told me that they wished to gain my aura ability. That it was a gift from the gods and that whoever was able to use the auras correctly could see into the future.

Why was I just now remembering this?

Uncertainty filled me and I swiped a hand over my eyes. "I need to learn how to use the auras."

Charlie dipped his head in response and his eyes were back to normal.

"*Yes*, you do." He flew back to the window, his little back to me. "While I know you've got far too much on your plate, this is non-negotiable. You must learn, for all of our sakes. Or mistakes will be made that could be life altering. This is your rabbit in a hat."

Eagerness filled me to the brim, even while the dread still lingered from the dream. I pushed the vision of evil that had stood in front of me from my thoughts and scooped Star up.

I needed some time alone to work on this, with no distractions, but I'd need her help.

I walked over to Charlie and kissed him on his little parrot head. "Thank you for the insight and reminder. I wonder if you could do me a favor?"

He turned to look up at me, silent. I took that as a yes.

"Could you please tell everyone I'm not feeling well and want to be alone for a little while?"

His look of disdain at me wanting him to lie had me rushing on. "It's not really a lie. I am shaken up by my dream, and if I'm to learn how to use my auras, I need some time by myself. All these distractions here won't help."

He seemed to believe me and left to do what I asked.

I looked down at Star. "Now, let's hope I don't make too many people mad."

I found my beanie and slipped it over my hair. Instantly, I became invisible. With Star wound around my neck, I slipped out the door and looked around. Not seeing anyone I left it cracked and hurried down the stairs and out the door.

I snuck past all the fairies who milled around outside and walked out to the training grounds where I knew the Titans were. They came out here every morning with the Elves to practice and stay on top of their fighting game.

As I rounded a corner around a corpse of trees, I spotted Amarie and Rhea in hand-to-hand combat.

Both women had immeasurable strength, so while I came out here to practice on the auras, I'd also enjoy watching them spar.

I quietly backed up to a nearby tree and slid down it to sit.

I didn't see any auras-they seemed to come and go at will-and I wasn't entirely sure how to call them up. Concentrating I stared at the two women, focusing on the word aura, and pushing my power into it.

Nothing seemed to work, and I grew increasingly frustrated. How was I supposed to harness this if I couldn't figure out how to work it? Nothing ever came easy.

Four hours later after moving around the grounds and trying to get it to work while studying different people, not even a speck of light had appeared around any of them.

Star looked at me bored, and my head hurt from the strain. I'd give it up for today but decided to talk to Celeste about it in the meantime. She had to have some insight into how I could activate it.

I hurried back to my room and found the door closed.

Strange. I'm sure I left it cracked.

Creeping into the room, I hurried to take the beanie off. As I was placing it into the drawer, a voice sounded behind me.

"Feeling better?"

I jumped into the air and bit my lip to keep from crying out. My eyes met Hunter's in the mirror, and I don't know how I hadn't seen him sitting on the end of my bed.

"Umm..."

He chuckled and stood, walking toward me. "I knew the moment you left this room, and I've been keeping tabs on you all morning. Don't forget I've got an internal radar where you're concerned." He pushed a stray hair behind my ear.

"I would've helped you had you asked," he said more sternly.

I knew he would have, but I felt like I needed to master something by myself. I hadn't wanted to burden him or anyone else with one more thing I needed to learn.

"You'd never be a burden to anyone, Andie. You've got to stop thinking like that. We're all in this together."

A knock on the door interrupted us and I turned to see Celeste breeze in.

"A little birdie told me you weren't feeling well, so I thought I'd check in on you." She smiled, taking in Hunter and me. "He might have also mentioned that you had a dream. Want to talk about it?"

Both she and Hunter looked at me, their brows raised in question. I really didn't want to talk about it. I didn't want to remember it at all. But I supposed I must.

Their eyes met when I was done, worry clear in them but also determination.

"Well, if Charlie believes you must get the aura powers working, then it is clear we must figure out a way. He knows more than I can even explain." Celeste acknowledged. "Let's have lunch and we'll go from there."

Hunter pulled my hair gently as we walked out. *No more hiding from me either missy.*

I couldn't hide from him if I tried. That much was certain.

After lunch, Celeste led us outside and to another path that I hadn't seen before. It wound around the trees and emptied into a clearing where a bright blue pool of water stood, a small waterfall cascading from the rocks behind it.

"We'll start working on the auras here. This is the Well of Restoration. It's meant to heal grievous injuries that anyone in Fairy sustain, and Aine normally wouldn't let just anyone have access. But of course, in this instance, we have approval, and she agrees that our best chance to relax you enough to let your natural abilities shine will be from the waters."

I looked at the pool and back at her. "So, what do I do? Just get in and see if I can see an aura on you two?"

I wasn't sure how this would work, but I was willing to try anything.

"Yes, wade into the water, close your eyes, and just let it relax you."

She and Hunter sat on the bank as I slowly stepped into the coolness. The further I went, the more it seemed to warm and feel as if a blanket surrounded me. Hugging me in its embrace and relaxing my muscles. Easing the tension that always kept them tightened.

"Turn around now, darling. Close your eyes for a moment."

I did as Celeste said, feeling weightless in the water.

All of the worry, fear and insistent noise drifted away, as if filtered out of my body.

It was silent and peaceful.

"Now, keep your eyes closed and I want you to envision the auras you've seen before. Concentrate on those visions and study them. Try to remember what you felt as you saw them in those moments." Her voice was soft and low.

Each of the times that I'd seen auras filtered through my mind, and I stopped on each one, studying them, letting the emotions that I'd felt slide through me. During those times I hadn't been able to see anything other than the colors, but as I looked closer, knowledge suddenly filled me at what each color meant.

The white that I'd so often seen around my friends and family meant that they were sensitive and intuitive with high intellect and an ability to understand others in a spiritual way.

Sometimes I saw pink around Presley, and it meant she loved to be loved and around friends and family at every opportunity. She was very romantic and extremely sensitive.

I smiled to myself. *That's so her.*

The orange that had surrounded Jasper meant he was hot headed and quick to lose his temper. And the black that I'd seen around Freya indicated hatred, illness, and misery.

"Andie, slowly open your eyes now and focus on me," Celeste called out. I followed her instructions and blinked at the brightness. Blue light, the same color of her eyes glowed from her. It was gorgeous, and immediately I knew that it meant she was a peacemaker who prized truthfulness and clarity. The downside was that she could take on too much and neglect her needs.

"Wow," I breathed, not taking my eyes from her though I knew Hunter stood somewhere nearby.

She smiled at me, serene and calm. "You can see it now?"

I nodded.

"Good. We'll take it a step further. Keep your eyes on me Andie. Look into the aura, focus on nothing else. Feel the energy coming from it and immerse yourself."

Her body faded away as I intensely searched the light, my whole being feeling swallowed up by it. A sizzle of power ran through me, and a vision of Celeste standing beside Coeus and Aine holding a bouquet of flowers flashed by.

A wedding?

Pleasure at the thought ran through my bones as it faded, and Celeste came back into sight. My eyes cleared and relaxation still filled me.

Hope lit her eyes and I glanced at Hunter to see the same expression in his.

"Did it work?" he asked, his voice gravelly, a spark of hope lining the timbre.

"I... I think it did." Wonder laced my words as I floated, letting the joy run through me at mastering it. Well, I'd mastered it here. Whether I could outside of this body of water was another story.

Celeste looked pleased and gestured for me to come to her.

I reluctantly walked out, water dripping from my clothes, and as soon as I was on land, I immediately missed the feeling of complete peace.

"I won't ask you to divulge what you saw. I'd rather not know the future unless there's some way I can alter it for a better outcome," Celeste stated.

I squeezed the water from my T-shirt and only smiled. I knew the vision I'd had was one that would be for the ages. A happy time.

Hunter had been quietly standing off to the side with a lopsided grin on his face. It occurred to me that maybe I should try to see his aura now while I stood on land and outside of the magical water.

I focused on him and remembered the feeling the water had garnered. Slowly, indigo tinged the outline of his body. The deep purple glowed, and I sensed that he was in tune with himself, that he searched for higher truths and could see past deceit that people tried to pass on as truth. Strength was also a part of his aura. And passion. Passion for the ones that he loved and a sense that he would do anything to protect them.

His eyes widened as the feelings I gave off were transferred to him and in turn he felt what I saw. I could tell that the reading amazed even him. After all he'd been through and endured, he had grown into an amazing man.

This I'd known but could tell that he hadn't. Even with all his cockiness, he was a stand-up person. He had a good heart.

Elated at being able to call his aura up, I pushed further. Immersing myself in the lush color. Again, my vision tunneled, and I was swept away on a current that I had no control over.

He stood at the base of a mountain. A mountain on fire. While I stood high above, looking down. His arm was stretched out to me, his eyes pleading and his mouth turned down in agony. He shouted, but in the vision I could hear no noise, only see.

And like an elastic band, I was snapped back to the present.

I won't fear the unknown, I told myself, willing my mind to recognize that at any moment these visions could change depending on our actions. Whatever had led me to be on that mountain with him so agonized below, I would work hard to prevent.

At least now I had this as another weapon in my arsenal. It couldn't help me kill Helios, but it sure could help me be prepared.

An unnatural sense of calm came over me and I smiled into Hunter's eyes as he studied me warily, sensing but not knowing the vision.

"Well, I don't know about you two, but I am starving. Can we get dinner? Maybe Aine can have the kitchen whip up some cheeseburgers."

They stared as I calmly walked ahead, before following slowly behind.

I felt bad for all the whiplash I'd seemed to cause them and the others lately with my ever-changing mood. It wasn't something I could help, and I knew they dealt with it the best they could.

Aine did serve my request for cheeseburgers and as I watched Amarie and the Elves look at them with slight disgust, I laughed, dipping a fry into ketchup.

"I promise you'll like it. How could anyone not like cheeseburgers?" I asked as Killian stole one of Trela's fries off of her plate. She swatted at his hand, chuckling.

Those two were fast becoming close, and so were Bea and Shay.

At first, I'd thought that Bea was simply happy to have another dragon shifter around, but it became quite clear that their feelings extended beyond friendship when I'd seen the looks between the two so often.

I was happy for the two of them *and* Killian and Trela.

Coeus sat next to Aine and she giggled about something he whispered in her ear.

I pictured all of us together at Celeste's house in two days' time when we celebrated Christmas. I only hoped that all my presents arrived there on time. Amazon was an amazing service. They'd even gift wrapped them for me! I certainly didn't have time for that.

Which reminded me that I needed to pay Eira and Balwyn a visit. I wanted them to make sure to have food at the house when everyone arrived, and that they would be there too, regardless if Balwyn wanted to attend or not. I wanted him there.

My mind wandered to Teagan and Presley, hoping that they were okay, and wishing desperately that they would be with us to celebrate.

Shaking myself from the melancholy feeling, I decided to shake things up from the normal evening at the castle. I knew at least Killian would back me. He was like my partner in crime when it came to fun.

"Hey, what do you say to making gingerbread houses and singing Christmas carols?" I called to the table.

Everyone looked at me like I'd grown two heads, and I laughed. "Okay, we'll do this the easy way or the hard way. I am your leader you know. I could just order you to do it." I teased and they rolled their eyes or laughed, shaking their heads.

Killian got everyone up and used his enthusiasm to get the rest into the spirit. I always admired that about him. He was such a people person.

Hunter just smirked at me.

"You could always play the piano while we sing." I gave him a coy look, and he smiled and shook his head.

"The things you get me to do." He laughed but agreed. I wasn't aware that anyone else knew he played, and I hoped that I hadn't overstepped my bounds by forcing him into it.

He looked back as he turned to go. "I'll be right back. And Andie? No one forces me to do anything, least of all you."

With a wink, he disappeared, sifting.

While we got table set up and all the necessary items to make the gingerbread houses put out, I felt a change in the air and looked up to see Hunter sitting at the magical piano in a corner of the large room.

Neo stood on top of it with a small violin, and they both had cheesy grins on their faces.

Trela and Bea whooped loudly as the two began to play while the rest of the group stared in wonder.

Hunter played a haunting rendition, one that I was sure he wrote himself, before breaking into a lively round of Jingle Bells. Killian began singing, and everyone eventually chimed in, their voices rising and falling in tune.

Joy spread through me as I watched everyone laugh and tease each other about their versions of a gingerbread house and I challenged Aine and Celeste to a contest.

"Let's see who can make the best one, and the rest can judge once we're done! And," I gave them both an evil eye, "no cheating with magic! You have to do this without it."

Their eyes just twinkled but they agreed, and we got to work.

By the time we were done, I studied my house. It looked pretty pathetic. I hadn't been able to get some of the gingerbread pieces to stay put, so the roof sloped a little, the windows were a bit wonky, but hey, I was proud of myself.

Aine and Celeste's houses were vastly different. Aine selected to make a miniature version of her castle, and somehow it was absolutely perfect. She even had a silver candy suspended by a clear straw in the air to depict the floating orbs.

Celeste made a version of the Oak, and I was slightly jealous that I hadn't thought of that. She even made a little Brownie out of candy pieces that stood in the doorway.

"Are you sure you guys didn't use magic?" I asked skeptically as I stared at their creations. They both just snickered, praising one another's efforts.

"Whatever. I don't care. We're not even going to have the others judge because I'm awarding you both as the winners." I laughed as I walked away and over to Hunter who was having fun playing with Neo.

"You made quite the splash when you popped in here and began playing," I stated as I sat beside him on the bench, leaning my head on his shoulders.

His long fingers danced gracefully over the keys, and I recognized the song. "*All I Want for Christmas is You.*"

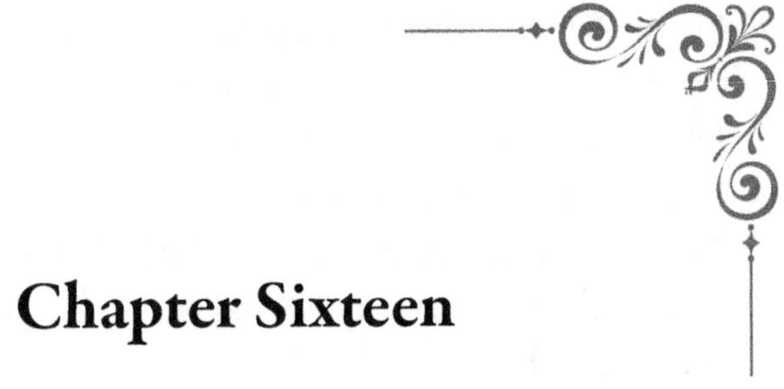

Chapter Sixteen

The next day was a whirlwind of activity. Hunter and I sifted with Celeste back to her house, meeting Eira and Balwyn there. We'd left the castle while Aine ordered the fairies to decorate for the holiday. They'd zipped right into action, and a giant Christmas tree was being erected on the lawn as we departed.

Here at Celeste's house, it was quiet, and cozy. I realized then how much I'd missed it. I proudly studied our handiwork on the tree and added some water to the stand. The pine needles gave the room a fresh scent reminding me of all the holidays with Nan.

She would have loved this, I thought as Eira landed on my shoulder, hugging my neck.

"I missed you, sweet girl. But I am so excited for tomorrow. I've never celebrated Christmas before, and I've been studying up on all the traditions!" she crowed, clapping her hands and proceeded to tell me all of her plans.

It was really overkill, but who cared? We were going to enjoy the day like it was our last because I had big plans on moving forward with this war after the New Year.

I insisted on making snickerdoodles with Celeste, and I could tell the fact that I did warmed her heart. It was always something that Nan had done, and I wanted to continue the tradition now with her.

We laughed as Hunter swiped some of the cookie dough before going back into the living room to help Eira and Balwyn. They were adding who knew what to the décor and setting up a huge table outside so that everyone would have a seat for Christmas dinner.

While I wanted everything to be perfect, most of all I just wanted everyone to enjoy themselves.

Much later that evening, we said goodnight to Celeste when she headed off for her room and waved to Eira and Balwyn as they sifted back to the Oak.

I looked around the house, and it was as if I were back in Fairy. It was a dream lit up magically from the tree to the fairy lights that danced around the ceiling, and the mistletoe that hung in every doorway.

Tomorrow would be a good day.

∞

And it was a good day. At least the majority of it. Everyone arrived early with beautifully wrapped packages that were placed under the tree. Laughter and conversation permeated the house, along with the smell of ham and all the other food that Balwyn had whipped up for us. He grumbled in the kitchen when he was interrupted, but I swear he was in his element and loved every minute of it.

Eira greeted everyone who came through the door and was playing hostess, happy as could be, while I just enjoyed everyone's presence.

When my dad came through the door, I threw my arms around him, knocking several gifts to the floor in the process. He chuckled, holding me tight before setting me back to scoop them up.

"Did you bring it?" I whispered into his ear.

He hugged me tighter and whispered back, "Sure did."

I pushed back to look at him. Happiness lit his face. I was so thankful that he was happy about my surprise, and that I had his approval.

When it was time to sit down for the meal, we gathered on the back lawn and Eira had us all go around the table and say one thing that we were glad about on this day.

"How do you just pick one?" I said aloud. Everyone agreed, but still participated.

When it was my turn, I turned to Hunter who sat beside me. "I am thankful for the Fates that brought us together. For second chances. *And,* for every extra hour that I get with you." I beamed into his questioning eyes while snickers came from Emric and Charlie. I faintly heard Eira hushing them.

"I know we have the bond, and we will forever be together. But," I pulled a small box out from my pocket, "like you, I want everyone to know you're mine, and that I'm yours."

I nodded at the tiny package, urging him to take it. His eyes were moist as his strong fingers grasped ahold of it. He already knew what was in it. I was really surprised he hadn't found out before now.

While he opened the box, I continued. "I wanted something special for us. Something that when you look at it, will always bring comfort."

I grasped his hand as a lone tear tracked down his sharp cheekbones, staring into his dark eyes that now swirled with gold. Just like the rings nestled in the box.

"Hunter, when this is all over, when we've won this war, and everything settles down, will you be my husband?"

My voice had never been steadier or stronger. Even though we were young, the trials and tribulations we had been through had aged our souls. We were meant to be together, and there was no reason to wait.

By now, everyone had quieted, waiting for his answer.

He didn't say a word out loud. His arms wrapped around me, pulling me into a fierce hug. His hands smoothed my hair over and over.

Nothing in this world or the next could keep me from being your husband. You are my heart and soul. I promise to always cherish and protect you.

We kissed, and the onlookers exploded in cheers. Tears of happiness flowed all around while Hunter slipped the thin band on my finger, and I did the same with his.

The rings were simple, nothing flashy, but inside of the strange metal, golden fire swirled, never resting.

That was the task that I'd asked my dad to accomplish. I had remembered him telling me of a precious metal that reminded him of the fire that lit when Hunter and I touched. It had never been far from my mind, and when I'd learned about it, the thought grew and built.

Dad did a fantastic job, and I pulled him to me once Hunter and I stepped apart.

Happiness glowed on his face as he looked at Hunter, and he stuck his hand out for him to shake.

"I know you'll make my little girl happy. You already do. And for that, I am thankful."

∞

The food was perfection and while we ate, Emric, Star, and Charlie played on the grass, further adding to our entertainment and excitement.

Just as I was about to raise a toast, Toni and Logan charged out the back door, spilling onto the patio. All conversation stopped, and I slowly lowered my drink.

The sheer terror, even in Logan's eyes, had my hackles raising.

"What is it?" Hunter stood, rushing to them and steadying Toni where she stood.

"There are monsters... in Junction," she gasped, swallowing hard as her eyes bounced around the table.

My heart beat fast, and my mind went to Sari. I couldn't find my voice, but Hunter took charge.

"Casualties?"

Logan shook his head stiffly. "None that we know about yet. Sari called the coven and we rushed over." He looked at me and Celeste. "Don't worry, she's safe. My second-in-command took her to the compound, though she was very shaken up."

He ran his hand through his hair and, distraught, he sat down on one of the steps, Toni following suit.

Hunter squatted in front of him, and we all moved closer to hear better.

"What kind of monsters are we talking about?" Hunter asked quietly.

"We didn't get close enough to get a good look, but they flew in the sky, like pterodactyls. The rest of the coven is there now, sequestering the humans and spelling them as quietly as they can. These things seem drawn to noise. I'm not sure that they use their vision."

Hunter nodded and stood up, motioning to the rest of the Titans. "We're going to check it out. If they're in Junction, they could be headed this way." He gave me a deep look.

I'm sorry, baby. I'll be back as fast as I can.

I only bit my lip, not worried about our Christmas plans, but worried about him and my friends.

He grabbed me in a tight hug, then quickly let go, gathering the team and then sifted.

Celeste and Aine hurriedly ushered everyone into the house while Charlie took to the skies to see what he could.

Eira twisted her hands back and forth while Balwyn spoke quietly to her.

I stood in front of the bookshelf looking at them all, the book where the Keys lay at my back. The dragonfly bracelet I wore lit up brightly as I stood so close to it, and I stared down. The dragonfly reminded me of the past three journeys and all we'd been through to conquer them. I remembered what Toni and Logan had said about those things being attracted to noise, so I kept my voice as quiet as possible.

"It appears war is upon us. Evil is at our door. It won't go away quietly, but neither will we. Just like every time we've gone face to face with it, this time will be no different. We need to prepare for anything."

My voice despite the low volume, held strength, and I hoped it assured them that we-or rather I-would do anything in my power to get us through it.

We gathered together as we waited for the Titans' return. Dad held my hand as we whispered our plans.

Today was mostly done, and no one wanted to venture out in the night, especially not knowing what those things were capable of, but we would get started at first light.

I knew Hunter wouldn't like it-heck, no one here but me liked my plan to hone in on the remaining two stones-but I felt it was vital. And the sooner I found them, the better chance we had. We needed to stop Helios anyway we could, and the more weapons in our cache, the better. It wasn't just Helios we were fighting anymore. It was also the demons that were being unleashed.

The air moved, and I looked up to see Hunter and the Titans standing before us in front of the Christmas tree.

Rhea looked a little shook up, but the others' faces were stony. Hunter's jaw was tight as he strode to my side.

"It's not good. There are hundreds of them in Junction, and it doesn't look like they're leaving anytime soon. They've roosted on the tops of houses and buildings. We can't move the citizens without rousing their attention, so for now the coven has put a sleeping spell on them. Any of the magical beings that called the town home have been sent to the coven. For now, it appears they aren't moving, so I think we'll be okay here unless there's a rouge in the midst. They seem to stay in packs, but they're killing anything that moves. We discovered a group of them feasting on the cows in a farmer's pasture, and there were several dead cats in the road."

I closed my eyes. I knew it would be bad. Any creature from hell would be set on destroying. I was only glad that no citizens had been hurt that we knew of and the coven had them all taken care of. One less worry for us. We still needed to get rid of them somehow.

"How can we kill them?" I asked aloud.

Lelantos stepped forward. "We plan an attack on them, see what they can stand and can't. Although I tell ya, if we had your friend Teagan here, his hellfire would come in handy."

I agreed, but it wasn't possible right now.

It was late, and everyone was exhausted from the festivities earlier and also from knowing the new threat that we faced.

Celeste got everyone set up in rooms and on pallets on the floor. Star, Emric, and Charlie holed up with me in my bed, and Hunter made a pallet out of covers and pillows on the floor, refusing to leave my side.

Amazingly, I fell right asleep, and no dreams plagued me. And it was a good thing, because I'd need to get all the rest while I could.

∞

The next day bloomed with sunny skies and a crisp wind in the air. Hunter still snored on the floor beside me, and I couldn't miss the opportunity to cuddle.

Slowly as to not disturb my bed mates, I slithered out of the covers and sank to the floor beside him. He was warm and slept on his stomach, his face turned toward me. I just studied how peaceful he was in his sleep. Rarely did you find his face so relaxed and almost childlike.

I wish he didn't have so much on his shoulders.

He sighed, and his dark eyes opened slowly, a soft grin rising on his lips.

"Well, this is a good way to wake up." He stared into my eyes before shifting slightly and running his hand over my cheek, the fire in his ring flashing.

"I just wanted to lie with you a while and watch you," I admitted.

He pulled me into his arms and nuzzled my neck, breathing me in. "One day we'll wake up like this every morning. Mark my words."

The bed covers shuffled and Emric's head popped out. He looked hilarious as his eyebrows drew down. "Well, isn't this cozy. But you know with all your chattering down here you could take it to a different room. Some of us are trying to sleep." He hmphed before turning around and cozying up with Star.

I mock-whispered to Hunter, who chuckled, "He's just jealous."

I heard a snort under the covers, but no retort and Hunter groaned as he stretched. "I guess we should get up and get some breakfast. It's going to be a long day."

I followed him downstairs, where everyone was already up and Balwyn and Eira were back and busy in the kitchen cooking up stacks of pancakes and bacon.

It was rather like feeding an army.

Celeste tried to convince Balwyn that it would be faster if he let her use her magic but he sternly and with no-nonsense told her no.

Toni and Logan left to report back to their coven and give them direction on what to do next. Everyone was pretty much in a holding pattern until we knew more.

My mind wandered to what other kinds of creatures were roaming around and where.

"Dad, how has it been going with getting the West Coast and other countries prepared?" I asked. He turned from his breakfast, swallowing fast and took a drink of orange juice.

"Really well, I think. At least everyone seems prepared for what we can handle. With some of the creatures, I have no idea what to expect, so we'll need to get the word out for the factions to be prepared for anything and at a moment's notice."

I nodded, satisfied that he had done, all he could. Now it would be up to the magical communities to protect who and what they could.

We filled up on food, and when we were done I made sure Balwyn and Eira packed our sacks just in case we needed to flee quickly.

The Titans gathered together and talked furiously, etching out a plan of attack. The fact that they had decided to set down their own comfort, despite the rules that had long been set in place, all to help us warmed my heart more than they could know.

It was a sacrifice they had been willing to make. And really, no one knew what the end result would be if they didn't, and Helios defeated us. No one knew the true amount of power he had built up, or who was on his side.

Right now, we had a strong suspicion that Hades was, and of course we knew the Fomori.

I thought it strange that we'd not seen any of the Fomorians recently, but I knew it was only a matter of time before they reared their ugly heads.

Like one unit, the Titans stood, and Hunter came to me, Coeus to Aine.

"It's time," Hunter said softly.

I nodded, biting the inside of my cheek and willing myself to stay strong. He was powerful, and I couldn't forget he still had his shifter abilities too.

His forehead touched mine, and I nodded. "Just promise me you won't take any un-needed risk. Learn what you need to, kick their butts, and come back to me." My smile wobbled a bit before I got it back under control.

He leaned back and with more bravado than I knew he felt, he gave me that cocky grin. "I've told you before and I'll tell you again, I'll always come back to you."

With that heart-melting wink, he turned and marched over to his team. With a salute, they were gone.

I fidgeted. My body was full of pent-up energy, and I thanked the stars that so far the darkness had stayed hidden. I couldn't deal with it right now.

I pictured the Titans waging war on those winged creatures and winning. I imagined them killing every last one of them and hoped that it would be so.

Dad patted my hand before I stood up and began pacing. I knew everyone watched me, waiting. I had to do something. I couldn't just sit here.

And then a thought came to me. I knew what I had to do. And I knew Hunter would be furious, but I'd deal with that later.

"I need to find the stones. Now," I stated to the room and everyone turned to me, waiting. "I know it would be best to wait on the Titans, but I don't know that we have time. Things are getting worse daily, and we need them. I'm certain of it."

Killian stood and walked to stand beside me. "I'm with you." He said, his voice strong and sure. Next came Trela, Bea, and Shay. Amarie looked uncertain but when my dad also stood with us, her group acknowledged that they would help as well.

Satisfied, I turned to Aine and Celeste. "If you could stay here in case the Titans return before we do, and explain, I'd really appreciate it. I'll have my phone with me. Please call me with any news."

The ladies both looked a bit worried, but knew it was better to let me do what I wanted rather than hold me back. I'd find a way regardless.

"Okay then. Let's get changed and get going. I have an idea of where to start first."

Chapter Seventeen

When we all stood together in battle gear, with magic and weapons on standby, we slung our packs over our shoulders and said our goodbyes..

I had all the confidence in the world in the team that stood around me. All of them harnessed different powers and abilities. They were strong and smart.

"Where to first?" Killian asked, his energy and excitement evident.

"To Germany. I have a strong suspicion one is there."

And we sifted.

We found ourselves atop Watzmann Mountain. Exactly where I wanted to go. I'd once read about a king, a tyrant really, who lived in the deepest corners of southern Bavaria. He enjoyed slavery and hunting local peasants. One day after he'd killed many of them in what was said to be a large blast of power, executing them all at once, a curse was placed on him and his family.

The book of tales had explained that he had found a stone with immeasurable power. That this stone had turned him into the horrible man that he was. It was the local coven who then put the curse on his entire family which turned them all to stone.

They were then entombed within a range of seven mountains, of which the Watzmann was one. It was also the tallest out of the seven, and I felt it a good starting point for the stone to call to me.

Now, the stone could have been stolen by anyone, even the coven that had cursed him. But I felt deep in my soul that it was still on his person. We just had to find him.

"Whoa!" Bea called out as she turned in circles, shivering. It was winter after all.

I agreed; the sight was something to behold. Majestic and beautiful. But we really had no time to appreciate it.

I closed my eyes and tuned them all out, though I knew they waited.

I searched for that feeling, that acknowledgment that the stone Kalie had given me put out when I'd first walked into the room. It was subtle, but distinct.

I was about to give up and suggest we move to another mountain when I got an itch, a feeling inside of me. The darkness stirred a bit and stretched.

Despite wishing I could find the stone on my own, I had known the power inside of me was needed to find it. Tentatively I let it out a little. My eyes turned black and as I let it come up a little higher, I noticed the veins in my hands standing out, almost as though black ink was running through them. I wasn't afraid. I had this.

For now, you do... the voice chuckled, but I ignored it. She-it-was too sure of themselves for me to take seriously right now. *Oh, you'll take me seriously. I promisssee.* It hissed at me, and again I ignored it.

When I'd let it rise all I was willing to, I let myself feel. And there to the west of us came a slight throb of power, a hum as if a note of music were on repeat.

That's it! Excitement filtered through me, and satisfaction ran through the darkness.

"Gather round," I told my team. "We're headed to that one over there." I pointed to a shorter mountain about three peaks over.

Our landing this time was much shakier, the ground under our feet pebbled and dotted with rocks and boulders. We searched the mountainside and before long Kit called out. He'd found a sealed cave.

This had to be it. I felt the magic pulse inside of me. The stone calling to Helios's power inside of me. We climbed up to where he stood trying to find a way in, but the boulder in front of it was just too heavy to move.

"Stand back," Killian said with authority. We did as he said, and I was proud of him for taking charge when needed.

With a few words, he threw his arms out. A blast of power rushed from him, hitting the rock and making it crumble to dust before our eyes. I'd half-expected to have to shield myself and the others from rocks flying, but he'd made sure to destroy it so completely that there wouldn't be any stray shrapnel.

The entrance was large and dark, and the Elves took point, leading us in, while I lit my light orb to bob ahead of them. Inside was just one chamber, and in the middle of it stood three tombs etched into the rock with heavy lids covered in dust.

We stood around them, and I felt power coming from the largest in the middle and motioned to it. Amarie's team used their muscle to move the heavy slab before stepping back for me to look inside.

An orange glow lit the stone body that lay there, and I grimaced at realizing we'd have to break him apart to get to it.

"Ugh. Anyone got a hammer and chisel?" I joked, but not really. This would have to be done carefully so as to not damage the gem inside.

Killian gave me a look that equated to rolling his eyes and saying, *Please, I've got this.*

I had no doubt.

I dipped my head at him to go ahead, and we stood back once again. This time, he used something different. Blue light radiated from his hands in a small beam like a laser. Intricately, he moved his hands to cut the rock away from the stone. It took a while, but then he had to be extremely careful.

Once he was done, he stood back and gestured to the tomb.

"There ya go." He smiled that boyish smile, and Trela whispered to him, which was really surprising for her. Shouting his praises seemed more her style, though I could tell that whatever she said made him stand a little taller.

I leaned into the small space and plucked the small gem out gently from where it nestled.

"Sorry, dude," I said as I looked down at the destruction we'd caused to his stony figure.

Holding the orange stone in front of me, the magical light inside of it beat like a heart every few seconds, and the darkness inside of me purred. I pushed those bricks down on it hard as I stuffed the stone into the pocket at my chest and zipped it closed.

I surveyed my team and saw that they were all impressed with Killian's ability and the fact that we'd found the third stone.

"One to go!" I said cheerily, just as my phone rang.

I hurried to pull it from the pocket on my hip and answered.

"Celeste? What's up?"

She filled me in that the Titans were still battling the monsters in Junction. Hunter had checked in and of course was angry with me. He'd asked to speak to me, so she'd had to tell him what I was doing.

"He wants you to know that you both will have a long talk later," she chastised.

"Oh, I can only imagine." I rolled my eyes but recognized that he had a right to be mad with me, even though it was for a good cause.

I filled her in about the stone we'd found and that we were about to be off to find the fourth and final one. "Wish us luck!" I said.

"Good luck, dear. I am impressed with your fervor to find these. And I hope you're right, that they'll somehow help in this fight." She sounded weary.

"Don't worry. It will."

I hung up and hurried to update everyone who patiently waited around me, and then we were off to the next location.

China.

We landed this time in what looked to be a desert. It was The Moving Sands, a place of spiritual journey.

Long ago, a monk and his companions had to cross over the sands in their mission to fetch a Buddhist scripture from India and return them to Tang China. There was said to be a sand demon and eater of humans who lived beneath the sands and that the monk had recruited it as his third disciple. When the creature had appeared above the sand, a diamond sparkled in its head like a third eye, pulsing with power. The monk had thought that this stone was what had given the creature its power and without it, the creature would be no more.

Eventually, the monk gave into greed and tried to kill the sand creature for the diamond, resulting in the creature eating him.

That diamond was the fourth and final stone we needed. How we'd get it from the sand creature, I had no idea, but we were going to try.

I filled in everyone, and as we stood there, I felt the power deep in the earth, radiating from wherever the creature resided.

"Trela, Bea, and Shay, I need you to shift to your dragons. Killian, Amarie, you're to ride them and mount an attack from above. The rest of us, will fight from the ground. This thing likes flesh, so make sure you don't let it get close.

The girls shifted to their dragon forms and the Elves climbed aboard. The air swirled the sand around us as their wings beat furiously, taking them high into the air.

I watched their magnificence in wonder.

To see the three of them swirling in a circle above us, the blue of their scales sparkling in the sunlight was a sight to behold.

Tearing my gaze away, I looked to Killian and then back at the sand where I felt the gem beating like a heart. "Do me a favor and aim one of those blasts you used earlier right about there." I pointed with my finger to a spot a little further than where I knew the sand demon slept.

Killian grinned. "You got it."

And in no time, the blue magic from before shot from his palms, rippling the air before blasting into the fine brown silt, sending a plume into the air at least thirty feet. The ground shook below us, and I shifted myself to stay on my feet, bending at the knees to prepare for what was to come.

And it didn't take long.

A roar could be heard from underground, and again the sand under our feet quaked and swirled in front of us, as if something were tunneling in, instead of out.

The power from the stone grew more intense, and within seconds the sand raged up and out with a creature that was as large as the dragons.

It looked like a cross between a bull and a centipede. Horns grew from atop its pale head, its body long, and I counted six legs. A whip-like tail protruded from behind.

Eyes that were milky and blind blinked in our direction, and in its forehead sat a sparkling diamond. Small compared to its body but noticeable, nonetheless. The sun glinted off of it and an inner light pulsed, grabbing ahold of the darkness inside of me.

It was that moment that the demon's head turned with a snap in my direction. Its bullish nose sniffed the air, and then it threw back its head, letting out another deafening snarl.

The blackness inside of me curled in pleasure, and I gritted my teeth, holding it back. Now would *not* be a good time to give it reign.

I looked to the sky and nodded, motioning Killian back a few steps as the monster took a tentative step in my direction.

I didn't have to wait long before Trela attacked furiously. She swept down with Amarie on her back, spewing fire at the creature while Amarie heaved her magic at it. As the dragon swept back into the air, Bea and Shay followed in synchrony, one after the other, spewing fire and magic as the demon screamed.

I watched the beauty of their attack and was mesmerized. If only their strikes had done damage to the creature in front of me.

Its body seemed to be impenetrable, at least to the fire and magic they had used. The only thing it did was enrage it. Its eyes glowed with hatred and the diamond pulsed brighter.

We had to destroy it before the power in the gem was accessed by this thing. I had no idea what it might do.

I shouted to Killian to be heard over its roar as it turned back in my direction.

"I'm going to try and stun it! Once I do, blast it with the power you used to get to the last gem. I'm going to tell the girls to do everything they can from above at the same time. We need to put our all into it!"

He nodded, and I concentrated on sending my thoughts to the group above us. I'd never tried to project my thoughts to them before, but I was certain they would hear me and understand.

I cringed as the demon crept closer and closer. It was in no hurry to reach me. It was as if it knew I stood no chance, that there was no place for me to go in this barren land to escape.

I projected to them all that no matter how close it got to me, they must keep up the assault. I felt their hesitation, but I knew that they would do what I asked, no question.

When the revolting creature was within twenty feet of me, its size seemed so much greater. I immediately threw my hands out and whispered the spell that would stun it, pulling on all my reserves of magic. I felt it fill me up, racing to my hands before exploding out of me and directly at the demon.

It bellowed again as if it sensed what was coming, the long tail whipping out from behind it and slamming into the ground right beside me. Heat from one of the barbs on its tail sliced through the leg of my suit, but I ignored it, hopping away at the same moment my spell connected.

The horned demon stopped mid-motion, it's mouth wide open, and razor like teeth lined the entire inside.

Immediately, the dragons swept in, and Killian readied.

"Now!" I yelled, and in synchrony flames and magic hit the wormlike creature, battering it mercilessly.

Killian let loose his power and aimed directly into its mouth. I momentarily had a second to admire how smart his strategy was. The fire and magic before it was stunned had been basically useless, its body repelling it.

But there was no way with it aimed directly inside of the creature that it wouldn't work.

And I was right.

I had a split second to realize as it exploded, the sand shaking around it, swirling and sinking in on itself, that I would need to grab the gem before it was lost in the vastness of the desert.

In that moment, it was as if I were seeing everything in slow motion.

Gore flung high and wide as the demon exploded into a million pieces, the diamond winking as it was dislodged amongst the chaos.

I couldn't run to get it; the sand was pulling in on itself like a whirlpool that would suck me in.

In an instant, I was running and leaping for all I was worth. My power, even the darkness, pushed to propel me high into the air while my eyes didn't leave the stone.

Spatter hit me from every direction, and I still didn't bat an eye.

Stretching my arm out as far as it could go, I snatched the diamond midair, holding tight as my body soared, before slamming into the sand on the other side of the destruction.

I landed hard, the breath knocked out of me, and I wheezed. I wasn't able to catch my breath. I didn't know if I was injured. I was paralyzed while my lungs strained to bring in air.

Killian dashed over to me as I rolled to my back, coughing and spitting sand. My hand still clasped around the diamond.

"Andie! Are you okay?" His voice was winded and worried.

The dragons touched down with a rumble in their hurry to check on me, and I turned my head to see Amarie slide off, running in our direction with the others fast on her heels. I felt slimy and gross, wiping away a piece of flesh that clung to my cheek and flinging it away as my breath eased back into me.

Satisfaction rang out in my bones as the power from the diamond filtered in amidst the many concerned voices that surrounded me.

"I'm okay." I took a deep breath and smiled as feeling came back into my body and I gently moved each limb to make sure there were no damages.

"Really, I'm okay. I just had the breath knocked out of me."

I sat up with the help of Amarie, as the dragon shifters bounded over after shifting back and dressing.

Stuffing the diamond into the same pocket where the other one rested, I felt them shift, nestling closer to each other.

"That giant bug was something else!" Trela exclaimed. "We gave it everything we had, and it *still* didn't seem to make a difference."

I stood and dusted myself off, picking off more pieces of goo. I could only envision what I looked like. My hair felt damp, and I didn't want to think about what was in it.

"You guys did perfect. I couldn't have asked for more. That demon was impenetrable, except for its mouth. Killian made a good decision to aim for it while I had it paralyzed. It didn't stand a chance." I smiled at the guy in question. "Smart move, bud."

He blushed and smiled big. "It was the only thing that made sense after our other efforts. It wasn't anything."

Trela laughed and hugged him big. "You're just too modest. If it hadn't been for you, that thing would still be alive, and who knows what would've happened? Just take the praise and roll with it," she whispered, though I heard it loud and clear, smirking at him as I walked to Amarie.

"Ready to go home and see what these stones can do?" She looked a little skeptical but agreed, and we gathered everyone together to sift back to Fairy.

Chapter Eighteen

Aine was outside in the courtyard when we appeared. All it took was one look at me and she was sprinting over. I'd never seen her move so fast.

Worry was in every line of her face and she moved to check all of my limbs.

I gently grasped her hands. "It's not mine, Aine. I'm not hurt, I promise."

She stared into my eyes with lowered brows.

"I promise. I'm not. This is just a mess from the demon we had to destroy to get the last stone."

She let out a breath, and her eyes turned from worry to incredulous.

"You found *all* of the stones?"

I smiled broadly at her and reached into the front pocket of my suit, pulling them both out. They twinkled in the light from the sun and her hands went to her mouth in shock.

"I... I knew that you were determined, but I never imagined you would have found them so quickly. How did you know where to go?"

I placed them back into the pocket and thought a moment.

How did *I know where to go?*

Some of the intuition that I had came from the stories I'd read before, but that couldn't have been enough to lead me to those distinct places. *Or* to even discern the stories would be linked.

It had to be the darkness. Maybe even the knowledge from the book that it had absorbed. Leif said that it needed that knowledge. And so, in turn, had I.

Hmm...

I explained my thoughts to Aine, and she agreed that it most likely had to do with the book and the link that the darkness had to the gems.

Celeste rushed outside then, and I explained everything to her too. By that time, I was exhausted and in really bad need of a bath. A scouring one that would get this filth that now seemed dried on, off.

As I walked to my room, my thoughts went to Hunter. I hadn't even asked for an update on the Titans' mission. The high that I had ridden from retrieving the two stones had overpowered me.

I'd make sure to find Celeste right after I got the muck off and ask for an update. Oh, and food.

∞

I didn't bother drying my hair, letting it hang loose to air dry. The coolness of it felt good after being in the hot dry desert.

Star purred as she ran up my body, settling in her favorite spot around my neck, her little nose tucked in behind my ear.

I hadn't noticed it before, but now when she did so, I felt a sense of peace. Like a puzzle put together. Without her there always felt like a small piece was missing. I knew lately I'd been leaving her here a lot, but I'd need to remedy that. I knew she needed me just as much as I did her.

I wound my way down the stairs, talking to her softly as we went, relaying all that had happened.

She simply snuggled in tighter.

I found Celeste in the apothecary, working with a lavender liquid. Curious, I went to stand by her side. "What are you doing in here?" I poked at a dish full of jelly-like clear balls, and she grabbed my hand, pulling it back, chuckling.

"Dear, you must not play with those. They're very delicate and the Naiads would have my head if you destroyed them."

I studied them closer and noticed something silvery moving around inside that I hadn't noticed before.

"Well, what is that? It's so weird." I frowned, my eyes watching the swirl of whatever it was inside.

"Dear, these are the Naiads' eggs. They've been having a lot of babies born that don't last a month. They asked me for help, and I'm working on a potion for the mothers to drink that will give them more viability and the babies a better chance to live. You could call it a favor for a favor." Her eyebrows went up. "They were a little less inclined to help us when they got a glimpse of the shades recently. I just gave them a better reason."

She was a crafty woman; I'd give her that. While I'd known that there were some factions that were still leery about helping, I hadn't thought about what would happen if they got scared off by the looming threats around us. It became more real when you were thrust into it. More so than just talking about it.

"Well, thank you for doing this. It is a win-win for us both, I suppose." I sighed as I sat in a chair nearby, watching her work.

"So, what's happening with the Titans? How is Hunter?"

She glanced up at me after pouring some of the purple liquid into a vial.

"They were successful in their mission and killed all of the demons that they could find, but in the process, it drained them of their power." She capped the vial and set it aside before coming to stand before me.

My shoulders stiffened at the serious look on her face.

"Hunter is okay, Andie, I promise. But when a Titan goes against their word to not get involved and uses so much of their magic, so intensely, they lose it for a while and have to return to their land to basically, well, power back up."

I had never even thought about what using so much of their power would cost them. They'd never explained, and I'd never asked. I only knew that it could cause them pain to go against their written law.

"Hunter was adamant about staying here, at least until you got back, but Coeus coaxed him into going. He would have been no use to you here in the weakened state he was in. And the sooner they have their magic back, the better."

"Do you have any idea how long that will take?" I asked quietly, staring at my hands and fighting the insane urge to cry. For some reason, being in Fairy made the urge, the want for Hunter slam back into me twofold.

"It could be a few hours, or it could be a few days. There is no knowing, darling."

I took a deep breath and nodded.

"When they do return, we will need to have them take the gems and forge them in some way so that they are together again for you to use."

I hadn't thought about what we'd do with them once I had them all, just that I knew I needed them to use against Helios.

∞

One day stretched into two, and I wondered aimlessly around the castle, feeling lost without Hunter there.

I knew that it was the bond pulling these feelings from me, and as the hours wore on, the darkness fought to rise.

I didn't have him here to help suppress it, and I began to have visions of Teagan and Presley being tortured. I knew these weren't real, at least the ones of Presley. We still had no idea where she was. No one had been able to get ahold of her or find her, but I felt it in my soul that she wasn't with Declan.

News of more shades being spotted around the globe along with other ghastly demons heightened my depression as I felt that things were slowly spinning out of control.

Get it together, Andie. It's all in your head. Things aren't as bad as they seem.

But they were getting worse, and it was only a matter of time before everything exploded.

I needed to find something proactive to do instead of moping around.

Or you could have a little fun... the dark voice taunted me, and I scowled.

I'd let it up a little this morning when I got ready. Opting for dark clothes again, but I drew the line at the outfit it wanted me to wear, choosing a black T-shirt and ripped black jeans.

I found myself turning to the room where the butterfly house was.

It was quiet in there, and for some reason it called to me. Maybe because it reminded me of Hunter and the moments we shared in there. The glow from the glass house lit up the library around it. The smell of old books tickled my nose and the fairy lights that danced near the ceiling gave it a mystical look.

As I neared the glass, wings began to flutter where they had been still before. As if sensing me the closer I came. When I reached out a finger to touch the clear wall that separated us, the butterflies took flight in an array of colors.

All except the same huge blue butterfly from before. It hovered near where my finger sat, its brilliant wings kissing the glass.

Time seemed to slow down, and a voice sounded in my head.

Leif.

They are reminding you of the magic in all life. You must embrace and be in tune with it. Quiet your mind and listen through your intuition, your subtle senses, thought and feelings. Sometimes the butterflies are magical winged messengers delivering guidance and love when you most need it. Step inside and let them give you what you need.

Her voice faded and as if pulled by her guidance and the blue butterfly in front of me, I stepped toward the door, opened it and stepped in.

Immediately, I was swarmed with the soft wings alighting on every part of my upper body.

I sat cross-legged on the floor and closed my eyes, opening myself up to them.

A tickle inside my head was the only warning before warmth rushed up my body and through every limb. A wealth of feelings swam through me. First relaxation, then calm, and an overwhelming sense of peace.

It reminded me of the time I'd spent in the Well. I slowly opened my eyes, and the butterflies took flight again, each one emitting a glow around them of different colors. *They had auras?* I had never thought to test it out on anything but another person and seeing all of their soft glows left me in awe.

The fact that the oily darkness hadn't dared to rear up in here-in fact, it had retreated rather quickly the moment I stepped in-also stunned me.

At least now I knew I could come here if it got overwhelming with Hunter gone.

I lay back and stared into the air around me. The winged creatures swirled and dipped, landing briefly on different flowers to feast on their pollen. It was magical.

While I laid there, I thought about Nan and my mom. Had they witnessed as much as I had? Had they experienced all of this beauty and wonder as I had?

Nan surely had at least before Celeste had rescued her.

I wondered where they were now, and if they were watching over us. Could they see all that we went through and did they have any knowledge of the outcome? I knew that wherever they were, it was a good place. For surely if there was a hell for these demons to rise from, there was also a Heaven. Somewhere peaceful and happy.

I fell asleep with a smile on my face, amidst the beauty of the butterflies and flowers.

When I woke stretching, I felt renewed. It had to have been the best sleep I'd had in a long while. I was warm and cozy and looked down the length of my body to find the butterflies had lined me like a blanket.

And as if noticing I was awake, even though I hadn't moved, they flew as one off of me, and the blue one hovered near the door as if saying, *it's time to go.*

I didn't really want to leave this cocoon of peace I'd found myself in, but I knew it was right.

I was sure someone would be looking for me.

And just as I had imagined, as soon as I exited the library, Star came running, pouncing into my arms.

"What is it, girl?" She looked a little stressed out, and the cause came scurrying around the corner of the hall right behind her.

"Let me at her!" Emric growled, his eye's spitting fire at the trembling ferret in my arms.

"Why would I do that? What's wrong with you?" I scolded him, holding him back with my foot as I clutched her to me.

"She ate my pancakes, and I'd only gotten one bite in!" He growled, his ears bent low.

I looked at him in surprise. Here lately he'd been eating more and more human food, and less of the disgusting raw meat he usually feasted on.

"I'm sure it was a mistake, and even if not, Aine's cook could replace them for you within minutes. Now, put your hackles down and back up a bit."

I walked around him, and he hmphed. "I wanted those pancakes. And she needs to learn some manners. You don't go eating off someone else's plate!"

I just giggled as I left him grumbling.

Aine had the fairies hard at work, and I stopped to chat with them for a little while after noticing them hanging streamers and balloons. All black, silver and gold.

They informed me that it was for the New Years' ball. Aine had one every year, and she vowed that this one wouldn't be any different, despite the challenges. Usually, she had a huge gathering, but this year it would just be for our small group, and the Titans should they make it back in two days' time.

Even so, she would still go all out for the festivities. She was never one to do something small, Neo told me, and I agreed. She was Queen of Fairy and Queen of excessiveness. At least when it came to celebrating.

I loved that about her, though, and I thought about the vision I'd seen. If it came true, that would be one heck of a party.

Feeling light and happy, I went outside, and that sensation dropped like a lead weight at my feet and shock gripped me.

Kneeling on the ground was Presley, her body swaying precariously. I rushed to her. No one else was around as I quickly took in her state.

Torn clothes and gashes all over her body. Cuts that were familiar lined her arms and neck, causing queasiness to roll in my belly. Dark circles lined her eyes, and her beautiful blond hair was matted to the back of her head, her eyes closed in exhaustion.

"Pres. Pres, it's okay, it's me," I whispered as she began to fight my hands when I touched her.

"Let me get you up and to my room."

Her eyes fluttered open, not really seeing me, but she nodded, and I gently pulled her up and wrapped my arms around her.

Sifting, we landed near my bed. I backed her up to it, prodding her to sit, and I lifted her legs so that she could lay down.

I called to Celeste with my mind and asked her to bring some salve when she came.

Kneeling beside the bed, I wanted to touch her and reassure her, but I was too afraid I'd rub one of the ghastly cuts.

"What happened, Pres? Can you tell me?" I asked softly. I needed to be gentle with her and not show any fear.

Her eyes opened again, and she stared at me with anxiety, her breathing became erratic, and her head shook back and forth. She reached into her pocket and pulled out a small piece of paper, letting it fall to the cover before she began sobbing.

Celeste rushed in then, soothing her as best she could with her healing light, while I helped to put the salve on the many cuts we found once we'd removed her clothing and cleaned her as best we could.

Quietly, I moved from the bed while Celeste sat with her once she'd fallen asleep.

I opened up the folded paper and saw harsh slanted words written.

You remember these cuts, don't you, Andie? This time we let her live, but we're coming for you both. next time I'll let the fomori make those cuts even deeper, and they will feast on your organs. You can't hide.

-Jasper

Anger seared through me. That little weasel had taken over Freya's position in the Fomori.

Seeing him human-sized months ago in Junction now made sense.

He was a depraved and disgusting fairy. My short time with him showed how low he would go in his quest to be more powerful. And he found it with Helios and the Fomori.

A million images of what he might have put Pres through filtered in, and the blackness rose inside of me. I knew my eyes turned dark as I walked to Celeste wordlessly handing her the note to read.

She was tired from expounding her peace to Pres, but at the sight of my eyes, she laid her hand on mine, and a trickle of her warmth ran into my veins.

It wasn't enough to stop it from rising.

I made myself lean down and kiss the top of her head before placing her hand back into her lap. Turning, I left the room and went out into the moonlight.

The air was cool, and the comets streaked across the sky. I made my way down to the pool that Hunter had taken me to, and sat, staring at the glow of the moon on the water, planning my revenge once

I got near Jasper again. I'd never let him get his hands on one of my family again.

Not if I could help it.

Chapter Nineteen

The next day, I was up early-well, I hadn't really slept. I'd stayed out by the pool until the wee hours of the morning, only curling up on a sofa in the study to catch a few hours of sleep before the noise of the castle woke me.

I rushed up to my room to check on Pres and found her still asleep with Star cuddled up to her. Emric and Charlie were at her feet. She looked so broken, and even in her sleep fright seemed to chase her.

Hatred at what was done to her fueled the darkness inside. I didn't even think twice before I grabbed my beanie and threw it over my head.

I had one thing on my mind.

Revenge.

I sifted to the one place I knew I could take my anger out on. Oregon. The mountain loomed ahead. All of the trees that surrounded it were black and singed from the fire that spewed out. Black smoke rose all around it and lava flowed.

Winged creatures circled in the air, and several perched on Declan's cabin. Sentinels watching for enemies.

The darkness licked inside. As the calls from the demons around me grew louder, it seemed to call back, rising inside of me past the point that I could push it down.

My feet moved of their own accord, and my subconscious pushed back to no avail.

Don't you want your revenge? the voice said.

Fire and anger licked in my veins. I did. I wanted to burn every one of those things. Declan first. The closer I walked to the scene of destruction, the more creatures I saw pouring from the widened crack.

Yesssss

My head snapped toward the cabin to see Declan leaning against one of the porch pillars, grinning from ear to ear, satisfied. I ignored him. I'd deal with him later.

My gaze went back to the demons who now inched closer. Each one was different in size, shape and ugliness. They howled and screeched and snapped their jaws.

I knew they were drawn to my darkness. It was playing with them, and I *let* it.

I wasn't afraid as they circled me, but I kept my eyes on their movements. These things might not yet hurt me, but I wasn't going to let them escape to hurt my friends.

They sniffed me, studied me. Growled at me.

And I let them. For just a moment.

When they felt comfortable that I couldn't get away, and when they least expected it, I bent down low and let out all the power I'd been building.

It blew the first ring of demons around me back. They were flung into pieces that smacked the others around them.

Stunned, the demons looked at the gore, then back at me, and they charged.

I should've been afraid, but at this point I was mindless with rage as Pres kept filtering back into my mind. Not to mention Teagan who was trapped in the house behind me.

One by one, they came at me, and I hit them with all the spells in my arsenal, using the darkness to fuel the power behind them.

It laughed and ate it up. My anger powered it to rise.

Then the demons got smart. Or so I thought until as I turned a circle, I saw Declan in the background weaving his hands in the air.

I didn't have time to dwell on him as the creatures came at me faster and faster. A wave of the ones pouring from the crack came to join until I was surrounded by hundreds of them.

I couldn't keep up with them now. And I felt slash after slash to my back as I fought the ones in front of me.

The darkness in me sighed and egged me on.

Keep fighting. You can't give up now.

And I didn't until I felt a burning in my gut and looked down to see a long horn sticking out from my stomach and pain bloomed all through me.

No. No, no, no, no, no!

My mind screamed at me as I pushed myself off the horn stumbling as hands grabbed at me from all around.

I've got to get out of here!

I didn't waste any time and sifted. I had no idea where I was going, but I couldn't fight them, not with an injury like this. My hands pressed to my abdomen, and blood gushed around them as I slammed into rock and all I could see was black.

∞

Images of Presley with the Fomori.

Teagan pleading with me, his hands stretched out and agony written on his face.

Jasper laughing, his evil face looming.

Declan smirking as he pulled Teagan behind him. Demons surrounding me in terrifying waves.

I woke briefly, the sky above me before my vision blurred and sleep dragged me under. This happened multiple times.

My body felt numb and cold, and I wondered if this is what it felt like to die.

I was in an out of consciousness until I woke to darkness, stars glittering above me. A noise sounded beside me, and I strained to turn my head toward it.

There on the ledge beside me sat two panthers, one dark as night and the other as white as the moon. In fact, the black panther had a white sickle moon on its forehead, and the white panther had a sun on its head. Yellow eyes blinked slowly at me from the black cat and light blue from the white cat.

As if one unit, they moved closer until they were only a foot away. I felt no animosity from them as they lay in front of my view, their eyes on mine.

They were majestic and beautiful. Full of power.

The white one laid its paw on the arm I stretched out toward it, and instantly a voice resounded in my head.

My dear girl, you've gotten yourself into a pickle this time.

Nan?

Her laugh lilted in my mind as she chuckled.

I know it's rather startling, but yes, it is me.

"But I don't understand. Is this reincarnation, or am I dreaming? Why are you a panther?"

The black panther laid its paw against my hand, and an unknown female voice filtered in.

We were given a choice in this fight that you're up against. For it's not just your fight, but a fight of good against evil. There are higher powers at work here too. Limited, but there. Oh, Andie. I never wanted this for you, sweet girl. I tried to keep this from happening, but fate is a greater magic than a mother's love.

My soul clenched at the knowledge that this was my mom. She was here. Sort of. I rubbed my finger against her paw as tears pooled in my eyes.

Shhh, baby. It's going to be alright. Nan and I are here now. Even though we can't be in our old forms, we will help you through all of this when we can.

Nan cut in, and her blue eyes, so different than they gray ones I was used to, twinkled just like before.

First, we must heal you. Sleep, darling. We won't be here when you wake, but I promise you we will be back.

Magic raced into my skin, and I was drug into the dark abyss again, even though I fought it.

The dreams this time were filled with butterflies, fairies, and Hunter.

∞

Wings sounded around me, and I pried my eyes open, squinting at the light filtering in from a window.

A head lifted from the bed beside me, and Hunter stared into my eyes. He looked exhausted, and worry was etched into his face.

Above me, blue dragonflies swarmed, some landing on me now and again, others simply happy to soar.

I reached out a hand and cupped Hunter's cheek. He instantly nuzzled it, the rasp from his five o'clock shadow tickling.

"What happened?" I croaked, my throat parched and tight.

He grabbed my hand in his and leaned down to kiss me quickly before reaching for a glass of water.

"Here, have a drink."

I took it and sipped it slowly, the cool liquid soothing the scratchiness that I felt.

"I should be extremely mad at you," he started, and I bowed my head, knowing full well he should be. "But I also know you had a rough time with me gone, and then with all that happened to Presley, it just caused something in you to snap."

I started to argue, but he held up his hand, his eyes stony.

"No. It did. That darkness in you fed on your anger and despair so much that it tricked you into going to Oregon for revenge. I had Celeste filter out your memories while you slept so I could see what happened. You had a scar on your abdomen that was recently healed, and I had to know if something horrible had been done to you."

He heaved out a breath, swiping his hand across his mouth, and stopped for a second to control the emotion I felt coming off of him.

"I had to know you'd be okay. That you were still my Andie."

I sat quietly, feeling guilty for what I'd put him through.

"I arrived shortly after you left, and we couldn't find you anywhere. Star pestered me so much that I picked her up, and the strangest thing happened when I did. A picture, a flash of you on a ledge with two panthers. And I knew where I had to go. The Titans and I sifted to Oregon and scoured high and low for you. When I found you, you wouldn't wake up. You were covered in blood, but I couldn't find a wound. And now I know why." His eyes softened.

"You had someone watching over you. They healed you and kept you safe until I got there. And then they just... disappeared."

I swallowed thickly, the image of the panthers clear in my mind and the words they had spoken. I wished they could be here now. Even though I'd rather them be in their old forms, the thought that I still had Nan and mom in this way was a miracle.

I knew I didn't need to explain anything to him. Even if he hadn't seen my memories, he would have now.

"Did you hear what they said about the fight having higher attention then? I don't know why I hadn't thought of that."

He smoothed my hair back. "It's always been a fight of good against evil. But this time the stakes are higher, and if they don't help in some way, all that they've worked for could be destroyed. Good would be gone and evil would reign. That can't be allowed."

He sat me up in the bed and other than a few sore muscles, I felt well.

"I'll be right back. I'm going to get you some food." He was halfway to the door when he pulled back and tossed something on the bed. "I figured you might want this back."

It was my beanie. I'd forgotten completely about it.

He smiled before turning again. "Don't worry. Celeste had it magically cleaned for you. It stank badly of sulfur and brimstone."

I imagined my whole person had smelled something horrible when they brought me back. The stench permeated the entire area around Declan's mountain.

After a bowl of soup and some sweet tea, I felt my energy return. While I'd ate, everyone came and checked up on me, filling me in on what had been happening for the two days I'd been out of it.

Presley was doing better, and Coeus had been working with her on controlling the night terrors that plagued her. She wouldn't be up for a fight anytime soon; they had warned me.

I had a feeling she'd prove them wrong. She was a lot stronger than many gave her credit for. And I knew she'd relish in taking down this evil once she was healed.

In that, we were a lot alike. We just needed to be smarter about it and do it together, not alone.

Trela and Bea were fast to fill me in on the New Year's ball that just so happened to be tonight.

It was the worst timing, but I suppose it would be a new year with or without it. I tried to get out of going, I really did. I had no desire to dress up and act happy, but I knew I needed to. Not just because I was their leader, but because it would make them happy.

So, after talking to everyone, Hunter shooed them out and gathered me in his arms as we lay on the bed.

"Take a little nap, and I'll wake you when it's time to get ready."

He kissed me sweetly, and I snuggled into his arms, while Star cuddled at my back.

∞

I was quiet while the fairies raced in a flurry, fixing my hair and makeup. The dress I wore tonight was bright red and *so* out of my comfort zone. I think that was Aine's intention, though.

New year, new things, yada yada. I think I'd had my fill of new things over the last year to last me a lifetime.

But I must say, the dress reminded me of the one Julia Roberts wore in *Pretty Woman*, and it was absolutely gorgeous. My hair was even done up like hers had been.

Trela, Bea and Shay filtered into my room then, each one dressed elegantly. Trela wore a light blue dress that shimmered when she moved, Bea a deep plum one, with a long slit up the thigh, and Shay wore a tailored white suit with a deeply plunging neckline. One that Bea's eyes kept gravitating to.

"You all look gorgeous!" I exclaimed, as did the fairies that had stopped to take them in.

Bea stepped forward and grabbed my hand, twirling me around. "Yep, we sure do, but look at you! Hot, hot, hot!" She whistled low and winked. "Hunter isn't going to know what hit him."

They all laughed, and I smiled. I had to admit that all of this was always worth the looks he gave me when he saw me wearing a dress.

We chatted a bit before Celeste came in with my crown. "Do I really need to wear it tonight? It's just us. None of the factions will be here."

212

Her eyes twinkled as she settled it on my carefully done up-do while the fairies secured it with bobby pins. "Yes, my dear, you do. One thing Aine didn't mention is though the factions won't be here tonight, you will be televised to them ringing in the New Year."

She rolled her eyes slightly. "You know Aine."

I groaned. The last thing I wanted to do was pretend on a televised video. "Couldn't someone else do it?" I pulled Trela to my side. "Trela's great at public speaking!"

She gave me a look like I was crazy before folding her arms in front of her. "Nope. Not me. I ain't doin' that. I love ya, girl, but this is all you." She pulled away from me, calling over her shoulder as Bea and Shay followed. "Knock em dead, girl!"

Laughter followed them and Charlie landed on my shoulder. He'd been hiding away lately, and I hadn't seen much of him.

"This will be nothing. Don't worry about it. You should just say a little spiel about how proud you are of all of them in this fight. But be truthful and let them know it won't be easy. But you have faith in them and that good will win."

His smooth voice soothed by my ear.

Emric wound around my legs, his fur tickling them. "And be sure and say that you see only good things to come for this New Year. That always gives them the feel-goods." He tittered. "It doesn't have to be a long speech. Most of them won't care, anyway. They'll most likely be too deep in their drinks by then." He sniffed the air.

And that was probably true. The magic community loved to drink and party the night away.

Their words made me feel slightly better.

"Well okay then." I eyed Celeste in her white gown. "By the way, you look stunning."

I admonished myself for not telling her that to begin with.

"Why, thank you, sweetheart. Shall we go?" She held out her arm, and I looped mine through it.

"Yes, let's get this over with."

I found myself biting my lip to keep from rolling my eyes, as we paused at the top of the stairs and heralds announced us.

Celeste the Moon Goddess and Andie, Leader of the Fae.

The Titans, Elves, and dragon shifters stood below us next to Aine and Killian, all looking up.

Was that really necessary just for our friends?

And then I remembered the televised part of this party. Was the entire thing being televised? Neo flew around Celeste and I in a circle, a small camera on his shoulder, and my suspicions were confirmed.

Dang Aine!

I'd have to watch my every move the entire evening, not just when making the speech.

We slowly descended and my eyes sought out Hunters. He raptly watched, a small smile on his face as he took me in.

When we reached the bottom, Killian stepped forward for Celeste's hand with a small bow, and Hunter reached for mine, bending over it and placing a soft kiss to the back.

"My lady." His eyes met mine with a devilish air and I looked him over.

His tux was midnight black, and he wore a blood red tie that matched my dress. I imagined we made a stunning couple, and the thought alone made me smile.

"There's that beautiful smile we've been missing," he teased and turned me around to go into the ballroom ahead of everyone else.

A large table lined the middle of the room, with a New Year-themed tablescape. Black and white roses with golden tulips sat in vases, while fairy lights flickered in jars. Balloons and streamers hung from every available part of the ceiling, and orbs lit with little lights bobbed in between.

The dance floor was set up in a circle around the table, and Neo had someone else positioned at the DJ booth this time. A cute little girl fairy who hadn't seemed to take her eyes off of him as he swirled around with the camera.

Hunter took me to the seat at the head of the table where Aine usually sat and pulled out the chair. I didn't question it, although it felt strange to take her spot. She had made the seating arrangements, so it was what she wanted.

Hunter sat to my left, and I was pleasantly surprised to see my dad filter in through the doorway and come to stand beside me.

"Dad! I didn't know you were coming." I smiled and started to rise, but he pushed me gently back down, instead leaning over to place a kiss on my cheek.

"I wouldn't miss my first New Year's with you. This year will be a fresh start and full of amazingly normal time with each other once we get over this hump." He smiled genuinely at me, and I smiled big back.

He sat down on the other side of me across from Hunter, and they struck up a lively conversation of all the things that the communities across the globe were doing to shore up their security.

I watched as everyone else was seated and found it interesting that Aine had chosen to seat the Elves in between the Titans. It was a good move. Oftentimes they tended to stick to their own groups and unless we were on a journey together, didn't interact much.

She sat at the end of the table directly in my vision and I gave her a nod and a smile. She just winked, knowing full well what I was conveying.

One by one dishes were magically flown out to line the table and crystal glasses filled. Aine had reverted back to the food from the magical world, but I wasn't disappointed.

Each and every bite that I tried was delicious and I found myself relaxing and joking with my friends and family as we ate and drank.

My favorite dish, though, was dessert. Once the dinner dishes had been cleared, individual plates with dessert were flown out to land in front of us, and they were epic. I mean, if a dessert could be a work of art, this was it.

In front of me sat a whimsical confection made to look like the crown that sat on my head. It even had a magical light that raced back and through the moons and stars, mimicking the moonbeams.

I was stunned, and a little afraid to destroy it by digging in.

I glanced at Aine and she beamed, satisfied with her surprise. Everyone had the same reaction as I did, gasping at the beauty of it.

"Well, it's meant to be eaten, so please, enjoy," Aine called down the table, and I knew it would be bad form not to eat it.

Lifting the spoon that sat on the dish, I tentatively broke through the strands of gossamer and cream. Lifting it to my lips my eyes almost rolled back at the taste. Words couldn't explain the sheer pleasure that ran through me as the sweetness touched my tongue.

Hunter groaned beside me and his thoughts filtered in.

That good, huh?

My eyes flew open, and I smirked.

So good. Only one thing would be better...

He licked his spoon, his eyes on me, and I blushed looking back down.

"So how is it you didn't have the same reaction as me?" I asked, taking another bite and shivering.

"Remember, I told you Sari's magic doesn't work on me. This dessert is her creation. You didn't think Aine would settle for anything less than some extra magic for this special night, did you?"

I should have known.

The rest of the table, all except the Titans, enjoyed their dessert just as much as I had. No one talked as everyone took it in. The Titans merely smirked at each other as they watched.

It was truly an experience to taste Sari's magic.

When everyone had their fill, and their bellies were happy and satiated, the dishes were whisked away, and music began playing. No one moved to dance, but rather turned toward Hunter, who then stood, his hand out to me.

"Shall we?"

I placed mine in his and let him pull me up and lead time to the dance floor. We danced forever, and others finally joined in. I was even surprised to see Coeus moving Aine around the floor in a waltz.

During a break in dancing, Aine found me and declared it time to make my speech. She steered me over to a display she had set up with the black and white roses in the background.

"Just say what you feel. It doesn't have to be long," she whispered as she moved off, leaving me alone in front of Neo and his camera.

I took a deep breath and began.

"Good evening, friends. I want to first start by saying thank you. Thank you for all you have done in the past few months to secure the communities all over the world. Many of you have done so without complaint and regardless of your affiliation with the communities. Your actions have kept so many people safe, and without you it wouldn't have happened. I ask that you keep up your vigilance. Be steady even in your fear. With this New Year will come the fight of our lives, and I implore all of you to help us. It won't be easy, but I have all the faith that we will overcome. That evil will be destroyed, and we can rest easy and return to the lives we wish to lead. Let us use that as our driving force. Do not let your guard down, be brave, be fierce and love each other with all you have. I wish you an incredibly Happy New Year. Better things are coming. Goodnight and bless every one of you."

I hadn't realized that I was holding my breath until it left me in a woosh. Neo's camera light turned off, and his arm hung down beside him while he smiled at me.

"Great job, Andie!" he said. "We're done with the videoing now. You can go relax and be yourself now."

Relief ran through me and I held my hand out for him to high five.

"I'd kiss you right now if that little cutie running the music wasn't staring holes in me." I laughed as his face turned red.

"How about you go over there and dance with her? I think she's been waiting long enough." I winked at him, and he immediately headed in her direction.

I loved it!

The sand timer hovered at the front of the room, and I saw that it was only five minutes until midnight. I searched out Hunter to see that he stood near one of the balconies, waiting on me.

I rushed as quickly as I could in my heels over to him.

"You did brilliant, baby." He kissed my forehead as he pulled me through the curtains and out into the night air.

"I've been waiting for this moment all night." He breathed as he gathered me to him.

"Me too. The moment Neo turned off that camera, I felt like I could breathe again. I was dreading our midnight kiss being recorded." I laughed as I looked up at his face.

He smoothed a stray tendril of hair that hung into my eyes away.

"They just need to get used to it. I'm going to be kissing you a million-no, a billion times more over our lifetime, in front of them all too."

And he kissed me again, just as I heard our friends counting down from five to one.

My eyes flew open at the boom that echoed around us, only to witness the entire sky fill with fireworks as Hunter continued to kiss me.

Maybe this year would be the year we made ours. It wasn't the first time I'd been submerged in danger and adversity. And it wouldn't be the last. I just hoped whatever we encountered in the future would be nothing as terrible as what this past year had been and the next month would be.

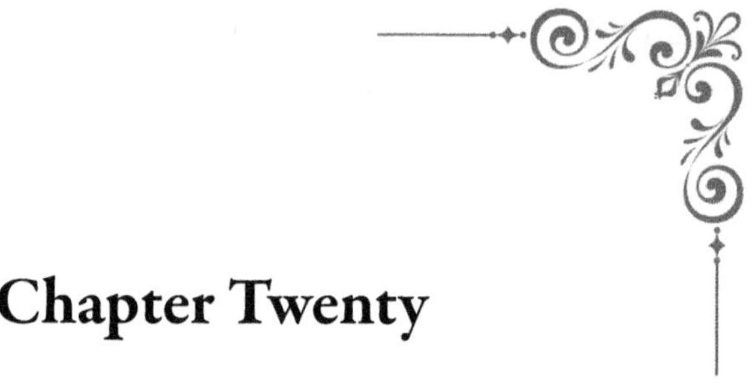

Chapter Twenty

The next day bloomed bright and beautiful. Memories of the night before lingered as I stretched in bed.

"Watch the foot, missy." Emric growled from the end of the bed where he curled up in a quilt. I stroked Star's fur, and she purred, stretching much like I had the moment before.

The ceiling showed blue skies with birds and bees flitting between flowers blooming on branches that swayed with a breeze.

Everything inside of me felt happy and content. Even the darkness was strangely quiet.

I frowned to myself because that usually didn't bode well. It typically meant that it was waiting in the wings to rear its ugly head when I least expected it.

Sighing I moved Star off of me and swung myself out of the bed.

I wanted to find Pres and see how she was doing. She'd refused to come to the celebration last night, preferring to hide away in her room.

I worried about her and her mental state, especially with all that was going on. I needed her strong for what was to come. A part of me knew that it would take every last one of us to destroy Helios. I also needed her whole, well, simply because she was my friend and I loved her. The thought that Jasper and the Fomori broke her was not acceptable to me.

I quickly dressed and got ready for the day, much to Emric's disgust as he tried to go back to sleep and failed miserably.

As I bounded out the door, the patter of his and Star's feet sounded behind me, and Charlie landed on my shoulder.

"Today will be a big day, Andie," he stated in a soft voice. "I think things are progressing faster than even I could have imagined," he muttered, looking off into the distance as I descended the stairs.

Just as I was about to quiz him on what he meant, he took off, flying through the open door and outside into the courtyard. He had been acting rather strange lately, and as I stood puzzled, staring outside, Emric stopped at my feet and looked up.

"Don't mind him. He sees more than we know. It's weighing heavy on his old soul. I'm sure he'll reveal what he knows soon. And if he doesn't? Well then, I'll just have to tickle it out of him." Emric chuckled, and I knew he endeavored to lighten the mood for me.

Patting his head, I turned toward the dining hall, searching out my friends.

I didn't find Hunter, but in a far back corner, Presley sat alone staring out of one of the large windows above the flower gardens.

Tentatively, I walked toward her, not willing to startle her.

There was a plate full of food on the table in front of her, and as I slowly slid into the seat across the table, I snatched a piece of melon, popping it into my mouth, smiling as her gaze was drawn to me.

I could see the alarm in her eyes before they fully focused on me and my smile. I grabbed another piece of fruit and chewed on it before pointing at the plate.

"Aren't you hungry? It appears you were when you loaded up, but don't worry. I'm here now to help you eat it."

Her mouth slowly tilted up and her eyes brightened. She shook her head gently and laughed, pushing the plate to me.

"You eat it. I'm not really hungry. And I didn't load this plate up, your boyfriend did." She laughed again.

Hunter had been here?

I frowned at her, but in a playful way. "You mean a Titan wanted to feed you and yet, here I am eating it instead? Come on, Pres, at least eat some toast."

I grabbed said toast and put my hand out, so the bread was directly under her nose.

She tried to ignore it at first, her gaze going back outside, but I was determined to get her to eat it *and* get her to laugh more.

"You know you want it," I teased and moved it even closer keeping up with my one-sided banter. It was only after I'd tapped her nose with it several times that she finally huffed and looked back at me, swiping the toast from my hand and biting into the bread hard.

With a mouthful and eyes that seemed to shoot flames at me, she chewed noisily.

"Happy now?"

I was shocked at first, and then I couldn't help the peals of laughter that rose out of me. Crumbs were dropping from her mouth onto her shirt, and the dirty look she gave me was just too much.

Her eyes slowly lost their heat, and before long they twinkled and she chuckled, shaking her head. "You can't laugh like that." She playfully scowled. "You know I can't stay mad when you do."

I grinned widely and leaned forward. "Yep! Why do you think I did it? Now, eat up. I have plans for us today."

Her eyebrows rose, and to appease me she took another piece of toast, munching on it slowly while I waited.

I hadn't really made any plans, but after seeing her sitting here so morosely, I decided that I had to do something to get her out of this funk. Even if it was only for an hour or two. She needed it.

I did too.

"So... what's the plan?" Pres asked.

"Well, how about you tell me what you want to do?"

Her eyes twinkled with mischief, and she looked much more like the Pres I first met.

Groaning, I stood. "Let me grab a coffee really quick. I have a feeling I'm going to need it."

She giggled and followed me to the coffee bar. "Oh, come on, Andie. I won't pick out anything that bad, but..." I shot her a quick look while I put the lid on the to-go cup. "Aine has a salon, and I want us to have a girls' day." She clapped her hands, ignoring the look I gave her and continued.

"Manicures. Pedicures. *Ohh*, and a massage! We definitely need a massage!"

The thought of sitting through all of that had my insides twisting, and Emric pounced over to join us. "What's this about mani-pedis's? I could go for one! Girls' day!" He screeched and jumped a little in the air.

Presley laughed as he raised his paw for a high-five and she obliged him.

I supposed I could sit through the torture for a little while if it brought her back from the abyss.

The things I do for my friends.

∞

Hours later, I scowled as I sat reclined in a chair while the fairies circled around us.

Some sort of green goo was plastered on my face, and my fingernails and toenails were dark blue with speckles of silver glinting on them.

The massage hadn't been bad, but afterward Pres had talked me into a skin treatment where the fairies used tiny little lasers. I was *not* a fan, hence my current attitude.

Emric sat in a chair nearby, his furry body splayed out rather indecently while he sipped some blue drink as two fairies filed his nails.

It was the most ridiculous sight.

Charlie and Star slept on a bench against the wall having decided that none of these machinations were for them. I didn't blame them, I wished I could do the same.

I hadn't even known that Aine had a salon in the castle. But really. What didn't she have?

"Oh, this has been the best morning. Thank you, Andie." Pres's hand reached over to grab mine, and she smiled serenely.

My heart softened, and the disgust at all of this melted away. It was worth it to see her be her old self. I beamed at her and squeezed her hand before leaning back and closing my eyes, only to be startled when the door to the salon banged open, Killian rushing in.

His eyes darted around, as if searching out someone.

"Who you looking for, Kill?" I asked lazily.

His eyes focused on me and grew wide as he took in my appearance. I'm sure having my hair up in a towel, green goo, on my face and painted nails were a bit of a shock to the system.

"Andie?" His incredulous look changed to one of amusement as he stepped closer.

"Uh... yeah. What is it?"

His boyish grin swung between me and Pres." Well, why wasn't I invited to this girls' day? He swiped at the green stuff on my face and sniffed it before leaning forward again and wiping it on my robe.

"Maybe because you're not a girl," I said dryly.

He pointed to the Phooka who was now snoring while the fairies worked. "He's not a girl. Yet here he is."

Pres giggled, and I shook my head at him. "He's just different, so there's that." I shrugged.

Killian turned to go.

"Wait. What'd you come in here for to begin with?" I asked, puzzled.

Killian stopped and turned around. "Oh yeah. Hunter wanted me to tell you that when you get done, you're both to join him and the Titans in the meeting room. That's all." He grinned and slipped out the door.

Well, at least there wasn't some kind of emergency. And if I were lucky, we'd get through the day without one. At least until tomorrow.

After his proclamation, I got antsy, wondering what the Titans wanted. After voicing the question several times, Pres sighed. "Well, let's go find out."

I felt a little bad about cutting our time short. And when I mean short, I mean short for her. It definitely hadn't seemed short to me.

Once we'd showered and gotten dressed, she smiled and hugged me tight. "I needed this so much. Thank you."

I hugged her back and felt so much better about the mental state she was in now. Until she opened her mouth again.

"But next time, we're going to go shopping too. *Oh!* And get our hair and makeup done..."

I grimaced, biting my tongue against the words I really wanted to retort with.

"Uh, yeah, sounds like a blast." The flatness of my words reached her, and she just laughed.

"Come on. Let's see what they want." She grabbed my hand, and we were off to the meeting room.

Celeste, Aine, and the Titans sat at the round table deep in discussion, their conversation stopping as we walked in.

Coeus rose and greeted us at the door. "Well, don't you both look refreshed and beautiful." His eyes twinkled. "Nothing like the fairy treatments to get you right on your toes again."

He led us to the table, and I took my normal seat, while he pulled up an extra for Pres. My eyes sought out Hunters where he sat next to Lelantos.

Humor lit his eyes as he looked between me and Pres.

It seems you did your good deed for the day?

I wrinkled my nose and if I hadn't been surrounded by others, I would have stuck out my tongue.

I think I did my good deed for the month. Why do people put themselves through all of that torture?

He laughed softly, and Aine turned to me once everyone was settled.

"With the New Year's celebration and everything else going on, we haven't had a chance to discuss the stones that you found." She gestured to the people around the table. "The Titans had an idea, and I think it makes the most sense for you."

She nodded to Rhea, who looked toward me.

"Since you and all of us," she swept her hand to the other Titans, "are the only ones that are able to touch the stones, we think it best to keep them as close together as possible, *and* with you. We'd like to take them to Olympus and forge them into a bracelet with adamantine."

I took in her words and thought that it was the perfect idea.

"What's adamantine?" I asked, curious.

She smiled. "It is the metal of the gods. It is unbreakable and resilient. The perfect housing for stones this powerful. Once we make the bracelet, Coeus will seat it in your arm, much like the dragonfly one that you have."

My hand ran over the silver metal that I oftentimes even forgot was there.

"And there will be no way for anyone to take it from me then?" I asked.

Her eyes met mine, serious and deep.

"No. Not unless you're killed."

A shudder ran through me, but I brushed it away immediately and made sure my voice took on a light tone.

"Well, that's not ever going to happen, so we don't have to worry about that. When will you leave?"

My eyes found Hunter's again, and I knew he was against leaving me for even a second, but they had to do this together.

"Within the hour," his voice rumbled.

I resigned myself to it and knew he'd do anything to expedite the process and get back to me as soon as possible.

Nodding, I stood and walked to him while the others began to filter out and get ready to leave.

"How long will you be gone?" I asked quietly.

He tilted my chin up so he could see my eyes. "We'll be back late tonight. I promise."

"Okay then. Be careful, and I suppose I'll see you first thing in the morning."

He hugged me tight and kissed my temple.

"I'll wake you up bright and early. That way we can get the bracelet on you and breathe a bit easier."

I bid them all goodbye and watched the powerful group of gods as they sifted.

How is this my life?

Presley didn't leave my side for the rest of the day. Emric took great pleasure in teasing her mercilessly, and satisfaction that things seemed back to normal ran through me.

That night, I suggested a slumber party. I felt the need to be surrounded. Which was really strange. I guessed it had something to do with Hunter being gone.

Trela, Bea, Shay, Pres, and Killian all squeezed onto my bed with me, Emric, Charlie and Star at our feet and a bowl of popcorn in the middle.

While there were no TVs here in Fairy, Killian was able to talk Aine into letting us borrow her magic projector, and we were currently enjoying *Twilight*. I'd never really been into vampire books or movies before, but I was surprised by how much I was enjoying this one now.

"Guys, are vampires real?" The thought struck me as we watched. I mean, here we were in Fairy. Shifters and dragons *were* real. Why wouldn't there be vampires?

Emric snorted. "Sure there are, but not like the ones in this movie. There are what we call psychic vampires. They feed off of others energy. They may be a little faster than an average person, but other than that they have no magic. They simply must take the energy to survive. Then there are others who do drink human blood, but not by biting them. They usually get blood from blood banks and only take a little at a time. They have a disorder, you see, and they need the blood to keep their bodies from failing."

He waved his paw at the screen. "All this is an accumulation of drama and myth."

His explanation was interesting and made sense. It wouldn't be the first time Hollywood got it wrong or expanded on legends and myths weaving it into their own versions.

After a while, the dragon shifters made a pallet to stretch out on the floor and Killian got himself comfortable on the chaise lounge, while Pres and I snuggled into my bed. We were barely able to hold our eyes open.

Sleepily, she hugged me close. "Thank you for today, Andie. I needed it more than I knew."

I yawned and closed my eyes, the movie playing softly in the background. "You're welcome. I needed it too."

Chapter Twenty-One

Red hair clouded my vision before Leif's face came into view. She sat back on her haunches and held a white rose to her lips.

Blinking slowly, she looked past me as if seeing something that wasn't there.

"Soon the earth will shake, and fire will rise. There will be death and destruction... Pain."

Her voice was soft and woeful before strengthening.

"You will have to make choices that will seem incomprehensible. It will be a battle of power, but also a battle of wills. Is your will great enough?" Her blue eyes stared into mine stonily. "It must be if you wish to win. Sacrifices will be expected."

In her eyes, I saw blue flames rising with gold flames twisting through it. What did it mean? Why did these flames make me think of Teagan and Hunter?

My body was racked with tremors.

Leif leaned forward and placed her palm against my forehead and my vision flashed to white.

I was looking into a sky, the blue completely covered by clouds. Something moved slowly through the fluffy air, wings scattering the mass away as it came closer.

It was majestic and beautiful, it's body sleek and all white. Powerful wings extended on either side.

I caught only a glimpse before Leif's face looked back into mine, her ruby red lips opening to speak once again.

"Strength and healing will come, but only if you have faith and devotion. Use your courage and energy wisely."

Once again, she leaned forward, this time reaching out her hands. She placed them on my shoulders, and with a small smile, she pushed.

I fell backward, my body tumbling through time and space. Darkness.

Strong hands pulled me into a warm embrace.

"Shh... it's okay." Hunter's voice grounded me, and my eyes snapped open.

I didn't feel as though I'd even slept a minute, but my body hummed with nervous energy.

Pres sat beside me, studying me with worry.

I pushed back gently from Hunter and looked around to see that I had woken everyone up with my dreams.

"I'm so sorry. What time is it?"

Killian was quick to let me know that it was seven in the morning and they'd all slept fine, well until the last few minutes.

"What was the vision about?" Charlie landed at my feet, his eyes seeming to pierce into my soul.

I knew that Hunter had seen everything as it ran through my mind again, yet he kept quiet, knowing it was mine to tell. I quickly outlined the dream or vision to them, making sure to keep my voice neutral and unafraid.

"It's really not anything new. We know the battle ahead is going to be dangerous and..."

"It'll just plain suck," Emric finished, licking his paw, while everyone agreed.

I was determined to steer the topic away my vision. I didn't want to talk anymore about it now.

Smiling brightly with a happiness I didn't feel, I looked at Hunter.

"Well? Let's get that bracelet on. I'm excited to see it."

Everyone got up and put the room back to rights, filing out to get ready for the day. Hunter lagged behind, snagging my hand as I headed to change.

"Hey. I know what you were doing. It's okay to be worried. It's even okay to show fear. At least with me." He ran his finger over my jaw.

"I know. But right now, they," I jerked my thumb over my shoulder, "need strength. I can't show them fear, not right now. And if my vision was any indication, we should be scared."

He frowned at me, but I pulled away fast before he could say anymore. I needed to hold onto my feigned strength. If I didn't, I feared I might drown.

∞

After a hot shower, the darkness decided it was time to rise and shine. It hit me quick and without any warning.

I was brushing my hair out, and when my eyes fell to the mirror in front of me, they were black like the night. I watched in horror as tendrils of black crept through the veins in my neck and fire lit my stomach.

You never know when evil will rise...

The thought flew through my head, and I frantically worked to push the oiliness down.

Now, now. Is that any way to treat me? You need me. I need you. It's time you realize thissss...

I didn't want to listen to it. How could I work with this evil? My fear rose as the darkness did, feeding it, making it laugh and preen inside of me.

You can't do this, I pleaded with it. *You don't own me!* I pushed harder and ignored the door as it flew open. Star raced to my shoulders, while Hunter hugged me around the waist, his eyes molten and veins lit gold.

"Fight it, Andie. Fight it." His voice was steady but his face fierce. Star's magic coasted into me and wrapped with the energy of his, both helping me slowly push the blackness down.

We could have stood there a minute or an hour, but it felt like a lifetime before the black in my eyes faded and my veins returned to normal.

I breathed heavily; my body worn out from the strain. I could see in the way that Hunter and Star took in air that they were just as taxed.

If it took that much out of the three of us to contain this evil, I worried what would happen when it rose further.

I turned to Hunter, my jaw clenched. "It's getting stronger. We've got to do something soon to get rid of Helios. I can't take living with this thing one more minute," I seethed.

"Easy." He ran his hands up and down my arms. "We will get rid of it, somehow or some way."

"It said I needed it and it needed me. It's talking to me more and more," I said shivering.

He looked thoughtful as he steered me out of the bathroom. "Isn't that pretty much what Leif already told you? Maybe at some point in the upcoming battle, you can tap into it, use its knowledge."

I knew that was what Leif said, but I still hadn't been able to come up with a logical way that it made any sense.

"But why would it help me destroy Helios? It's his power, after all. Destroying him would mean destroying it too."

He shook his head, his brows lowered. "I haven't been able to figure that out yet. But there has to be a reason. There just has to."

He took me once again to the meeting room, where all of the Titans were seated. Every time I saw them at the round table, visions of the Templar Knights filled my head. Though they were my friends and guards, I often forgot their power and age, and all that they stood for.

Celeste and Aine stood nearby, while the girls and Killian came in behind Hunter and me.

On the table in front of my seat lay a silver box. Engraved on top of it was a butterfly.

I glanced at Hunter and he just shrugged before smirking. I knew what the butterfly meant. He had done it to remind me of the time when the butterflies drew us together. It was almost like a rebirth of our relationship.

"Open it," Coeus boomed from the table jovially. "I think you'll be very happy with how it turned out."

I slowly lifted the clasp that held it closed, pushing the top open. Inside the box, nestled in white silk lay the most beautiful piece of jewelry I'd ever laid eyes on. And between my crown and the butterfly bracelet, that said a lot.

The four jewels winked at me from atop the band, all nestled in the silver metal that they said was impenetrable. Intricate designs were carved into the delicate circlet and I leaned close to study them.

What I saw took my breath away.

Amidst etchings of dragons, Were shifters, fairies, and the moon were tiny words. They read: *Victory, family, love, strength, and unity.*

Everything on this bracelet embodied my family, my friends, and this fight we were all in.

A tear slipped from my eye as Coeus walked around the table, picking the box up while Hunter turned me toward him.

I swiped at the lone drop and smiled at the Titans around me.

"Thank you for doing this. I... I can't explain how special you've made this for me. And how much each and every one of you mean to me," I whispered.

Everyone in the room grinned, bowing their heads. Including Coeus.

"It was our honor, Andie. Now, let's get this seated." He kneeled before me, and I extended my arm. Gently he clasped it around my wrist. It was strangely warm and though snug, it felt right to have it there.

The jewels' power seeped into me, and the darkness purred but didn't rise.

Weaving his magic around the bracelet, Coeus spoke in an ancient language. Sparkles lit the air around us, dancing before zapping into my skin at his final utterance.

There was a slight burning, just as before, but nothing I couldn't handle, and it was soon gone. I stared down at the bracelet, now essentially a part of me, amazed again at its brilliance.

It was time to get to work. I had the stones, but I needed to find the final Key. Having all of those in our possession when we battled Helios was a must.

Hunter pulled me aside as everyone around us began conversing. "About the winged horse, do you have any idea what it means?"

I hadn't really thought much about it. The other parts of my vision had clouded out that particular one. Frowning, I shook my head. "No idea. Though I'm sure it must mean something, or else Leif wouldn't have shown it to me."

He looked just as puzzled as I felt, pondering on it. "Remember when I told you months ago that you'd be able to shift at some point?"

I did remember now that he mentioned it and hope lit my blood on fire.

"Do you think I'll be able to shift into that? Into a white horse with wings?"

He smiled and his eyes twinkled. "Well, nothing is impossible, apparently. I guess we'll have to see."

Visions of flying through the air clouded my thoughts, and excitement ran through me.

"How do you shift? Can we try it now?"

He laughed at my excitement. "It takes a lot of practice, especially for someone who isn't part of a shifter clan. How about we focus on what's going on now? After it's all over, we'll train you on how to shift." He winked and disappointment flowed over me.

Pouting a little I agreed. He was right. There was just too much on our plate right now to add more to it.

Hunter's phone rang just then startling us both. It still amazed me how even though we were on a different plane, they'd been able to magic their phones to work.

Gotta love those powers.

He spoke to whoever was on the other line, and I stiffened as his face fell, his eyes turning serious.

"We'll get ready," was all I caught of the conversation before he ended the call, his body tense.

"Stay here," was all he said to me before striding over to Coeus and the rest of the Titans. Their voices were low and fervent, and I strained to hear them.

It wasn't long before they turned as a unit, the entire room watching them.

Coeus cleared his throat, his eyes on me as he spoke. "It seems that things have escalated. The coven has just advised that the Fomori and more demons have converged on Junction, essentially taking it over. They're making a statement to us. To *you,* Andie. I'm afraid our battle has begun."

Cold ran through me, and my spine straightened. We knew it would be soon; I just hadn't expected it would start today.

All eyes were on me as they waited for my instruction. It was still difficult at times to remember I was their leader. Well, the Fae's, not the Titans.

"Right. Are the humans in Junction protected?" I asked first, looking at Hunter.

"Yes. Logan and Toni were alerted when the Fomori were in route and activated the coven to get all of the humans out of town. They've taken them to the compound where there is plenty of room in the underground shelter. Whenever this is over, they'll be spelled so as to not remember any of it."

I nodded, satisfied.

"I need to find the last Key. Please call my dad and have him meet us at the Oak," I said to Celeste, who agreed and hurried out. I looked to the dragon shifters and Killian. "You're with me. Emric, Charlie, you are too." Then I turned to Hunter. "Is it possible you can go with me this time?" I asked softly, the leader hat gone, and I cringed at the pleading that bled through in my voice.

He grabbed my hands and brought them to his chest, his eyes serious and somber. "You don't seriously think I'd let you go without me, do you?"

I shrugged, feeling a little helpless. "I don't want you in pain. I know what breaking your law means."

"That law went out the door when each one of us agreed that this battle was far more important than an archaic treaty. There might be pain, but it would never be from defending you and our world from evil." He winked before turning to his team.

"Make sure while we're gone that you defend all portals to Fairy. We cannot have any evil slipping in unawares."

They all agreed quickly.

Aine called to her fairies, and thousands of them swarmed into the room. It was a sea of color and wings. While they lived and worked here, they were also her army. Even though they were small Fae, they were also magical and full of power.

The group I had declared would be with me gathered around, and my attention was taken from the orders Aine doled out.

Their faces were serious and solemn as they waited for my instructions. I noticed that Presley hung back, awkward and nervous. I hadn't called her name to go with us, but only because I wanted to give her the option to decide for herself. I wasn't convinced that she was healed enough from the torture the Fomori and Jasper had put her through.

She noticed my gaze, and I watched as a myriad of emotions swept over her face. I gave her a few minutes, and the moment she decided was obvious. She didn't even have to say a word and I knew.

Her back straightened, and she set her shoulders. Lifting her head higher, she took a deep breath that rippled through her.

With two firm steps forward, she occupied the empty spot in our circle, her eyes never leaving mine.

"You sure?" I asked lightly.

Her nod was stiff, but she didn't hesitate. "I can't sit back and watch while everyone else fights this evil. After what they did to me, I need to have a part in it. So yes, I'm sure."

I smiled, happy with her response, as did the rest of our group.

"Good." I clapped my hands and turned to leave the room. "Get your suits and meet me outside. We're going to the Oak."

Everyone went their separate ways, and Hunter promised to wait outside my room for me.

Rushing inside, I flung my clothes off and used my magic, the sleek purple suit soon lying against my skin. I grabbed my beanie, stuffing it in a pocket.

Rather than feeling anxious, excitement rippled through me. This was it. It was now or never and the last journey to find a Key.

I swung open the door to find Hunter right where he said he'd be.

As he leaned against the wall in his black suit, I admired how muscular he looked. He reminded me of a sexy ninja. *My* sexy ninja.

The darkness inside me purred right along with me.

He just smirked and grabbed my hand. "Let's go."

Down the stairs and out the door we went, and I could feel the energy bouncing from him just as much as it was for me.

Our group stood waiting, and it surprised me to see Bea holding Emric and Shay holding Star. Both of the magical creatures looked content and happy. At the arch of my brow, both girls just shrugged.

Charlie landed on my shoulder and dryly stated, "They fed them cookies, and now they're best friends."

I chuckled. It didn't take anything but food to endear someone to those two.

Emric snuggled deeper into Beas arms, but Star licked Shay's face and then jumped down, winding herself around me. My familiar only liked to sift with me.

"Everyone ready?"

They all agreed, and we sifted.

Just like all the other times, our feet landed with a thump on the wood floor of the Oak. Balwyn and Eira stood at the ready, obviously having been alerted that we were coming.

The moment we appeared, Eira was zipping around, chatting everyone up, while Balwyn lugged packs to each of us.

"Don't know how long ya plan on bein' gone, but I's put enough food an water in ta packs as I could fit," he said,

"Thank you, Balwyn. I hope we won't be gone too long. You haven't seen anything strange around the woods, have you?" I asked, weary that the Fomori and the demons might infiltrate the magical woods too.

He shook his head back and forth slowly. "I's not seen a thing other than the birds an wild animals. Don't ya worra, I's keepin' my eyes out for tha Fomori. Ain't nothin' getting to my Oak!" His voice rose in anger.

I kneeled down and, to his surprise, wrapped my arms around him. He stood still in shock but eventually patted my back, uncomfortable.

"You're the best. Take care of Eira for me while we're gone." I winked at her, and she rolled her eyes from where she hovered behind him.

Balwyn stood up as straight as his little Brownie body would let him, the pompom on his night cap bobbing in tune with his nod.

His fist hit his chest, and he bowed quickly. "I swear ta ya tha I won't let nothin' happen to her or ta tha Oak." He turned then and scurried to his hidey hole, and I turned to my friends.

"It's time to go. We'll use the fairy portals to get to Finias. We'll find the last Key there."

They followed me as I went up to the portal room, disabling the force field that protected it with Star's help. It hadn't changed a bit, and like before, Star hopped down, sniffing as she went until she came to a frame situated low to the ground.

The scene in the portal was much like the one we'd traveled through that took us to the Stone of Destiny. Rolling green hills and purple heather stretched as far as the eye could see. Not a soul moved.

Shay stared wide-eyed around her at all the different portals, and Bea filled her in on how they worked.

I turned to them all, laying out the plan.

"We know the last Key is the Spear of Lugh. I've actually given it a new name though, the Spear of Victory. Because I know that finding this last Key will help lead us to victory. I want you all to keep that in mind as we go on this journey. Like always, we have no idea what creatures we'll encounter. What dangers we'll face. More than likely when we get close to the Key, I'll have to continue the journey alone to find it. And that's okay. But to get there, we have to trust each other, work together, and if I ask you to do something, only question it if you see the darkness in me rising."

They all listened raptly, nodding their understanding. Hunter only smirked. He always did what he wanted. I stuck my tongue out at him.

"I'll go first. See you on the other side!"

I hurried to scramble through the portal as fast as I could before Hunter could stop me. Knowing him, he'd want to go first to make sure there were no threats waiting.

Too bad.

I tumbled headfirst into the tall grass, letting my body roll before finding my feet. Standing, I looked around, and one by one my friends appeared.

I couldn't see a thing but hills. Looked like we were going to be walking for a while.

When everyone made it through the portal, I set off with Hunter by my side.

"How do you know this is the right way to go?" Trela called from behind.

"I don't, but we have to start somewhere. And most times, if I'm not heading in the right direction, the Fates somehow steer me there."

As our feet trampled the grass and flowers, white butterflies scattered, filling the air around us with wings. Presley laughed and held her hand out while some of them proceeded to land on her.

They stayed with her for a while as she walked, and I could hear her talking to them in a low voice, as if they listened.

We trudged up and down hill after hill, and I finally spotted a tree line ahead.

The sun was beating down on us, and I felt relief at seeing the thick forest, knowing that the shade would be a reprieve. Even though our suits were breathable, the darkness of the fabric drew the heat of the sun right to you.

As we approached the woods, Hunter stopped us. "Let's let Charlie fly over first and make sure there's no one waiting to surprise us," he said as he turned to me.

It was a sound idea and I looked to Charlie who promptly took to the air, his bright blue wings stretching and soaring.

He wasn't gone long and landed on my shoulder, addressing everyone. "I didn't see anyone lying in wait. There is a pool of Selkies not far from here, next to a monument of some kind."

I tried to place Selkies with anything I'd read about Lugh, but nothing came to mind. It couldn't be where the Spear rested. *But* they might have some information on it, so I figured it was worth checking out.

I stepped forward to enter the trees, and once again Hunter stopped me, his face turned down in fake menace.

"*I* will lead for now."

His statement didn't broker a response. I knew if I did, it wouldn't matter. He'd still find a way to dominate. For now, I was fine with that.

We filed into the brush, and Hunter knocked away anything in our path. Pres breathed in quick excited breaths behind me as we trampled through the vegetation.

Charlie quietly gave direction on which way to walk to take us to the pool, and before long the splashing of water reached my ears.

Through branches that hung down heavy with leaves, I saw large gray bodies swirling through the water, while others lounged on the rocks lining the pool.

Hunter made sure to make some noise as we exited the forest, so as to not startle them. I don't think we would have even if we'd been quiet. At the breaking of twigs and rustle of leaves, they lazily turned in our direction, studying us without a care in the world.

It's almost as if we were expected.

One of the larger Selkies in the pool swam toward the bank where we stood, and with a shimmer of magic, the seal skin slid into the water behind it and out stepped a gorgeous male.

He was naked. *Of course, he is. He just shed his selkie skin, Andie,* I admonished myself.

It took all I had to stare directly into his moss green eyes and not anywhere else. They alone were captivating.

He came to stand before me, and I felt Hunter move closer. "You've come for the Key." The deep voice resonated throughout the clearing, echoing off the rocks behind him.

I nodded slowly, at a loss for words.

He didn't smile. Well, there really wasn't a lot of emotion that showed on his face at all. "You'll find what you seek in there." His finger pointed toward the monument that Charlie had spoken about earlier.

It was a large statue of a lynx, its mouth open in a growl.

"May I?" I gestured toward it, asking for permission.

The man nodded, and Hunter was glued to my side as I strolled over. The rest of the group stayed in place, their eyes watching the Selkies for any untoward moves.

I searched the statue for an opening, and only when I looked inside of its open mouth, did I see a small handle. I knew the Key wasn't here, my bracelet hadn't lit up and I hadn't felt any power. It wouldn't be that easy. It *never* was.

Cautiously, I opened the small door and reached inside. I pulled my hand back out quickly at the touch of something only to see that cobwebs covered my fingers.

Squinching my nose up in disgust, I stuck my hand back in.

There! Paper touched my fingertips, and I slid it out slowly. There was no telling how old the paper was, and I couldn't have it falling apart in my haste.

When it lay in my hands, I didn't understand what I was seeing.

Hunter leaned over my shoulder. "Huh. It's written in the language of dragons." His look was puzzled before he waved Trela over.

"What ya got there?" she asked as she looked at the paper.

"Think you can read this?" he asked, pointing to the writing.

She whistled low. "It's been a long time since I've seen the language of our people, but yes, I can read it."

She took it from my hands and studied it before looking up again with confusion. "This doesn't make any sense. All it says is that the answer you seek is in a box at the bottom of the water."

I groaned and stared at the pool lined with Selkies. I absolutely hated the journeys that took me underwater. There was always something sinister in the water.

"Great," I said, walking back to where the male Selkie stood.

"I'm going to have to dive into your pool. Do you grant me that request?"

He didn't hesitate, turning to the side, his arm stretched out to the water. "Be my guest."

And *finally*, emotion showed in the form of a smile. It made me slightly uneasy. Why was he so happy about me swimming into his pool?

Hunter pulled me back away from him, whispering in my ear. "He'll try to lure you in. Not to hurt you, but to claim you. That's what Selkies do. I'll go to the bottom."

There was anger and jealousy all wrapped up in his voice as he hissed the last.

I only shook my head, adamant that if we didn't do this right, we might not get whatever was in the box below.

He felt that through our connection and sighed, stepping back away from me. "I'll be here waiting. If you're not back up very soon, I'm coming in after you."

I knew he would too. "I'll be back soon. I promise."

And with that I pushed past the Selkie and dived in.

My suit kept me mostly dry, and the water that surrounded me was cool but not cold. The further I pushed myself down, the clearer the water became.

I could see baby Selkies swimming around the bottom, playful and enjoying themselves. They swam around a large branch that had at one time fallen into the deep. A ray of sun shone through the water and onto the branch, and a tiny glint of something sparkled back up at me.

That had to be the box.

My lungs were already straining from holding my breath so long, and I pushed myself harder, ignoring the little Selkies who spotted me. I brushed by one and stuck my hand down to where the small box lay, grasping it tight and it pulled from the muck on the bottom.

I pushed off and back up as quick as I could, my lungs screaming, my focus solely on the light above. As I did, the male who had stood above splashed into the water, swirling around me, his green eyes trying to capture mine.

I knew he was trying to captivate me with his gaze, and I slammed my eyes shut. He didn't know who he was trying to mess with, but I wasn't falling for it.

My head broke the water, and I sucked in a deep breath, wheezing as I heard splashes near me.

My eyes opened to see Hunter's hand reaching out and I grasped it with my free one, the box held snug against my chest with the other.

"I was about to come after you. That took way too long, Andie." His eyes seared into mine. "Especially when ol' green eyes jumped in."

I laughed through my coughing and stepped onto the bank.

"He never stood a chance."

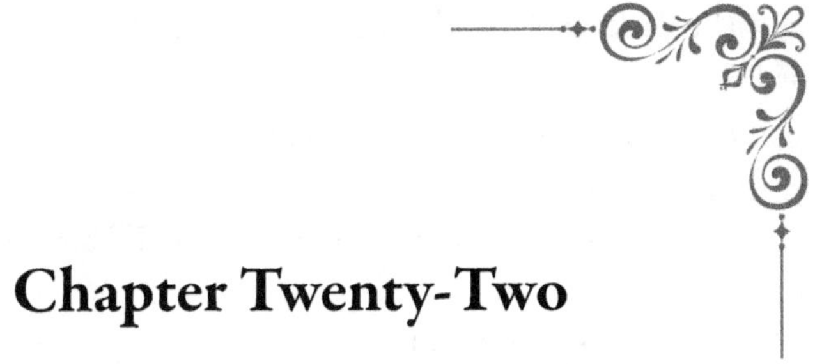

Chapter Twenty-Two

I thanked the Selkies properly, as any leader would do, and then we walked out of the clearing and back into the woods.

When I felt that we were far enough away, I sat against a tree, my team hovering over, and stared down at the box.

I had to have faith that this would lead to the Spear.

Lugh was known as a trickster, and it hadn't surprised me one bit that he was leading me on a scavenger hunt. I just hoped it wouldn't be a long one.

The box was green and made out of a polished stone. Smooth and slick. There was a small indention under the lid, and I put my finger on it, which automatically triggered the lid to open.

Inside, something was wrapped in a leaf that had forever stayed green. Magic must have kept it preserved. I lifted the leaf bundle out and sat the box aside on the dirt beside me, carefully unwrapping it.

Shock gathered inside of me as I stared at the object in my palm. It was an exact replica of the Oak. There was no question.

Why in the heck was this what he left? I turned it in all different directions, looking for some sort of clue.

Nothing came to me.

I looked up at the group around me and their faces reflected my confusion. "What would the Oak have to do with the Key?" Killian asked, his eyes puzzled.

We sat silent for a few minutes, and I racked my brain, searching for something that would make sense.

The darkness chuckled inside of me, and I felt my frustration rise as I told it to shut up.

You don't see what is directly in front of you.

Anger rose.

Well obviously, I said back to it. Or else I'd already have figured it out.

"Andie..." Hunter said.

I felt the darkness rising even as he laid a hand on me. This time, his touch didn't help, and the darkness crooned.

As my eyes changed, my vision went black, and instead the image of the Oak flashed in front of my eyes.

Now I was inside of it, yet it wasn't the same as I remembered. It was *bigger.*

A huge spiral stairway wound around a tree inside of the tree. Gods and mystical creatures walked slowly up the stairs, and magic floated in the air.

See? the voice in my head said.

I watched as a young deity held a book as he marched up the stairs, and whatever form I was in followed. I watched as he placed the book in a heavy wooden cabinet in a hidden room at the top of the Oak.

His hands weaved magic much like Celeste had done to seal our book in its resting place. As I watched him go back down, he stopped every so often at different doors, weaving more magic before he returned to the bottom of the stairwell, a satisfied smirk on his face.

It's Lugh.

And now the object made sense.

I was thrust back into the present, the darkness slowly descending on its own and I was left gasping for breath.

Everyone was up in arms around me, and Hunter grabbed me to him.

"What happened? You weren't breathing, and I couldn't sense you at all." His voice was strained and upset.

Killian thrust a water bottle into my hand, and I took a deep drink.

"Somehow the darkness inside of me helped. I don't know why, but it put images inside of my head, showing me where we need to go."

I wiped my mouth and stared at the tree that was still clutched in my hand and then held it up. "The Key is where it all began. It makes sense that it would be where it would end too. The Oak. It's in the *Oak*."

Shock lined their faces, and Emric smirked while Charlie looked chagrined.

"You knew?" my voice rose as I looked at the two of them.

"Well, of course we knew. But you had to find out on your own, or it wouldn't work. The Fates have set things up in order. If we'd disturbed the natural order, it would be chaos. Who knows what would happen?" Emric said snootily.

"It doesn't mean it's going to be easy either," Charlie said quietly. "This will be the biggest challenge of all."

And I believed him. After what I'd seen just now, I worried about actually being able to get to it.

We decided to eat something before heading back to the Oak, and we planned.

Presley came up with a brilliant idea to lure Declan to Celeste's house while giving me time to find the Key.

We already knew I'd have to go in alone. It wouldn't be any different from the other times. And we would still have to end Helios and the Fomori.

I thought her idea was brilliant. Hunter? Not so much.

The plan was to have a party with the coven and Were shifters in attendance. They would drop the protection around the house, knowing that he and the Fomori wouldn't be able to resist it. There would be too much temptation.

By the time it got into full swing, I'd have the Key and be ready to rumble.

Jokingly, I came up with a secret phrase that I would use during battle if I needed everyone to focus their power to help me. They all laughed at first with me, but in the end, we figured it wouldn't hurt.

Once we'd gotten every detail down to a T, we packed up and sifted back to the Oak.

∞

My feet touched down on a bed of leaves and I stared at the outside of the Oak in confusion. We'd never landed outside. We'd always landed inside.

I pulled the necklace that held the small key out and went to place my hand on the nodule where the hidden doorway was. It hit an invisible barrier, and a sting lit my hand as if I had been bitten by something before it bounced off.

"What the heck!?" I cried out, and my friends ran to my side. "Don't touch it. There's some kind of field around it."

They got as close as possible, searching every inch for an opening. There wasn't one.

My mind went to Balwyn and Eira. Fear for their safety caused a ball to form in my throat.

I voiced as much to Hunter as he came to stand by me.

"I'm sure they're fine. They're the keepers of the tree. This field, it's the tree's magic encasing it."

"How do you know that?" I asked curiously.

He gave me a look and I realized I should know better. He *was* a Titan, after all.

"Okay, but why is it trying to keep me out? That makes no sense. It has to know the reason I'm here and that I have to find the Key to save everyone and everything."

He shrugged, just as puzzled as I was. "Let's call Celeste and fill her in. We need to get everyone on the same page about the party, and she might have suggestions on how you can get in."

He gestured toward the tree.

He was right, of course, and I wondered if she had known like Emric and Charlie, that the last Key was here.

Surely not. I couldn't see her sending me on a goose chase if she'd known.

Within minutes, Celeste and Dad sifted to the clearing, both looking just as bewildered by the tree's protection as the rest of us.

So I guess that answered my question. She hadn't known.

"I've never seen anything like this happen here before." She stared, her mouth open. I couldn't help but press the matter some though.

"Have you ever seen the inside of the tree change? Like I mean, completely look different inside?" I asked, probing.

Celeste was extremely old; she had to have been around when Lugh was here.

She looked away, biting her lip before looking back at me and sighing. "Yes, the Oak was completely different thousands of years ago. It wasn't until the Fomori raided these woods and I had to escape with your Nan that it changed."

She gestured for me to follow her over to two tree stumps where she sat down and continued her story.

"Before the first battle with the Fomori, the Oak was a majestic place. It was the entrance to our world. It took our people to all of their homelands. Consider it as if it were a huge place full or portals to anywhere. Oh, it looked the same on the outside, but the inside was massive. A huge stairwell resided in the middle, stretching up as far as the eye could see. Some said to the heavens." She picked at her skirt.

"But when the Fomori found these woods, it had to be protected. Its magic changed; the portals were hidden. Don't get me wrong, they're still there, but haven't been used since. It, my dear, was the real reason that all of the Fae were so despondent when the woods were invaded. They lost not only the woods, but their beloved transport and favorite place to come together. That also led to the anger between the Fae and other magical communities, for they relied on the Oak as well."

My head spun with all this new information. It was incredible, but I still had no idea how to get in. And I really needed to.

She patted my hand. "I have a feeling it will let you in, but not with everyone else here. It's in defense mode, and it knows you to be the One. Not everyone else. I suggest that we leave you and get everything ready for this deception for Declan. And once you are here by yourself, you should be granted access."

My team began to argue that I shouldn't go alone. Even bringing up the idea that it could be a trap.

I stopped that talk quickly. I knew Celeste was right, and I knew I needed to get going and fast. There was something in the air that told me evil was coming.

The darkness agreed.

The group waited off to the side while Hunter told me goodbye. While I didn't want him to leave, I was ready to get the Key and get the upcoming battle over with.

He pulled me close and ran his hands over my face, before resting his lips on mine. It wasn't a long kiss, but it was the sweetest one yet.

"I know you'll be okay," he kissed my nose, "but please... please come back to me. Don't take unnecessary risks and have faith in yourself."

He looked into my eyes, and I leaned further into him. "You be careful too, and take care of them." I nodded to the group.

They waved, and I smiled, blowing my dad a kiss.

"You know I will, baby." Hunter hugged me tight again, then let me go. "Go get that Key." He strode back to the others and they clasped hands, staring at me with love as they disappeared.

I let out a slow breath and turned back to the Oak.

"Okay, are you going to play nice now?" I tentatively reached out. As my hand neared where the force field had been before, some power grabbed me, and I was sucked in.

I stumbled to find my footing as my gaze raced around. It looked exactly like the vision that the darkness had given me, except there was no one walking around. The majestic space was empty as a tomb.

It gave me the creeps really. There was no warmth in here now. No cozy fire or warm blankets. No friends or family.

Just me.

I stared up at the huge stairway that spiraled up and up. It was a bit daunting.

In the quiet of the space, I heard a faint noise, but I couldn't tell where it came from. It seemed to bounce around in the expanse.

Well, now or never. I pumped myself up. It had become a ritual each journey, and this time was no different. As I swung my arms from side to side, I noticed the dragonfly bracelet glowed very faintly.

That assured me that the Key was here, but I still had a long way to go to even get close to it.

Starting forward, I took the first steps, slowly, counting each one. I didn't trust things to always be what they seemed, and I wanted to know how many steps it took to get up, so that when I had to come back down, there'd be no surprises.

Oh, there will be surprises.

The darkness had snuck up on me this time.

You'll be happy I'm here shortly. Keep going.

I gritted my teeth and walked up more steps, the noise that I'd heard earlier was louder now as I came to a large platform.

Immediately, the stairs above me disappeared, and I had no place to go unless I wanted to descend. I turned to look back, only to see the ones going down had vanished too.

Well, now what? I asked the darkness, admonishing myself for doing so.

It purred and curled itself inside of me.

I looked around the expanse of the room below and above me and didn't see a thing. A few minutes passed, and my frustration grew.

Should I try to sift up?

The option was taken away from me as the platform rose on its own, shifting to the side as it went higher. It moved slowly, but I bent my knees and braced myself. Falling to my death would not be an option.

All of a sudden, it stopped with a little bounce, and it reminded me of an elevator. Just a magical one.

A table sat before me, with three small jugs of milk and a note set out across the middle.

What the heck was this? I'd expected a monster or something magical to jump out at me.

But milk?

I reached for the notecard. The paper was old parchment, brittle and yellow with age. Carefully, I opened it and all it said was:

Two are sweet and taste divine. One is sour and will leave you blind.

I stared at the small containers and dropped the note back to the wooden tabletop. So this was a game of chance? Leave it to Lugh the Trickster to leave crazy tests for me.

How was I supposed to know which one was poisoned and which ones weren't? They all looked the same.

I picked each one up and sniffed them. They all smelled the same too.

You've got magic, powers beyond what most have, and you're relying on your senses? the voice inside my mind hissed at me.

Well, yes, I did have powers, but how was I supposed to use them to figure this out?

The darkness sighed and began to rise. I resisted the feeling, pushing it back down. But it was insistent, like a constant poke to my brain and I finally relented.

Watching from the inside, I saw my hands rise into the air to hover over the first cup of milk. My finger pointed down and began swirling in the air above it, and I could see my magic twisted in the dark magic that flowed out.

The power inside of me had joined our powers to figure this out, and I watched in amazement as the milk in the glass swirled so fast, but nothing happened.

This was repeated on the second cup that sat beside the first. Again, nothing changed.

At that point, I realized what the darkness was doing. But it wanted to show me even though now we knew it was the last glass that was poisoned.

My finger swirled above it, and as the milk moved like a cyclone, faster and faster, the liquid was separated and the poison, a clear, thick liquid, sat on the bottom, the milk on top.

My hand pulled back, and the darkness yawned, slithering back down into my stomach. I got the distinct feeling it was insinuating that I was an idiot.

I felt like an idiot. I should have thought more about this, and like it said, used my magic. But I was used to using my magic to fight and do menial things, not figure out tricks and mind games.

I sipped both of the unspoiled milks and turned around, waiting to see what other tricks Lugh had up his sleeves.

That must have been what he was doing in my vision as he stopped so many times on his way down the stairs. Setting up games, or traps.

I didn't have time for this.

The platform began to rise again, and so did the darkness, quicker this time as if in preparation for something it knew was coming.

A new room appeared around me, dark and long. It was a huge hall with stone walls on either side and at the end of the hall stood a statue. I couldn't make out what it was of from here, it was just too far away.

Tentatively, I stepped off the platform and began to walk. But the darkness stopped me.

And it's a good thing it did. The spot I had just been about to walk into suddenly lit up in flames. Fire shot out from the cracks in the floor and the surrounding walls.

Use your magic...

I took a deep breath and opened up my powers. I let it flow out of me without restraint. Again, the gold light of my power was twisted with the dark.

It slithered around the room, searching out all of the traps as the fire that had shot up died. The black and gold wisps of power hit the wall ahead of where the fire had been, and a giant piece of concrete fell from the ceiling, hitting the floor with such force that the entire room rattled.

It broke upon impact, and I shuddered at the thought of what would have happened if someone had been under it. My gaze at the huge piece of rock was pulled away as daggers were thrown across the room, and then next came an onslaught of boiling hot water.

The magic bounced around, touching every available surface of the room before slamming back into my body with force. I felt drained from expending so much power, but without the help of the darkness, it could have been worse.

Again, I wondered why it was helping me.

You'll find out in time. Keep going, it muttered.

I began to cross the room, my heart thumping hard in my chest with each step I made. I trusted the magic that had searched the room, but still couldn't stop the fear that there was something it missed.

Sweat rolled down my face, and my legs felt heavy and shaky.

I held my breath as I reached the end of the hall and stood before the statue. It was none other than Lugh, a smile wide on his face as if laughing at the demise of whoever chanced that hall, *or* celebration for those who made it through.

Reaching out, I touched the cold stone face, and the room spun around me. I felt my body being turned upside down in a black haze. My stomach dropped before I was righted again, but the room I was in now looked like a dungeon.

It was dark and dank. The only light available came from two candles that flickered on either side of the room. They illuminated instruments of torture and blood stains on the floor. I shivered as I heard noises from behind a guillotine.

Standing still, I prepared for whatever was coming. My magic was at the ready.

Out stepped a lynx and a dog, side by side, their eyes focused on me. Drool dripped from the dog's mouth, and the lynx licked its paw.

What could be the test with these two? I racked my brain about Lugh and all I had studied on him. I knew he'd had a hound and lynx as pets, but what could he have planned?

I panicked as they slinked forward, their movements mimicking each other, and menace glowed bright in their eyes.

Lugh wouldn't want me to hurt his pets, surely? My mind flew a mile a minute as I tried to figure out what to do.

I attempted to talk to them gently. I crooned and told them I wasn't here to hurt them. It didn't stop their charge toward me.

Dogs and cats liked meat. *Food.*

An a-ha moment lit my brain, and I conjured up fish and raw beef. They landed in front of the two animals with a flop, causing the two to pause.

In a flurry they were on it, chewing fast and gorging themselves.

I didn't wait, hurrying around them while sticking to the wall, as far away as I could get while they were distracted. I moved fast around the devices that littered the room, searching for a door, a sign-something!

A growl sounded low behind me, and I turned to see the lynx extremely close to me, ready to pounce. The dog must have still been eating.

Fright ran through me as I reached out to try and find a weapon of any kind. There were none.

"It's okay kitty. I'm not here to hurt you. I promise. Please don't make me." My voice trembled as its nose touched my leg, sniffing. I didn't have time to react when its mouth opened and sharp teeth bit down. Even the magic of my suit didn't stop the lynx's bite.

"Please, please!" I screamed out. "I don't want to hurt you!"

Still, I did nothing, for surely I'd be punished if I hurt Lugh's beloved pets. This was his machinations after all.

The pain bloomed up my leg as the cat shook its head, his jaw still closed tight on my shin bone. I slid down the wall, biting my lip, only to fall back into space.

The pain was gone immediately from my leg.

I had passed the test.

Again, my body was spun around, dizziness chasing me as I looked to see a ceiling above me as I lay on a cold floor.

Sitting up, I looked at my leg and it was as if nothing happened. No pain, no marks in my suit. It was just another trick on my mind.

"Ach, the mind is a fickle thing, isn't it?" a deep voice sounded, and my head snapped up to see twins standing in front of me.

Wait... Not twins, Lugh. Two identical versions of Lugh.

He stood tall, a giant of a man. A green and white kilt covered his bottom half, and furs over his top. Red hair waved down to his shoulders, and a slight beard and moustache graced his face.

He smiled. Well, *they* smiled, their eyes twinkling with mischief. I stood waiting. So did he.

I gave in and asked, "Why are there two of you?" To which he smiled wider and bowed slightly.

"I thought you'd never ask!" With a chuckle, they spoke in unison. "You must tell me which one of us is good and which one is evil. Choose wisely, or you might not like what happens next."

His laughter echoed off the walls.

Good versus evil. Good versus evil.

There was really only one way I could do this. With auras. And that was assuming these two had auras. I mean, he wasn't real, was he? Surely not. He'd been long gone, but somehow manifested himself here for this task.

Stop it, Andie. You don't have time for this.

The darkness agreed. *Hurry up!*

I gritted my teeth, wishing there was some way I could stop it from infiltrating my head with its words, but at the same time I knew that I probably wouldn't have made it this far without it. It knew things...

I concentrated on the two figures in front of me, breathing deep and thinking about the Well and how I'd felt in it. I pictured my night with Hunter at the lake and also when Nan and Mom had healed me.

My shoulders relaxed, and slowly light began to outline both figures, growing with each inhale that I took.

Both were consumed now in bright white light, and I was confused. Neither one of them put off an evil or dark aura. What if I wasn't doing something right? What if this was another trick? He had to be playing with me and tricking me to make a mistake. He wasn't called the Trickster for nothing.

Oh, for God's sake, go with your gut. Quit overthinking.

The darkness was right. I really didn't see any other choice.

"Umm... neither one of you is evil," I said quietly with bated breath, staring and bracing myself for retribution.

Surprise lit Lugh's face before he busted out laughing, and both versions shook their finger at me.

"You are good. So very, very good. On to your next and final task then." He chuckled, and that mischievous glint was back in his eyes, but he let his smile fall.

"Evil is all around. It is ancient and primitive. It is powerful. You must stop my blood, just as I did." He turned to the side, both figures swinging their arms back as the wall behind them faded and a majestic room appeared.

Their eyes followed me as I passed them, trying to keep my eyes on them and at the same time watching ahead of me.

The wall sealed as I entered the new room. It was all gold and black, a huge throne sitting in the center of the room.

A quick glance at my bracelet showed that I was awfully close to the Key. So close, in fact, that the light in the dragonfly pulsed.

I scanned the room for a threat, but it was empty. I seemed to be the only one here.

Just wait... the darkness sounded cautious this time, and it stopped me in my tracks.

I didn't have to wait long, for a giant dropped from somewhere above, huge feet crashing to the floor and splintering the tiles below us. Debris was flung every which way, some of it hitting me in the face before I could deflect it, and I felt blood start to ooze.

My eyes traveled up and up. This creature was huge.

He stared down at me with three eyes.

Yes, three eyes.

The two normal ones were black as night and full of evil malice while a third stood out prominent in his forehead. It was a golden color and moved differently than the other two. It was unnerving.

He had horns coming out from the sides of his head, sharp and long. Pockmarks littered his face, and he had the distinct look of the Fomori.

I knew who this was, and boy, it wasn't good.

Balor.

Lugh's grandfather whom he killed with the Spear of Victory, thrown right through Balor's two evil eyes. I knew that if I was to go behind him, I'd see another eye in the back of his head. One that would shoot fire and magic, incinerating his foes.

"ARGHHHHHH!" his voice boomed as he screamed down at me, his giant meaty hand following in an attempt to scoop me up.

I dodged it, my eyes searching around the room. I didn't have but a small knife in my pocket, and that just wouldn't do. The best I could manage with it would be just a nick to him.

Near the throne stood a candelabra. Not ideal, but at least it was something.

He swiped down toward me again, his pinky grazing me as I ran and slid between his legs, pumping my feet as fast as they would go. I would only have seconds before the eye in the back of his head spotted me, and then it would be certain death.

My hands reached the tall metal pole, and I yanked it as hard as I could out of the floor. Turning back, I saw that his eye had spotted me, and I knew I needed to hurry.

As I ran, I noticed a huge chandelier on the ceiling. That must have been what he had hidden on. It was so large that even it spanned bigger than the giant.

I sifted quickly, still gripping the long pole, and clutched the chains on the chandelier with my free hand as soon as my feet landed securely on it.

Balor roared, turning this way and that, searching for me, but he didn't look up.

I needed him to, so I'd have the perfect angle to pierce through the front and directly into the eye in the back. Just as Lugh had done all those centuries ago with the Spear.

That isn't going to work, the darkness said plainly. *You need to add power to the weapon.*

Of course, it won't work, I growled to it, furious that this couldn't be easy.

I felt the darkness rise and my hands turned black where I held the metal. *Just like before, feed it your power entwined with mine. Put everything into it that you can.*

It was at that moment when Balor looked up and spotted me. I hadn't even had time to get started.

Faster than I would have thought possible for the giant, his hand snatched at the chandelier, knocking it to either side and I held on for dear life. That was, until he began smashing at it with his fists, and one of his large knuckles caught me in the side.

I felt my ribs crack, pain instantly blooming.

I didn't have any time to think about the pain, and somehow I sifted to a corner, away from the giant just as I began to fall. Gasping, I grabbed my side, and I did something I never imagined I would do. I asked the darkness for help.

This time it didn't gloat. It didn't purr, it didn't even laugh. It rose with a surge, and with it came the absence of pain. I let it take over, but I felt it grasp ahold of my power as it stood my body up.

The darkness was unafraid of this monster. I could feel the ancient wisdom unfold inside of me, though I had no idea how. It was as if the darkness was finally opening itself up to me.

It was a strange and exhilarating feeling, not at all what I'd expected.

My body sizzled with power; electricity ran through my veins as the darkness took us from the shadows out into the light.

Balor tried to smash his foot down on us time and time again, but we ducked and dodged, and then with a mighty leap we grabbed onto his leg, before scurrying up like lightening.

He tried to swat my body off, but it moved so quickly he only ended up hitting himself each time.

By the time we'd climbed to the top of his greasy head, the monster was seething in anger.

The darkness wrapped my legs around one of his horns before dropping me to my stomach, the candelabra raised and now on fire with our magic. Swiftly my arms swung up and then back down in an arc. Every last ounce of power we had pushed in and through the front eye with such force that it shot clean through and out the back.

Balor's scream ricocheted off the walls of the throne room before turning to a moan as his huge body began to sway.

The darkness was depleted, and I found myself still clinging to his horn, the pain in my ribs stabbing and excruciating. I had only a second to use the last bit of magic that I felt left as his body toppled over.

I landed on my butt next to the throne, choking on bile that threatened to rush out while my vision darkened. Before my eyes closed, I saw Balor hit the floor.

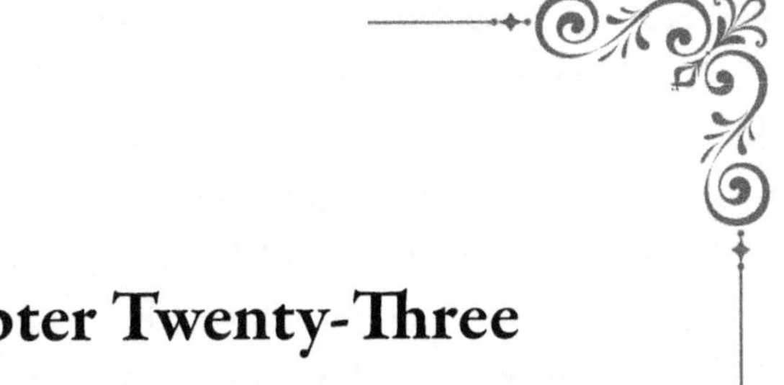

Chapter Twenty-Three

Soft fur tickled my nose as I came to.

"Don't move, darling. We're almost done." Nan's voice crooned to me and I felt warm all over.

"It's not perfect, but we can't stay." My mom's voice chimed in, and I willed my eyes to open despite wanting to stay in the peaceful state I was in.

The black and white panthers sat on either side of me, their paws each touching my head, and the sun and moon symbols on their foreheads were lit up with magic.

"What are you doing here? How..." I croaked out before my mom interrupted.

"We can't stay. The Fates only allow us to come when we're most needed. Your fight is far from over, my girl. We were able to heal your ribs some, and Nan restored some of your magic. You must claim the final Key now."

I stared at them both, my lips trembling.

Nan removed her paw and sat up straighter, and she gave me the same look she'd given me countless times when I was being a brat.

"Andie." Her voice rang strong. "Now is not the time to let your emotions get the best of you. There's a battle already raging outside. Your friends and family need you. You must hurry."

Shock ran through me. "The battle has already started?"

They both nodded, and I sat up quick, their figures disappearing as I did so.

Fear ran cold through me. My family was out there, fighting for their lives without me. What had I done? How long had I been in here?

My bracelet fairly hummed as I gripped the arm of the throne, only to see a book with the Celtic knot sitting atop the seat.

It hadn't been there before while the darkness and I battled Balor. I knew it hadn't, I would have seen it.

This was my prize for killing him, but I had no time to spare.

I reached for it, and in my hands it instantly changed to a long spear. The bronze tip glowed blue as I grasped the wooden handle, and its power ran through me.

As soon as I stepped away from the throne, it changed into the smaller version of the book and I tucked it away safely in my pocket as I had done with all the Keys before.

Now I just have to unite them.

The tree immediately let me out as I sifted, and when I landed in Celeste's living room, I could hear the battle raging and the house shook from the loud booms.

I worried about everyone out there, pleading with anyone who might be listening, any higher power, to let my family and friends be okay.

Striding over to the bookcase, I said the words that Celeste had taught me, and the field around the book that held the rest of the Keys slipped away.

I grabbed the old book, shuffling to the page where the other three Keys lay, while taking the Spear out of my pocket. Without hesitation, it flew from my hand and onto the page.

Once it was seated there, the large book in my hands shook and a glow lit from within. The four Keys rattled on the page and, like magnets, began to slowly inch toward each other.

I willed them to go faster as the sounds of screams echoed from outside, and fire lit the sky, illuminating the dark living room.

As soon as the small books touched on the page, I was thrown back in a blinding light, my head hitting the bookshelf. The four Keys spun in the air as one. Their light so bright that I could barely make out what was happening.

They flashed as the sword, the cauldron, the stone, and the spear twirled together.

The darkness spoke quietly, as if to keep the Keys from hearing it.

Hold out your right hand.

I slowly lifted it into the air, palm up and I didn't have to wait long. The Keys forged together in a ball of that celestial light, even brighter than before and it shot right into my hand.

Burning pain scorched my palm, before racing into my veins and through the rest of my body.

I screamed in torment; my body was on fire. Power that I'd never felt before raced through me and instantly so did the knowledge that it was Nemed's power. The original leader and King of the Fae, from whom I was a descendant.

As the light faded and the burning stopped, my eyes fell to my palm. There lay the Celtic knot, each Key nestled in between the dark lines. It merely looked like a tattoo. The color was the same as the Unalome on my arm, but I knew deep inside that I could call the power from all of them out. I could use each weapon how it was intended, or I could use them together, uniting their magic to suffocate all evil.

Even so, Nemed's knowledge that now lay inside of me showed me that it wouldn't be easy.

Outside was a battle between good and evil, and it wouldn't be so simple as blasting the evil to kingdom come.

Evil was crafty. Downright despicable. It would take hostages and it would have no mercy. I had no time to waste and running full speed out onto the front porch, I was greeted with hell on Earth.

Fire lit the skies. Trela, Bea, and Shay flew erratically, their tails swirling behind them as they rained down fire on the hordes of demons that raced across the pastures. At the same time, they battled the pterodactyl-like demons that circled around their broad bodies.

I could see the winged demons swoop in and bite at the dragons' scales. I only hoped that they could hold them off.

Searching with our bond I tried to locate Hunter. I felt his essence somewhere in the throng of the battle directly in front of me.

And I knew the instant he felt mine.

Don't come out here. It's a trap, he pleaded. *We're holding them off, but I've yet to see Declan or Helios.*

I raced off the porch and stayed to the shadows, my eyes seeking out the rest of my group.

Witches and warlocks battled the mass with magic, while Were shifters tore into the demons. Dad stood with the coven, his magic blasting relentlessly and my breath heaved out in relief. He was holding his own.

I knew the Titans were in the main throng where Hunter had been, and as I glanced back that way, Celeste was on a slight hill behind them, calling lightning down to strike the multitudes. I wasn't sure where Aine and the fairies were, but I knew they were here and fighting as well.

It was a mass of bodies in the night, only lit by the magic being tossed around and the fire from the dragons. Evil and good twined together in a horrific war.

I had to find Declan. I knew if I did, I'd also find Helios.

The battle stretched around the house and into the backyard. Still creeping along and out of sight, I spotted the man I was looking for. His eyes were directly on me, and a devilish smile lit his face. Beside him stood Teagan, still chained, the leash in Declan's hand.

He looked terrible, and anger flared inside of me.

I strode through the group of Fomori that stood in my way, lashing out with my newfound power, immediately turning them to ash.

As I moved closer, leaving a trail of destruction behind me, the bracelet with Helios's stones lit up, and Declan's eyes widened at the sight.

He laughed then, as I came closer. Waving his finger in my direction.

"Uh, uh uh!" he said, yanking the leash tighter, bringing Teagan in front of him.

"Stay right there, or this one you seem to care so much for will experience more pain than even you can imagine."

His eyes glowed with fervor, and as I stopped in place, his body began expanding, morphing into a larger, more muscular, more dangerous being.

Helios.

He had been Declan all this time.

The darkness growled inside of me and began clawing to get out. It wanted to sink its nails into the god in front of us.

Why though? If it were Helios's own power, wouldn't it be set on destroying him?

You'll find out very soon... it crooned with an evil laugh.

Now that Helios's transformation from Declan was complete, I stared, transfixed.

He was tall, at least ten feet, and his shoulders spanned at least four. His head was bald, and his skin was gray, but as a fire god, flames rushed through his veins and golden fire licked from his eyes.

I wasn't sure what to do as Teagan stood warily at Helios's feet. His eyes were on mine, watching my every move.

If I could just get the chain out of Helios's hands, Teagan might stand a chance.

It was as if the god read my mind because in the next second, he dropped his hold on the leash, looking down at Teagan and then back at me. Teagan didn't move, not an inch. He stayed put, his eyes now downcast, and I realized the leash hadn't really mattered. Helios used his magic to tether him to him.

Helios recognized the moment I figured out, laughing and sneering at me.

"You didn't think it'd be that easy, did you? I've watched you. *Oh*, I've watched you countless times. I had you pegged for smarter than that." He put his finger to his mouth, mocking. "But you never figured out who Declan was either. So maybe you're not." He chuckled before the merriness on his ugly face dropped and his hand shot out, slinging fire in my direction.

I had a scant second to jump and roll, the heat from the fire licking behind me.

Time to see what this bracelet can do.

I held it up in front of me, and the darkness inside laughed before pushing out and up, rising with the power that gathered in the stones.

The power that burst forth was enough to push me back. Sparks and silver power thrust through the air, smacking into his chest where it exploded.

A great crater that spewed fire now opened inside him, and he looked down at it with a frown.

Inside, I did a little jig, happy that it was able to do damage. It was short lived, though, as he looked back at me, ran his hand over his chest, and when he was done, the damage was gone, his skin restored. With a wink he snatched Teagan up in his large hands and leapt through the air.

He soared over the crowds of Fomori and Elves that fought. My eyes scanned over the bodies that littered the ground before backing up to track where he had landed.

And my heart stopped.

He didn't hesitate but scooped up the white tiger that fought mercilessly against the demons surrounding her. She yelped in surprise and then her body began transforming back to her human form. He laughed, his eyes on mine over the crowd and I took off running.

He leaped again, and my heart stuttered as I watched him grab ahold of my dad. The three of them bundled against his chest as he yelled to me over the fray.

"Shall I keep going?"

Fury rose inside of me, a vengeful and destructive anger. At that moment I knew rage like I've never known before. Hot and boiling, my vision red and set on the god.

He laughed and he laughed as he hopped further away with my family clenched in his hands.

"Andie!" Hunter shouted, running up behind me, fending off the demons that surrounded me.

I hadn't even noticed them, so intent on Helios I'd been. The other Titans joined in, knocking them back and circling me.

My eyes were still on the fire god as he got further away.

While Rhea and Lelantos finished off the ring of demons, Hunter pulled me to him. "It's not going well. We're losing a lot of people," he whispered. I only nodded. I felt the desperation and the decline of energy from my people.

"Declan was Helios. This whole time he's been there, and we did nothing. I let this happen." I stared after him in horror.

Hunter shook me. "Stop! This wasn't your doing-it was his. It's been his plan the entire time."

I logically knew this, but it didn't stop the guilt.

"He's got Dad, Pres and Teagan. I have to do something to stop him, but I don't know how. Not with him using them as shields. I'll kill them."

Charlie touched down in front of me in his Peryton form, majestic and sure, not a scratch on him. His eyes met mine before looking back at Helios as he retreated.

"Sometimes victory requires sacrifices you're not willing to give." His eyes were sad. "Victory doesn't come without sacrifice. Love doesn't come without pain."

Every bit of my soul screamed at his words. I didn't want to believe him. I couldn't sacrifice them. I just couldn't. I didn't have it in me.

He looked at me knowingly and took to the air. The darkness inside me agreed with him. I felt it.

It wasn't going to happen.

I turned to Hunter and the Titans. "I'm sifting to the rift. He and the demons will follow, I know they will. They want the Keys too badly. Spread the word to everyone on our side, make sure they sift there and get the ones who can't sift over there too. We're going to end this battle once and for all. No more games."

I gritted my teeth as Hunter argued. He felt my decision immediately. He *rebelled* against it.

I pulled him to me, kissing him with all I had. "I'm sorry. But you know this is the right thing to do." I made sure to say it loud enough where everyone could hear.

I hoped it would make it back to Helios.

Smoke and mirrors.

I left Hunter then, sprinting in the direction Helios had gone. Flinging my power out around me, I disintegrated all the evil that stood in my path. I had no mercy except for those demons still in the throes of battle with my people. They could finish them off.

When nothing stood between Helios and me, I shouted.

He stopped his measured steps and slowly turned around, his three captives hanging limp in his hands.

"What did you do to them?" I ground out, my fists clenched.

He held them out and shook them, adding to my fury. "Who? Them? They're simply sleeping. I couldn't have the great sorcerer trying anything now, could I?" He pulled them back in, a long snakelike tongue reaching out of his wide mouth, licking Presley's slack face.

I was so glad she wasn't awake.

"Well, you can have them," I said harshly, even though my mind warred with my words.

Waving, I sifted, but not before his mouth went slack in disbelief.

Chapter Twenty-Four

I found myself at the foot of the mountain, directly in front of the rift as wave after wave of demons poured out.

The crack had opened up so much that it took up the span of the entire side of the mountain. The air was thick with black smoke, sulfur choking out any vegetation around it.

I looked around, but it didn't appear as if anyone else had made it here yet.

When the demons marching out caught sight of me, they turned in my direction. I sifted out of their line of vision and to the top of the mountain, looking down on the rest of the valley below. It was littered with evil.

As I gazed around, others began showing up. The coven with the Were shifters, the Titans with Aine and Celeste. Hunter and the dragons' shifters, still in their dragon forms, even the trolls. I'd have to ask Hunter later how he did that.

They continued the fight here, cutting down the leagues of monsters that rolled at them.

I knew they were confused about why we were here. But the end *had* to happen here. We needed to send Helios back to Tartarus, and we also had to close the rift.

As the dragons once again took to the skies, Helios finally appeared. He stood directly in front of the opening in the mountain, his eyes scanning the crowd in front of him before looking up.

I let him come.

I didn't fire magic at him, even though I had oodles at my fingertips. He scaled the mountain with one hand, his other still clutching my loved ones. And when he stood before me grinning, I bargained.

They were now awake and fought him every second. There was no fear in their eyes, only determination.

I understood that feeling. I was determined that he would free them.

"If you free them, you can have me. *Please.*"

He laughed and set them down, the three of them yelling at me to stop.

I ignored their shouts.

"Who says I can't keep them and have you anyway?" He asked, his face turning serious. "Why would I strike this bargain with you?"

I smiled, the darkness in me taking over, and I let it rise. It stretched and crooned, laughing its wicked laugh.

"Because if you had me, the Keys would be yours." I shoved my hand out, showing him my palm.

It would be so easy to blast him right now with all of the powers I held inside me, but he had to be in front of the rift for this to work.

"And these? Don't you want your crown back? I showed him the bracelet, the gems glowing in the dark. "Well, I suppose you can put them back in a crown." I chuckled.

I saw when the greed took over. He couldn't help it. Gods were greedy for power, and he was the worst.

I heard my name called over and over, and when I couldn't bear it anymore, I looked down the side of the mountain and saw Hunter trying to climb up, his hand stretched to me, pleading. *Just like in the dream.*

I think at that time, I'd known it would come true. I had known I'd have to do this. I just hated the torment that it caused everyone else.

I smiled at Hunter and murmured, "'Til the stars go dark, my love."

Then I turned back around.

"Do we have a deal?"

He didn't think long on it. "We have a deal."

I nodded swiftly. "Then follow me down," I pointed in front of the rift, "and we'll declare it to everyone."

The darkness inside of me shifted and exclaimed. It told me to wait a moment. And so, I did.

Helios looked at me strangely as the darkness rose. I wasn't able to explain because in the next moment my head was thrown back to the heavens as I stood on that tall mountain, my body straining. My eyes opened wide as my mouth stretched. Dark, oily smoke poured profusely from me to rise into the air.

The last of it filtered out and my body suddenly felt lighter as I watched it waft away to join with the smoky air. I didn't know how or why it left, but I had a feeling it wasn't done with us just yet.

Straightening back up, I looked at Helios. "Okay, I'm ready now."

His eyes were incredulous as he stared at me.

"What..." I didn't let him finish-I wasn't about to explain to him. I owed him nothing.

"No time to explain now," I said breezily before my eyes turned stony. "Let's go."

"You first," he said, grinning. I only shrugged and sifted.

Once again, I found myself standing in front of the opening, but this time the demons rushing out had stopped. It was if Helios had put up a barrier.

But he looked just as confused as I did, when he sat Teagan, Pres, and dad down beside him.

His eyes squinted in anger as he looked at the crack. "Did you do this?" He turned, anger seething out of him.

I put my hands up and shook my head. "It wasn't me. I don't think any of us could stop this. I thought it was you."

Was it the darkness that did it? And who or what exactly was the darkness that had filled me?

I'd have to save those questions for later. I could feel Helios's frustration building and I needed to squash it before it got out of hand.

"Let's get on with this then." I turned to the crowd and shot magic into the air. Sparkes reigned down over the crowd stopping their battles. They looked toward the two of us as we stood in front of them.

"I've struck a bargain with Helios'" My voice rang out strong and sure. "In exchange for these three," I gestured to them beside us, "I'm giving him myself."

Shouts rang out. Screaming ensued. I knew my people were angry and scared. They probably felt betrayed. What I did made no sense to them.

It had to be this way.

I tried to reassure them as best I could without giving myself away. I honestly had no idea how this would work. But it had to. It just had to.

Because the darkness had imparted an especially important piece of information before it departed. Information that no one knew but me.

I'd gone about trying to use my powers the wrong way.

My thoughts on needing the gems were correct. So was the knowledge that I needed the four Keys. But what I hadn't realized was that I would need to use them both, together to send him back to hell and the rest of his demon friends too.

I hoped by now that Hunter had read me, and knew my intentions were not what he originally thought. I hoped he wasn't furious with me. And I knew he'd understand my words when I had stated his back to him.

Despite the pleas and screams around me, I turned back to the god.

His patience surprised me. But I guess when you thought you were about to get everything you wanted, you could afford to be patient.

"Will you allow me to say a few words to my family, and give them a hug, before this happens? I asked him, gesturing toward my dad.

He smiled again, signaling for me to do so, my request making what was about to happen seem more real.

I rushed to them and flung my arms around my dad, hushing him as he tried to talk.

"I love you, Dad, so much. I'll love you until the stars go dark." I pulled away from him and smiled as I saw the struggle he had to keep his face from changing from despair.

I repeated it to Pres. Even though she couldn't help in the same manner, at least she had an idea of what was going on.

When I got to Teagan, his eyes were fearful, and his voice choked as he told me to let Helios have him. To not give myself to the god.

I leaned back and looked into his eyes, murmuring *hellfire* before leaning in and pretending to kiss his cheek. "When you hear '*til the stars go dark*,'" I whispered fervently, hoping he understood. He hadn't been around during our planning. He didn't know I had jokingly given a phrase to our group that I would use when I needed their magical help.

But now he did, and I could only hope that Hunter was able to alert everyone else. I needed them. Even with all the power I had, I needed us all united in magic, just like the Keys.

I strolled back and positioned myself in front of the rift, gesturing for Helios to come stand by me.

I turned my body toward him but called out to those surrounding us.

"It's time now. You've all been wonderful, and I cannot thank you enough for your fealty. But now it is time to hand my powers over to Helios," I gestured toward him. "He will have the four Keys. The stones from his crown," I held up my bracelet and my breath caught at what I was about to do. I prayed that it worked.

Catching his eye as both my hands raised to show him the tattoo and bracelet I shouted at the top of my lungs. "And I will love you all 'til the stars go dark!"

And then I slammed my hands together, activating the bracelet and Keys. At the same moment power came from every direction, and hellfire burned behind him.

Helios screamed in agony and fury, his body lit up like a candle by all of the power while fire rained down on him from the dragons above. The power that slammed out of me was orange, blue, purple and green all mixing together. I stared in horrified fascination as it swirled around him and chunks of flesh began to fall off.

Even then he still attempted to get to me, his voice a continuous roar.

I backed up as close as I could get to the rift without it scalding me, still aiming the power at him. As his body disintegrated slowly, I watched him stumble.

The next moments happened in slow motion, and I knew real fear. Real pain.

He toppled like a tree, still alive but unable to move. As he fell, his remaining hand raked against my ankle. No amount of magic fabric could keep the fire and power that still ran through him from scalding me.

I screamed as I fell, his hand grabbing me, and my eyes bulged in pain and regret.

Somehow, I had screwed this up.

In that same moment, the blackness that had been inside of me soared down from above, twisting and turning around Helios's giant body. What appeared to be a hand formed out of the oiliness, grabbing ahold of him, and it yanked his blazing body toward the chasm.

I felt myself being pulled along, as his hand still wrapped around me and my fingers scrabbled to find purchase. Something, *anything* to pull me away from him.

I looked back in time to see the majority of his body swallowed up and my foot was about to be also.

Out of nowhere, Charlie swooped in, stomping on the hand that held me, and I felt it let go. The pain was overwhelming, licking up my leg, further and further. I rolled over just in time to see Helios grab ahold of Charlie, yanking the Peryton into the flames with him.

"No!" I screamed loud and long as demons poured around me going back to where they had come from as if called by their master.

Hunter was by my side in an instant, but I couldn't make out what he said through my sobs and pain. He laid his hands on me, and instead of talking to me, he whispered the words of a spell I'd never heard before.

Immediately, more pain joined as my joints began dislocating.

Through whatever transformation I went through, the darkness called as my eyes strayed to the closing rift.

Helios has always been mine. He thought to cheat me out of my kingdom. In his greed, he believed himself more powerful than me, Hades. The voice scoffed, before softly whispering as my body stopped changing and the pain began to melt away.

'Til we meet again…

The rift closed completely, and I realized how strange I felt.

Was I dead?

I looked around and all of my people stood before me shocked. Their mouths hung open and some even fainted.

But not Hunter. He stood beside me, smiling, and when he reached out and ran his hand over me. I knew.

He'd forced me to change. *To shift.* To do what I hadn't known how to do.

I looked down at the ground and saw white hooves below me and my body stretched out behind me. My gaze flew back to his, and the air shifted, feathers catching my attention from the side.

I have wings!?

That was the last thing that went through my mind before passing out. The exhaustion of the powers, the sacrifice of Charlie and now *this*.

It was just too much.

Epilogue

When I woke up, I was in my bedroom at the Oak. Star slept beside me. Emric was curled around her. And Hunter laid beside me, snoring softly.

If I hadn't known any better, I'd have thought everything that happened was a dream. A horrible nightmare of a victory.

But as I scanned the room, there was no Charlie in it.

He had really died saving me.

A soft sob tore from my mouth, and I immediately covered it, biting my lip to keep from full on crying.

"Hey." Hunter had woken, reaching over to grasp my face and turn it toward him. "It's okay. Everything's okay." He pulled me to him, enveloping me in his strong arms and woodsy scent. I let a few more tears fall and nodded into his shoulder.

"You did good last night, baby. But you had me so worried."

I pulled back and looked into his dark eyes.

"I know, and I am so sorry. I knew you'd figure it out somehow. You had to know that I would never give up so easily. I'd never doom both of us to an eternity in hell. I just had to make him believe it."

He smiled softly. "Well, you did, and now he's back where he belongs. And you also got rid of the darkness."

I shook my head, recalling what it had said before I passed out.

"I didn't get rid of it. It left me. And Hunter, it wasn't Helios's power. It was Hades."

His eyes grew round at my words, and I pressed on. "He told me right before he closed the chasm. All this time, he was furious at Helios for wanting to take over the magical world, because in turn that would mean he would rule over Hades. So all this time, I had Hades helping me." I laughed a little at the craziness of it. I still couldn't believe it, but it was true.

"How is everyone else?" I hurried to ask, my mind on my friends and family, praying we hadn't lost much of our community.

"We've lost some fairies, quite a few shifters and coven members." He frowned. "Most of the deaths occurred early on in the fight before you came with the Keys. Helios somehow knew of our plans and came early before everyone got here."

It didn't surprise me that he'd found out somehow. He was devious in that way, and if he was in his Declan form, some of the magical community might not have even known who that was. All it would've taken was for him to ask some questions.

"What about Teagan and Pres? The rest of our group?" I asked, worried.

He smiled his brilliant smile and slid out of the bed, grabbing my hand. "Why don't you come and find out?"

He pulled me from the room and into the main area. Everyone was there, and somehow the tree had stretched to accommodate them all.

My eyes ran over Celeste and Aine, who stood by Coeus and the Titans. They all looked whole and healthy as they smiled at me. Killian, Trela, Bea, and Shay sat on the couch, and other than a few scratches here and there they too seemed to be fine.

Amarie and her bunch all sat around a large table that hadn't been there before, while Balwyn and Eira flew around putting cups and plates before them. I was happy to see none of the Elves injured after the losses they had endured on our second journey. It took a while for Amarie to really talk to me after that.

Presley sat in a recliner near the fire, a blanket thrown over her, but her smile told me she was just fine.

It was when I saw movement near the door that I stepped further into the room. It was my dad, and he had his arm around Teagan's waist, helping him move forward.

His body was still emaciated, but the light was back in his eyes. I knew Balwyn would have him fattened up in no time.

I let go of Hunter's hand and moved forward, holding my breath. Teagan did the same as he stepped away from Dad.

"Andie, I am so sorry."

I threw my arms around him. "Don't be. None of this was your fault, and I think you've been punished enough. You thought you were doing the right thing when you took the magic from Declan. You didn't know it was Helios at that time. You had no idea it would do what it did."

He held me tight.

We would be okay.

The rest of the day was spent in the Oak. None of us wanted to leave each other's side; we just wanted to sit as a group and relish the victory we'd had and the terror we'd overcome.

While Pres and I played a card game with Hunter and Dad, I asked, "Does anyone want to tell me about that transformation that happened last night?" I raised an eyebrow at Hunter.

He blushed slightly, dipping his head. "I had to do it, Andie. It was the only way to get rid of the hellfire consuming you. When you shift, it heals your body. If I hadn't done it, you would have died."

I placed my hand on his. "And I am so glad you did, baby. I just want to know what exactly I shifted to." I laughed, and everyone cut coy looks at each other.

"Okay, enough already," I joked, laying down my cards, laughing. "Please tell me."

A voice sounded behind me, and I couldn't move for fear I was hearing things.

"I'll tell you what you shifted to, my dear. A beautiful white Pegasus. It is a high honor for the Fates to bestow someone with this as their animal, as it is the offspring of the great god, Poseidon. A symbol of hope and beauty, of renewal." His voice tapered off and I sprang into action, twirling around.

There, on the back of the couch, sat the most beautiful sight I could have ever seen.

A phoenix in all its majestic glory. Red wings tucked to its side, a red crown of feathers atop its head.

"Charlie?" I whispered, blinking my eyes over and over again.

The birds head dipped down in acknowledgment.

"It's me, Andie."

"But... but I saw you. You went into the flames. You... *saved* me."

Again, his head dipped. "And I'd do it again and again, my dear. You see, I never got to tell you my story in all the madness that was going on." He waved his wing.

"This form is my true form. The phoenix. I will always rise from the ashes."

He hopped down from his perch to stand directly in front of me, and I reached forward, gently wrapping my arms around him, and he nuzzled into my neck.

"I am so glad you are okay. Thank you. Thank you for saving me," I whispered.

He looked around the room and in unison, they all raised their glasses, "Until the stars go dark!"

I hope you've enjoyed Spear of Victory: United in Magic. Thank you so much for reading! I would love if you left an honest review for Spear of Victory: United in Magic on Amazon, Goodreads, or Bookbub! Reviews help authors more than you know.
https://www.amazon.com/dp/B0952C88T4
As always, thank you so much for your support and enjoying Andie's journey with me.
Love,
J.C.

ALSO AVAILABLE BY J.C. LUCAS

The Four Keys – The Beginning (Prequel to The Four Keys series)

https://www.amazon.com/gp/product/B08H1CXTKL

Sword of Light (#1 The Four Keys series)

https://www.amazon.com/gp/product/B088DKTL4C

Cauldron of Hope and Sorrows (#2 The Four Keys series)

https://www.amazon.com/dp/B08LSNQXVD

IF YOU'D LIKE TO BE one of the first to know about new releases or sales, click below to sign up for J.C.'s newsletter. You'll also get a digital copy of The Four Keys – The Beginning (Prequel to The Four Keys series) for free, just for signing up!

https://landing.mailerlite.com/webforms/landing/h1f5i7

Let's be friends! I'd love to connect with you!

Instagram: @j.c.lucas_author

Twitter: @lucas_author

Facebook: https://www.facebook.com/j.c.lucas.author

Goodreads: https://www.goodreads.com/author/show/20415558.J_C_Lucas

Bookbub: https://www.bookbub.com/profile/j-c-lucas-7fadf941-1617-4680-b878-53409fa91e17

Pinterest: https://www.pinterest.com/jclucas20/

If you have any questions or just want to give me a shout, email me! I'd love to hear from you. And as always, thank you so much for your support!

jclucas78@lucasjc.com

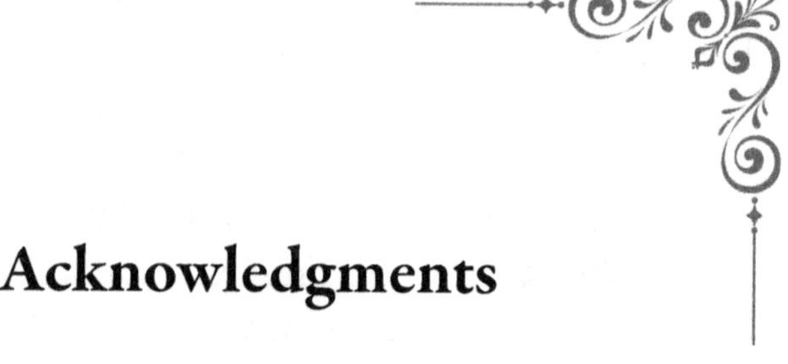

Acknowledgments

Where do I begin? There are so many people that I want to thank for their help with this book and all of the books in this series! First and foremost, thank you again to my readers and ARC readers. You are the ones that make my writing so worthwhile and enjoyable. I love the feedback that you give me, the ideas and inspirations, and your enthusiasm, it's incredible!

Thank you to my family. My husband and boys for cheering me on, giving me peace and quiet to write, and letting me bounce ideas off of them. To my mom who is my biggest cheerleader, Beta reader, and super fan, thank you!

Lindsay York, thank you so much for your beautiful editing, patience and for your polish. I've learned so much working with you and I am so excited to continue working with you on future books.

Maria Spada, what can I say? You have such beautiful talent and have never once complained about all the various ideas, changes I ask of you. The fact that all I have to do is tell you about my book, and you make the vision for the cover happen so beautifully, is a testament to you being a wonderful cover artist. I can't thank you enough!

Special shout-out to Makarena. You my dear, are such a bright light in my writing. I love the feedback you give and thank you so much for contributing ideas for Spear of Victory that I was able to incorporate. Your enthusiasm for this series has been outstanding and has brought me so much happiness.

And all of my author friends. Your support, inspiration, insights, collaboration, social media shares and enthusiasm has meant the world to me. You get me.

Thank you all!

Love,

J.C.

www.ingramcontent.com/pod-product-compliance
Lightning Source LLC
Chambersburg PA
CBHW060246100726
47907CB00003B/780